Praise for Catherine Czerkawska's previous novels:

'Beguiling and enchanting ... Czerkawska is an excellent storyteller.'
The Scottish Review

'Czerkawska tells her tale in a restrained, elegant prose that only
adds to its poignancy.' *Sunday Times*

'A powerful story about love and obligation.' *John Burnside*

'Moving, poetic and quietly provocative.' *The Independent*

'Heartwarming, realistic and page turning.' *Lorraine Kelly*

'Beautiful – lyrical and sensual by turns.' *Hilary Ely*

'A romance of Scotland's great Romantic. The Jewel finally gives
voice to Jeany Armour, the girl who sang as sweetly as a night-
ingale.' *Sunday Mail*

'Take any aspect of the novelist's art and you'll find it exemplified
here to perfection.' *Bill Kirton, Booksquawk*

BITTER ORANGES

Catherine Czerkawska

Published by Dyrock Publishing

Cover art by Alan Lees

Cover and book design by Lumphanan Press

ISBN: 978-0-9557364-6-9

You cannot think what figs
My teeth have met in,
What melons icy-cold
Piled on a dish of gold
Too huge for me to hold,
What peaches with a velvet nap,
Pellucid grapes without one seed:
Odorous indeed must be the mead
Whereon they grow, and pure the wave they drink ...
Goblin Market: Christina Rossetti

Those oranges – Gold! They're almost red.
They seem little chips just broken away
From the sun itself.
The Fruit Shop: Amy Lowell

CHAPTER ONE

Let the dove fly.
Let her gain height.
Do not worry about her
because she does not worry about you.

It was raining when a heavily pregnant Margaret stepped off the plane in Glasgow. Raining and windy and cold. The contrast between her home city and the sunny island she had left behind was stark.

'You'll be relieved to be back, Maggie,' said her brother, who had come to meet her, taking a little time off work to do it. He kissed her carefully on the cheek.

'Well, it'll be nice to see everyone again,' she said. 'I feel as if I've been away for ages.'

'That's because you have. And a lot's happened, hasn't it?'

'I suppose so.' She patted her bump. 'I've got myself a Spanish husband and a baby made in Spain as well. Who would have thought it?'

'Not me,' said Ian mildly, shoving suitcases into the boot. 'Not me, for one.'

She had not been back in Glasgow since early in January when, as the pandemic with all its rules and restrictions had eased, she had left to start a new job in property sales on Tenerife. Two years after her divorce, and having spent a large part of that time in lockdown with her mother, she had been ready for something new, so ready that she would have jumped at almost any change of scene.

El flechazo, they called it in Spanish. An arrow shot. The lightning strike of love at first sight. That was what had worried her family so much: that she had fallen in love with and chosen to marry a local man, so precipitately that she could hardly claim to know him at all. It was certainly what had made them feel that she was making the biggest mistake of her life. And yet everything about it had seemed right. It still did seem right. Everything including her pregnancy. The only thing that seemed wrong was the decision to come home to Scotland to have the baby. She had the uneasy feeling that she had been persuaded against all her wiser instincts.

So much had happened since she had first made that leap into the unknown. It was less than a year since she had met Luis Herrera Garcia where he was playing the guitar in a restaurant frequented by the property sales crowd. She had gone with him to see the almonds in bloom on the slopes of Teide, wary of all the warnings about 'holiday romances'. She had fallen out with him, briefly, only to be reunited with him in the certain knowledge that she loved him, that he loved her. She had married him, much against the advice of her friends and family, especially her sister-in-law Fiona who couldn't begin to understand how anyone, let alone Margaret, could do anything so rash, so foolish. Marry in haste, repent at leisure. She didn't say it out loud, but she was obviously thinking it. Well, Margaret had defied them all. The *flechazo* had felled her and now here she was, married and pregnant, with the prospect of returning to a new business and a new life on her husband's beautiful home island of La Gomera.

Once the baby was safely born.

But that event seemed like an enormous hurdle, fast approaching.

During the drive from the airport, the city already felt like some monstrous creature extending its tentacles around her, entrapping her. She wasn't relieved to be back. Not at all. Those months away had been so eventful, so crammed full of new experiences, that this place didn't feel like home any more. Fleetingly, she thought about demanding that Ian turn round and take her straight back to the airport. She could wait there on standby till she got a flight back to Tenerife. Only the sheer impossibility of it, that and the knowledge that her brother would refuse to do it, stopped her. She could feel tears starting behind her eyes, and blinked them away.

They were all waiting for her at her mother's suburban house to greet the prodigal. She was surprised they hadn't put up a banner saying 'welcome home'. Fiona had baked a cake. Even her niece and nephew, Lottie and Rory, were there, although she suspected that Rory, at least, was motivated by a desire to see what she had brought him in the way of gifts.

'My goodness – you're enormous!' That was Fiona. How like her, Margaret thought.

Annie glared at her daughter-in-law. 'It's probably a big boy.'

'Yes!' Margaret hugged her mother. 'Probably a big Spanish boy! Luis is very tall.'

Fiona frowned. 'You know I thought Latinos were quite small as a rule.'

Ian was unable to restrain himself from saying 'Shush, Fee.'

'Oh I know your Luis is tall. I was just a bit surprised, when we met.'

'Canary Islanders *are* tall,' said Margaret. 'But we don't know whether this is a boy or a girl yet. We decided to wait to find out.'

'Really?' said Fiona. 'We wanted to know as soon as possible.'

'Well we wanted a surprise.'

'How was the flight?' asked Annie, anxious to change the subject.

'It was fine. But I must message Luis. Tell him I'm here.'

'Safe and sound in Scotland, eh?'

'Yes, mum. Safe and sound in Scotland.'

During the next few weeks, Margaret caught herself saying, 'My husband is Spanish', all the time. On buses, sitting in hospital or clinic waiting rooms, wherever she started casual conversations with perfect strangers, she would say it, as though reaffirming the fact to herself, reminding herself about the truth of it. Not that she needed reminding. She was missing Luis with a constant ache, only relieved by the equally constant demands of late pregnancy. Every few days, she would have a video conversation with him that left her longing to touch him, to kiss him. Then she would dream about him, and wake up to an immediate sense of his absence.

Soon after her return, she was plunged into what felt like a continuous round of clinic and hospital visits. Although she had been well looked after throughout her pregnancy, there seemed to be a weird distrust of the care she had received on the island. She became all too used to the question mark that followed any pronunciation or mispronunciation of her new surname. On Tenerife she had continued to use her own surname most of the time, but here in Scotland, she felt compelled to call herself Mrs Herrera as a gesture of loyalty to Luis, especially in the face of Fiona's ill-disguised disapproval of her marriage. She was booked into a maternity unit with the stern admonition that she should have come home and done all this months ago if she wanted to give birth in Scotland. The truth was that she had been unsure at first about whether she wanted to come back to have the baby at all. Born in Scotland, she was a dual Irish Scottish national and an EU citizen. She was one more anomaly among many Brexit related anomalies.

'I didn't know what I was going to do. And I didn't know there was a waiting list,' she said, defensively. 'I only decided to come back a week or so ago. This was the earliest flight we could find.'

The receptionist raised her eyebrows, sighed, but said nothing more. At the clinic the midwife and the obstetrician were kinder and less judgmental. She had been referred to him because of her late registration, but – like her Spanish GP – he seemed much more laid back than anyone else.

'You're a wee bit older than average for a first baby, but nothing significant these days. Thirty five or six is nothing. I see women in their forties every week. You're a very fit and healthy woman,' he said. 'I take it you've had all the usual care on Tenerife?'

'Yes – and I had an English speaking doctor which made it easier. My Spanish is improving, but it's not quite up to childbirth yet!'

'You're healthy, and all your stats back that up, although we'll keep an eye on your blood pressure. Is your husband going to manage to come here for the birth?'

'I certainly hope so. That's the plan, anyway.'

'And you'll be going back afterwards?'

'We will. As soon as it's feasible.'

'I don't blame you. In fact I envy you! Will you be living on Tenerife?'

'La Gomera.'

'I hear that's a very beautiful place. My in-laws went there on holiday once.'

'It *is* beautiful. That's where my husband comes from. I have an Irish passport you see, so there'll be no problems for me moving there.'

'Lucky you. My wife's French. She's a vet. You have no idea of the problems. Or maybe you do ...'

She nodded. It was so nice to meet somebody who understood. 'It can be a nightmare. And expensive. But my mum was born in Mayo. Anyway, we'll be taking over a family business on La Gomera, a small restaurant. Luis – that's my husband – is a musician as well. He plays the guitar.'

She couldn't resist taking out her phone and showing him a picture of Luis, sitting outside the restaurant, guitar on his lap.

The doctor sighed. 'How idyllic.'

'Well I expect it will be hard work. But it's in a lovely place. The gardens are wonderful.'

'A good place to bring up a child.'

She nodded. She wanted to say 'tell that to my brother and his wife,' but she thought she'd said enough.

She signed on for ante-natal classes at her local health centre and listened to lectures about breast versus bottle-feeding, though she was determined that she was going to feed the baby herself. She had the birth process described to her in detail over and over again. She lay on cushions on the floor with other porpoise shaped women, some of them much younger than herself, and did her exercises and her deep breathing and her panting. She wished that Luis was there with her.

Nobody said very much about the pain, except that pain relief was available. Nobody spoke about it the way Luis's mother, Maria, had spoken to her about it.

'Margarita, you don't just feel the pain, you *are* the pain.'

She tried to put it from her mind as best she could. Perhaps Maria had been exaggerating in an effort to persuade her to have the baby in Scotland. Perhaps, thought Margaret, in her more uncertain and hormonal moments, Maria had thought it might be better if the child was registered in Scotland. In case things went wrong. That was what her own family was thinking. But surely Maria didn't feel the same?

Her blood pressure near normal, but her ankles had begun to swell up a little in the evenings. Every night, her hands would develop a peculiar prickling, tingling sensation that the midwife said went by the name of Carpel Tunnel Syndrome. It was less alarming than it sounded, but uncomfortable all the same. Her fingers swelled up so much that to her disgusted eyes they resembled sausages. She had to remove her wedding ring, sliding it off with washing up liquid and wearing it on a chain around her neck.

'Will I ever be able to wear it again?' she asked her mother, in despair.

'Don't worry,' said Mrs Sinclair. 'You'll be back to normal quicker than you think.'

Annie Sinclair had been delighted to see her daughter. Margaret felt it had almost been worthwhile coming home to experience her mother's intense pleasure at the prospect of another grandchild, and one from such an unexpected quarter too.

'I never thought I'd see this,' she said. 'You don't know how happy it makes me. Married again and expecting. And I'm so anxious to meet your Luis. He is coming over for the birth, isn't he?'

'Just before, if possible.'

'Are you happy, Margaret? This all came as such a surprise. Ian and Fiona couldn't believe it.'

'Could you believe it?'

'Me? Well, I know you better than they do. I'm very glad for you, you know. Just as long as you're happy with him.'

'When you meet him, then you'll know why. He's like nobody I've ever met before. He just came into my life like a ... I don't know.'

She thought about the mini twisters in Los Cristianos, dust devils they were called in America, swift winds that circled erratically along the beach, picking up anything in their path. As Luis had picked her up and swept her along.

'He certainly swept you off your feet. I'm not surprised though.' Annie had spoken to Luis online, seen pictures of him, including a short video of him playing the guitar and singing. She had been deeply impressed.

'What a very handsome and talented man!' she said, much to Margaret's gratification.

'Well I think so, mum!'

One wintry day, not long after her arrival, when they were comfortably ensconced in Annie's kitchen with cups of tea, Margaret ventured to ask, 'Mum, why has it upset Fiona so much? My marrying Luis, I mean.'

'Upset her? No!'

'Of course it has, Mum. If I can see it, you must be able to. You see a lot more of her than I do.'

Annie looked sheepish. 'Well, I suppose it has. A bit.'

'She seems to take it as a personal insult.'

'Perhaps she envies you, in a funny kind of way.'

'Why would she envy me?'

She smiled at her daughter. 'You know, it's quite nice to have somebody to pity. We all do it. I bet Alastair was enjoying doing it too.'

Normally a mild and kindly woman, in her darker moments Annie had felt like lying in wait for her ex son-in-law and beating him about the head with a heavy object. Or paying somebody else to do the job for her. She was sure it must be easy to arrange something like that in Glasgow, although she had told nobody else about these dreadful but somehow comforting thoughts and feelings, and the temptation had faded over time, especially after Margaret had met Luis.

'For the past couple of years, Fiona's been saying "Poor Margaret" quite a lot. Suddenly, she can't say that any more.'

'She can though,' said Margaret. 'I'll bet she still does. Poor Margaret, married to a suspicious foreigner who only wants her money. I bet she gives me a year with him at the most.'

Her mother avoided her gaze and Margaret knew that her guess had been pretty accurate.

'But it all rings a bit hollow now, doesn't it? It's just sour grapes, Margaret. That's what it is.'

Annie got on well enough with Fiona but she loved Margaret more. She couldn't help herself. 'You must be missing him, though. I'd miss him if he were my husband, and you've hardly been together any length of time. You must have just been getting used to each other.'

'We were. We were going to wait a wee while before trying for a baby. Wait till we'd moved to La Gomera. But this one had other ideas.' She patted the bump. 'And I am missing him. But we speak all the time. Even when he's working in some kitchen somewhere.'

Besides that, they sent messages and pictures: hers of grey Glasgow and the still-growing bump, his of flowers and trees, of rocky hillsides, blue skies and seas, and the red tiled roofs of *La Manzana Dorada*. His

Golden Apple. Their restaurant and the place where they would be living and working. He also sent the occasional smiling selfie, with the landscape of his island behind him. It was not hard for her to imagine him working in the sunshine, with the hibiscus, the oleanders, the almonds and the citrus in the gardens there. She took the opportunity of being at home to search for books about the cultivation of fruit and nut trees, to read up about essential oils and herbs and how to grow them. She made a Pinterest board for the restaurant, got him to send her lots of images including pictures of Paco and Carmen, his uncle and aunt who were passing the property on to them. She posted the images so that she could show them to friends and family.

'Oh Margaret,' said her mother. 'I can see what you love about it. How could you bear to leave it? How could *he* ever bear to leave it?'

'I don't think he could,' she said. 'And I sometimes think that I should have given birth there, followed my instincts. Even though his mum told me I should be in Scotland, should be somewhere where I spoke the language.'

She carried on wondering whether she had made the right decision in coming back to Scotland for the birth, but there was nothing she could do about it now. Here she was and here she must stay until the baby was born. Meanwhile, her mother's friends, from whom she had rented her apartment in Los Cristianos when first she had moved to Tenerife, had agreed that Luis could stay there alone until the little family moved to La Gomera, complete with the baby, in early spring-time. They were glad of the rent and besides, It would be a good time to move, a good time to start their new venture. Still, she missed her husband all the time with a constant, low-level sadness, a space in her heart that not even the fast growing bump could fill.

CHAPTER TWO

Inside my breast I have a casket
which won't open
because the master of this chest is away
and he has the keys.

The miserable weeks of winter progressed with bitter frosts and a chilly mist rising from the Clyde or – more often – howling winds and rain. She even began to wish for the Sirocco. The accumulated weight of Margaret's pregnancy insulated her from the cold, as surely as it had made her uncomfortably hot on Tenerife. The loss of her first Christmas with Luis would be a blow, but it was the coming of Christmas that allowed her to adjust in some measure to being in Scotland again. Christmas, after all, should be cold, so that you could light a fire and pull the curtains against the weather, making the rooms snug and safe. She had always enjoyed Christmas in the city.

One Sunday in December, she went to visit an old university friend. She and Suzie had always liked each other very much. They had met in their first year, when they had shared one of the raucous flats in the hall of residence, their rooms side by side. They had taken some of the same courses and had spent long nights drinking cheap coffee and not so cheap wine, and setting the world to rights. Margaret was transported back to Suzie's little boxed-in room with posters on the wall, Dougie McLean, Eddi Reader and Joni Mitchell blasting beautiful music from her speakers and an extensive library of the history of feminism and feminist thought on her bookshelves. Suzie had sometimes smoked small cigars with her head hanging out of the window since smoking was forbidden and there were smoke alarms everywhere, but the scent lingered. She would spray air freshener before the cleaner came in. Now she had stopped smoking altogether but nothing else was very different about her except that she lived more prosperously and successfully than Margaret. As soon as they met each other again, even though their interaction over the past year or so had been mostly online, they knew that they were still good friends.

They were an unlikely pair, Margaret and Suzie, but surprisingly enough they had hit it off right from the start. After their university days, they had seen less of each other. Latterly their main contact had been the odd lunch date in some city centre cafe, although Suzie had been very supportive when Margaret's marriage to Alastair was breaking down. Over the years her involvement with the women's movement had grown and flourished. Now, she was happily married to Laura, a senior buyer for a chain of high end interiors shops. They lived in a small, modern and fiendishly expensive town house, at the back of the Botanical Gardens, in the West End of the city. Margaret had never enquired too closely, but suspected that Laura – like her own ex-husband – had inherited money. Possibly considerably more money than Alastair. Glasgow house prices had risen astronomically over the past few years. Suzie had taken a Fine Arts course along with her English Literature, and moved on to a Postgraduate Masters. Over the ensuing years, she had gradually built up a successful career as an artist, specializing in children's book illustrations as well as exhibiting in galleries here and there. The pandemic had hit both businesses hard, but the interiors shop had moved most of its business online, with a certain amount of success, and Suzie had seized the opportunity of enforced isolation to focus on her illustration work.

When they had last met, Margaret's disillusionment with her ex had led to her agreeing with Suzie's cheerful generalizations about men. Now she felt quite differently, but she still loved her old friend.

'We're so different,' Suzie would say. 'Men and women. How can we ever find any point of contact? And it's always the women who suffer.'

Latterly she had begun to suggest, only half jokingly, that the entire male population of the world should be given something to dampen down their testosterone levels. 'Think of how much more peaceful things would be!' she would say.

The couple's little house was light, bright and stuffed with curios of one kind or another, since both Suzie and Laura were magpies by nature, and Laura travelled a great deal, bringing back suitcases full of esoteric collectables. Suzie herself never changed. She was small and dark, her face framed by short brown hair. She seldom wore make-up other than a slash of red lipstick, but invariably dressed in bright primary colours. She frowned at Margaret, more in sorrow than in anger.

'You've gone and done it again, haven't you?' she said, regretfully.

'I'm sorry,' said Margaret, humbly. 'I couldn't help it you know.'

'You don't have to apologise to me. It's you I'm worried about. You're like one of these creatures they turn loose from a zoo and the very next day there it is, back in its cage.'

If anyone else had said it, Margaret might have been offended, but it was impossible to be cross with Suzie. She began to laugh. Suzie's face was creased with worry.

'I'm not, you know!' Margaret protested, mildly. 'I'm a grown woman. I did something I really wanted to do for a change. Me and nobody else.'

'Well *he* must have had a hand in it! And now look where it's got you.' Suzie looked at Margaret's belly and frowned.

'I'm very happy with this, as well.' She patted the bump.

'You could have seized the opportunity and banished men from your life once and for all. You just lacked the courage to take it to its natural conclusion.' Margaret thought she was only half joking.

'Don't go on at me, Suzie. You know it won't do any good. And we both know you're not serious.'

'Well, not very, no.' She started to laugh. 'Some of my best friends are men. Isn't that what you're supposed to say?'

They were drinking lapsang. Margaret savoured its smoky taste for a moment and said, 'Do you remember that awful instant coffee we used to drink in the flat? Like gravy browning.'

'I know. It was cheap though. And that disgusting coffee creamer stuff.'

'I don't think we noticed.'

They paused, remembering their shared past with affection.

'I don't think I lack courage,' said Margaret. 'In fact I think I'm really very brave. I'm an explorer in a foreign land.'

'In more ways than one.'

'That's what we all are maybe, women and men. Lots of us fall by the wayside. There are casualties.'

'Too many, I reckon.'

'Some of us opt out altogether and take a different route. Some of us carry on. Feeling for footholds in the dark. Some of us make our home there.'

'Then you'll always be a foreigner. You'll always be a stranger to yourself.'

'Ah no. I'm a very happy citizen of nowhere, me. Poor old Teresa May. When she said that, I felt it described me exactly.'

'Well, I agree with you,' said Suzie. 'And it's certainly made Laura's job a whole lot more difficult.'

'I'm sure it has. If I didn't have my precious Irish passport, it would have made my job almost impossible too. Anyway, it's the trying that's so important. Having a go. Trying to make contact.'

'Hammering out treaties,' added Suzie, with a certain amount of sarcasm.

'If you like. But when it's right, there's nothing like it. It's the struggle to achieve a kind of transcendence.'

There was nobody else to whom she could have said this without feeling very foolish indeed, not even Luis, but now that the words were spoken, she felt the truth of them.

'I suppose I do understand you. I almost envy you that feeling,' said Suzie. 'I never felt that. Not with men, anyway. I don't think I could ever love a man in quite that way, not the way I love Laura, anyway.'

'But we all love everybody differently, don't we?' said Margaret. 'I mean it isn't a finite thing. The more you give the more you have.'

'You sound like a Facebook meme.'

'But it's still true.'

'Laura has a couple of brothers and I know she loves them to bits. But if I had been you, I don't think I would have been brave enough to try again. Not after such betrayal.'

'I wasn't brave. I was in love.'

'Or lust?'

'Oh, that too!'

'I think I would have left that kind of relationship behind after the divorce. Not gone looking for somebody else, not just tried to see myself reflected in some man's eyes.'

'But that would have been right for you. Not me. Besides, I don't think that's what I did. I think I see *him* in his eyes, nobody else. Aren't you even curious to know what he's like?'

'Your Luis? Very Spanish, I suppose.'

'Well of course he is. Canarian, anyway. He's a good man.' *Soy un buen hombre*, she thought. That was how he had described himself during their first disastrous date on the slopes of Teide. 'He's quite a vulnerable man.'

Suzie looked at her in exasperation.

'They all rely on women thinking that! So you married him out of sympathy. The usual excuse!'

'No. I married him on impulse.'

'God, that's worse.'

'I married him because I wanted to know him better. And I married him because I love him.'

'You should have come home to us. There's still time.'

Margaret looked down at her bump and patted it. 'There's no time at all. You sound like Fiona.'

'Heaven forbid.'

'And what if it's a boy? What if it's a lovely boy, Suzie?'

'Whatever it is, it'll come out with Made in Spain stamped on its backside.'

'Well, as far as I'm concerned, that's a good thing!'

'You're beyond hope!'

They parted on friendly terms, as always. Suzie hugged her affectionately. 'Let me know,' she said. 'Let me know as soon as it's born. Even if it's a little macho alien, I'll send it a cuddly toy. A pink one.'

Time passed slowly. She renewed more old friendships, went shopping for baby things with Fiona and her mother, took Fiona's children out for pizzas and bought Christmas gifts for the whole family. She managed to find a miniature of a lute player in Elizabethan dress in a West End antique shop, a detailed painting in a heavily carved wooden frame. She thought about sending it to Luis, but she didn't trust the post so she decided to keep it and give it to him when he came to Scotland, which should be very soon. She showed photographs of him on her phone to her mother's friends and neighbours and saw, with a certain amount of satisfaction, their surprise at his good looks, those high cheekbones, sensuous lips and dark hair. They hadn't expected it, she knew.

'Handsome is as handsome does,' said Fiona, a little sourly.

'Are you really happy?' she asked her sister-in-law over coffee and cake one day, but Margaret wouldn't rise to the bait.

She nibbled on a piece of densely sweet banana loaf. Too sweet. 'Yes.' She looked directly into Fiona's self-protective eyes. 'Yes. I love him, you know. I'm very happy.'

'We never thought ...'

'What? What didn't you think?'

Fiona stood up. 'I need more coffee,' she said.

'Fetch me another cup while you're there.'

'Are you sure?' Fiona frowned. 'You should be cutting your caffeine intake, you know.'

'They don't do that in Spain.'

'Don't they?'

'All these things vary according to the country you're in.'

'I never heard that. I'm sure it can't be true.'

'Some of it's true. Soft cheese. That's another one. We're allowed that in Spain.'

Margaret didn't know for sure, but Fiona always brought out the worst in her.

'I'm surprised you still like coffee. I couldn't even bear the smell of it when I was expecting.'

'I was like that for the first few months. Couldn't bear it. But I'm OK now. Still can't stand wine though. Just as well, probably.'

Cutting out alcohol had been no problem for Margaret. One of the earliest indications of her pregnancy had been an utter aversion to alcohol of any kind, and although she had been blissfully free of morning sickness, the smell of alcohol was still enough to make her feel queasy.

Fiona came back to the table. It was good coffee and it reminded Margaret of the coffee she drank while waiting for Luis in the small bars where he played, the rich, bitter taste of it.

'How could you take the risk?' Fiona persisted. She hated to take risks. 'We thought you probably wouldn't get married again, after Alastair.'

'Did you? I don't see why not.'

'He hurt you so much.'

'Well, I didn't think I'd marry either. But I came to my senses about Alistair. Put it behind me. You never know what's round the next corner, do you?'

She had already seen Jenny walking out with Alastair's baby, not so much a baby now but already a toddler, sitting up in a buggy and taking an interest in the world. She had been visiting her friends in the library, not far from the university. She had even managed to smile at the girl, who had clearly not known whether to say something or walk quickly past. Margaret had stopped her and asked her about the child, a wee girl called Chloe, and slipped a little money into the pram, as was still the custom in this part of the world. As she had done so, she had noticed the sudden surprise on Jenny's face when she saw Margaret's bump under the loose winter coat. Perhaps Alastair hadn't heard the news. Or perhaps hadn't seen fit to mention it to his new wife. It gave her a certain amount of satisfaction to be able to say, 'Oh yes, I married again. Didn't Alastair tell you? Maybe he didn't know. This will be our first. Just like you and Alastair.'

'What does your husband do?'

'He's a musician. He's Spanish.'

'Oh yes. We heard you'd moved out there for a bit.'

'For a lot, as it turned out! I met him on Tenerife. I'm just back here to have the baby. Then we'll be moving to the Canaries permanently.'

'Really?'

Did she see a flash of envy on the girl's face?

'We're going to run a restaurant on La Gomera.'

'La Gomera?'

'It's one of the smaller islands. Very beautiful. The restaurant belonged to his uncle and aunt. It's beautiful too. I can't wait to get back there.'

'How nice,' said Jenny. She still sounded surprised, clearly couldn't think of anything else to say. Margaret wondered what Alastair had told her about his ex-wife, how he had characterised her. Not adventurous, certainly.

'Yes. It's a big change for me but very exciting. And the weather's fabulous.'

Margaret hoped she would tell Alastair all about it. It was a little unworthy of her, she thought, prompted by her better nature, but when she moved on she searched her own heart and found, to her surprise and relief, that there was no bitterness left at all. She wished Alastair well with his new family. Even the ache of that wasted time seemed to have gone. All she wanted to focus on now was the future, with her husband and child.

'Well, you certainly didn't know what was round the next corner,' said Fiona, with feeling, when next they met, and Margaret told her about the encounter. 'Neither did we. What exactly are you going to do after the baby's born?'

'The plan is to wait a few weeks and then go back, of course.'

'Go back?' Fiona seemed very much surprised.

'Well why not?'

'With a tiny baby.'

'Why on earth not?' she repeated.

'But it was so dirty there.'

'It isn't dirty at all. And certainly not on La Gomera. Which is where we'll be going. Even the water's good there. Pure and clean. Have you looked at parts of Glasgow recently? I could hardly believe how shabby the place seems now!'

'But the smell of the drains, in all that heat.'

'All drains smell when the weather's hot. Even in Glasgow. Fiona, it isn't Timbuctoo, you know. And even if it was, we'd manage. They have babies and clinics and doctors on the islands. Good ones. And you can buy everything you need. Disposable nappies and ointments and everything else.'

'Oh I never used disposables.'

'Were you saving the planet, Fiona?'

'They're very environmentally unsound you know. I always had good old fashioned terries.'

'I'm sure you're right. I'll still be using disposables though. But I'll be breastfeeding so I'll be doing my bit for the planet that way. And there'll be very little danger of anything going wrong with the baby's health.'

'Breastfeeding? At your age? Have you thought that you might not be able to do it?'

Margaret wanted to take Fiona by the shoulders and shake her. 'Age has nothing to do with breastfeeding. And I'm not exactly ancient! God, Fiona, you teach food technology.'

'What does that have to do with anything?'

'Nutrition and all that. And there's nothing more environmentally sound than producing your own milk.'

'It's very difficult for most people, you know.'

'Fiona, if it was *that* difficult the human race would have died out long ago.'

'I was always squeamish about it. Bottles were good enough for my two. Breastfeeding was too much of a tie. I'd have felt like a cow. It always seemed unnatural, somehow.'

Margaret almost choked on her coffee. She began to laugh. 'Do you hear what you're saying?'

'I know it seems stupid but it always felt so primitive to me. I just couldn't bring myself to do it.'

'Well, never mind. I'm sure your two are thriving anyway. It's just a matter of choice.'

'Why did you come home to have the baby, Margaret?'

Margaret thought about it. It was a question she had asked herself many times.

'Sometimes I wonder. I think I'd have been OK there. But Luis's mother persuaded me.'

'Did she?'

'Oh she didn't want rid of me. She's lovely. But she told me I'd be better off having my first baby where they spoke my own language.'

Fiona gazed at her. 'I suppose she was right. Is Luis' – she still found it hard to say his name – 'Is he coming over for the birth?'

'He certainly is. Unless the baby's very early. And it isn't looking that way at the moment.'

'Why doesn't he come and live over here?'

Margaret sighed. 'Why *on earth* would he want to do that? Besides – he couldn't, could he? Not now. Your lot put a stop to that.'

Margaret knew that Fiona had voted for Brexit. She supposed her sister-in-law had her reasons, but they seldom spoke about it. Their views were so diametrically opposed that it seemed safest to avoid the topic altogether.

'Well, I thought that was what they all wanted to do. Come over here, I mean. Freedom of movement. People taking jobs. Foreign waiters.'

'He isn't a waiter. Not that it would matter if he was, but he isn't. And he couldn't live and work here. Not without a lot of expense and bureaucracy.'

'But you can live there.'

'I have an Irish passport.'

'Surely now you're married, he could come too.'

'I don't think you understood what you were voting for. Have you seen the cost of spousal visas? Work permits? Being married makes no difference at all. It's my Irish passport that's the prize. Thank God for mum.'

Fiona shifted uncomfortably. She hadn't really known what she was voting for, if the truth be told. Hadn't expected that Britain really would become a 'third country' but for that, she blamed the unreasonable Europeans, deliberately making things difficult for Britain.

'I don't know how many times I have to tell you that he isn't a waiter.'

'Well, you know what I mean.'

'No I don't know what you mean. He's a fine musician. And a pretty good chef.' She enjoyed detailing his rather ill-assorted talents in this fashion, proud of him. 'He's about to buy his own restaurant. We are. The place has been in his family for years. His Uncle Paco and Aunt Carmen run it now. Their kids don't want it, but they've always wanted Luis to take over. We're going to live there and run it together. It's a good place to bring up a baby. Babies. Maybe I'll have another one, now that I've got started.'

'Better get this one out first. And what on earth do you know about running restaurants?' asked Fiona. 'I expect I know more than you do.'

'Well you can send me recipes then. Besides, Luis will be doing most of the cooking, not me. We'll need help, of course, but he's worked as a sous chef for long enough. I'm going to grow things. Well, they grow anyway, but his aunt has promised to teach me all I need to know. And then there's the marketing. They haven't even begun to tackle online marketing yet. I'll learn. Fiona, it's so lovely there. There's a citrus plantation too.'

'What about schooling? For the child?'

'He can go to a local school. Or she. He'll speak Spanish and English too, because I'll teach him. Or her. Whichever.' She patted her stomach affectionately. 'And what they don't teach him at school, I'll teach him at home. We'll manage,' she said. 'Besides – it's just a lovely place to have children. They like kids there. Make room for them in all kinds of ways. I love it.'

Fiona shook her head in disbelief.

'Listen,' said Margaret, seeing all this though Fiona's critical eyes, but lacking the energy for real argument. Besides, the cake had given her violent indigestion. 'Listen, Luis was born and brought up there. His family are not rich. Not at all. But he was bright, like his mother. She's a lovely woman. One of his sisters is a teacher. They're a wonderful family. And he's turned out just fine. He's a good man. I love him very much.'

Fiona put down her cup, pulled out a tissue and dabbed at her mouth, faintly embarrassed by this passionate declaration.

'Besides – there would be a kind of freedom for me there.'

'Freedom? Tied to that man?' said Fiona dramatically.

Margaret smiled. 'Sounds quite good to me at the moment. I've really been missing Luis. He can tie me down any time. Mind you, the bump might object.'

'Margaret!'

'Well, you are *daft*. If anything, I was beginning to feel more at risk here.'

'At risk?'

'Well, worried about walking alone at nights. And not just at nights. You can't let kids go to the park. Not like we used to.'

'We didn't go to the park much either. Besides, it must be the same there. It *is* the same there. Your Luis said that there were muggers everywhere. Gangs. Drugs.'

'I think it might be a bit different on La Gomera. Where we're going to live anyway.'

'But it would be the same in any small Scottish village, wouldn't it?'

'Maybe it would. But then there's the sunshine.'

'And besides, how long will it stay like that?'

'I don't know. Until the developers get their claws into the place. Oh but they like children there more than we do, you know? I may be idealising it. I probably am. But I think my child might have a few more years of real innocence there, and that would be very precious.'

'Well I'd like to see the statistics.'

'I don't care about the statistics. It's a difference in attitude. I've seen Luis meet friends with a new baby in a pram. He bends down and picks it up, talks to it. Would Ian do that? Would any man do that here without being afraid of being accused of something horrible?'

'Indeed he couldn't,' said Fiona. 'Just as well, if you ask me?'

'We're paranoid. It's not healthy. It's all so different over there, and honestly, it seems better.' She could see that Fiona remained unconvinced. 'I have to give it a try.'

'I suppose so,' said Fiona, doubtfully. She stood up. 'Come on,' she said. 'I think maybe we ought to get home. You must be tired.'

Margaret didn't tell Fiona that they had only delayed moving to La Gomera because of Luis's pride; that they could have bought the restaurant six months ago if he had agreed to use her money; that he had insisted on doing it himself, doing it the hard way, and so she had spent an uncomfortable summer in a small apartment in Los Cristianos. She didn't say any of this because she knew that Fiona would see it as sheer, foreign, bloody-mindedness. Ian generally did as he was told, always taking the easy way out. They were a happy enough couple, but she knew that Fiona would never understand Luis's fierce and occasionally arrogant independence. For her part, she loved in him precisely those qualities that could most irritate her. Besides, unlike Alastair, he never made less of her than she was, never denigrated her on the grounds that she was a woman. The outrageously macho pronouncements he occasionally made were mischievous rather than malicious, combined with an unerring instinct for what might be most infuriating, rather than from any firm convictions. He saw her as his equal in all possible ways. In those first few months of their marriage, they had begun to hammer out a kind of respect for each other.

Nevertheless, as the weeks progressed, Margaret was gradually drawn into her Scottish surroundings again, following a familiar routine. She began to see that both proverbs were true. Absence did make the heart grow fonder. When people asked about Luis she felt full of love for him. But pregnancy seemed to have numbed her brain and in this state, out of sight was indeed out of mind. It took her all her time and energy to function on a day to day level. She could not worry about the baby and worry about Luis at the same time.

'I'll probably go back to Tenerife six weeks after the birth,' she told Annie and Fiona. 'That should give me plenty of time to get into the way of looking after the baby. I don't think it's fair to leave Luis any longer than that, do you?'

Fiona glanced at Annie. 'We'll see,' she said. 'You may not be fit. And we'll have to see how Luis feels when he comes over here. We'd better just wait and see.'

CHAPTER THREE

This is the prettiest landing-place, port or bay, in the archipelago.
One comes on it suddenly, around a corner as it were. The bay is
horseshoe in shape. The town or village of San Sebastian is built on a
flat piece of land about half a mile broad, entirely surrounded by
mountains , except at the back where it contracts into a barranco,
twisting and narrowing until it is lost in the recesses of the mountains.

Olivia M Stone, 1887

Over the Christmas period, Luis drove his sister Cristina round to *La Manzana Dorada* where, if all went according to plan, he and Margaret and the baby would soon be living. Their uncle and aunt, Paco and Carmen, had bought their house in Vallehermoso and they were anxious to hand the restaurant over to their nephew, impatient for everything to be finalised.

Much as Luis enjoyed his sister's company he had missed Margaret badly. The feeling of loss wasn't so acute while he was working but whenever he stopped, longing for her presence swamped him. He remembered the last visit to the restaurant, remembered her sleeping in the shade of the garden, her arms curled protectively around the bump, and the sweet rosiness of her skin. His desire to see her was an ache in his heart. He could feel the reality of all the miles that lay between them.

'Do you miss her very much?' asked Cristina.

'Very much.' But he wouldn't discuss it and instead began to talk about his plans for the restaurant.

Cristina sighed. 'I do envy you,' she said. 'You've got so much going for you.'

He didn't know how to reply.

'Have you thought of moving to the mainland for a while?' he asked. He suggested this occasionally, but she never seemed to respond. Perhaps she was afraid of the change involved. Once she had wanted to go, but the family had thought her too young then.

'You could maybe get a transfer,' he suggested. 'From the bank. Look at what Margarita did. Moving here on her own.'

'I expect I could.'

'Don't you want to?'

'I don't know what I want, Luis.'

'I often wonder if the bank is the right place for you. Fashion. You like fashion, don't you?'

'Yes. I do. And art. And photography.'

'I could see you as – I don't know – a buyer in a store? Working in a gallery?'

'On these islands?'

'You could always go to the mainland.'

'I should have done that years ago. Now it's become quite hard. Sometimes just lately it's been like ...' she paused. 'I can remember when I was thirteen. The year I was thirteen. I couldn't sleep at nights. I wanted everything. And yet if you'd asked me, I couldn't say precisely what. I was so restless. I used to wish I'd been born a boy. There seemed to be so many more possibilities for boys. I used to wish I was you, Luis.'

'But not now, surely?'

'It was the freedom I wanted. I envied you that.'

It made him feel obscurely guilty. He put his arm around her slender shoulders and hugged her. He wasn't aware that he had ever excluded her from anything. Now he wanted to help her but didn't know how. Each time he saw her, she seemed increasingly restless, as though some idea were gnawing away inside her, but because she didn't quite know what was wrong herself, there was little he could do. Besides, his longing for his wife made him selfish. There was hardly any room for Cristina in his heart.

'I'll sort something out for myself,' she said. 'You should worry about your new family.'

He managed to video call his wife on Christmas Day. He had been trying to get through for hours, he said but the signal kept dropping out. The broadband was dodgy at the best of times and the images kept freezing. He was on La Gomera, spending some time with his mother and the rest of the family, but he would have to go back to Tenerife in a day or two because he had a gig. And cooking. There was always work. The sixth of January, the Epiphany, was the most important time for the children in San Sebastian, because that was when the three kings came to the village bearing gifts. Rather than risk sending parcels from Scotland, Margaret had gone onto Spanish Amazon and ordered toys for the younger children, Miguel and Marie Carmen, and a few more grown-up gifts for Domingo.

'I wish I was with you,' she said. Their first Christmas as a married couple and she was missing it.

'I would like to have been there for a Scottish New Year.

'It's not just as good as it used to be.'

'What will you do?'

'Not much. The family comes round for a bit. We'll see in the New Year. The bells, we call it. I might manage half a glass of bubbles, although I'll probably be asleep by midnight.'

Even the sound quality was bad. Usually he might have been standing next to her but today his voice was remote, with a strange bubbling echo, as though he were at the bottom of the sea. There were just too many other people trying to speak to their loved ones. She could almost hear the whispers out there, in the ether.

'I love you,' she said desperately and he said, 'I love you too, *mi corazon.*' There were tears in her eyes. She had to go into the bathroom and splash water on her face before she could rejoin the family for turkey and Christmas pudding. She picked at her dinner. The baby had left very little room for eating.

Margaret went into labour towards the end of February, exactly a week before she was due. Luis had booked his flight for that same day. He had left the number of the restaurant where he was working, in case his mobile was out of power or signal, and he had given Annie instructions to phone him or message him if anything began. Two days earlier Margaret had gone to the hospital for yet another check-up. The young doctor had felt her bump with chilly hands and said, 'I expect he'll want to keep you in,' referring to the consultant. 'You'll be induced if the baby doesn't come soon. We don't like leaving things too long at your ...' she stopped.

'You mean at my age?' asked Margaret, reflecting that this young woman had yet to learn the rudiments of tactful doctor-patient communications.

'Yes,' said the doctor, apologetically.

'I don't want an induction if I can possibly help it. It's there on my plan.'

'You'd better ask Mr Blake,' the doctor said, shrugging off the increasingly common problem of a mutinous older mother and moving on to the next cubicle.

When the consultant came round, Margaret immediately asked him, 'Can I go home?'

He felt her bump too, though his hands were much warmer, and listened to the baby's heartbeat. 'You may as well go home. There's nothing doing yet.'

Relieved, she had the plastic bangle cut off her wrist and telephoned for Ian to come and get her. It was a couple of days later that the first real twinges came. She had expected something that gradually increased in intensity; contractions that she would be able to time until they were a certain number of minutes apart. She had seen so many films and television programmes in which women would suddenly clutch at their stomachs and groan. But this began so mildly that you would hardly have noticed it. By evening, the pains were definite but still mild, still very erratic. She phoned her midwife who told her to make the journey to the maternity unit.

'Don't leave it any longer,' she warned Margaret. 'The weather's likely to turn bad in the night and you don't want to be stuck in labour at home with a first baby, do you?'

Margaret added a few things to her ready-prepared bag. She felt a mixture of excitement and fear. Annie was coming with her. She had tried messaging and phoning Luis, but it had gone straight to voicemail. Just as they were leaving, he called back. She heard him, clear and anxious, at the other end.

'Where are you?' she asked.

'Still in Tenerife. At the airport. But I'm coming. I'll be there as soon as I can. Margarita, are you alright?'

'I'll be fine. I'm going to hospital right now. Mum's coming too.'

She heard him swearing fluently in Spanish.

'I'm on my way. I'm on the last flight tonight. I'll be with you by morning. Can you hold on?'

She laughed. 'It isn't really a case of whether I can hold on. It's whether your offspring can wait a bit longer. This baby has got the hang of the foetal position and isn't going to leave in a hurry. And mum says it isn't usually very quick with a first baby.'

'Oh, *Madre de Dios*,' he said. 'Listen, I must go. Take care. I'm coming. I love you.' She heard the phone go dead, but still she held it, staring at it.

'I never told him I loved him,' she said, to nobody in particular.

Ian was standing in the hallway holding her case. Annie was fussing about in the kitchen, locking the back door, unplugging the kettle. She came through.

'That was Luis. He's on his way. He'll be here before morning.'

'How did he know?'

'He'd already got a flight booked. He didn't want to wait any longer.'

All the previous week, people had been asking her, 'When are you due?'

'Then he'll probably be here in time for the birth,' said Annie, relieved.

'Good!' Margaret got into the car, gritting her teeth.

'Is the pain very bad?' Ian asked.

'No. It isn't bad at all. I'm just terrified. Maybe we don't need to go just yet. Maybe I could stay at home for a bit longer.'

For once, Ian asserted himself. 'Christ,' he said. 'We're going right now and that's that.'

At the hospital she was admitted by a doctor who looked young enough to be her son. His extreme youth was embarrassing.

'I wonder what he's doing out without his mammy?' whispered Annie. The white cotton hospital gown was much too small for the average pregnant woman. Margaret wondered what misguided male spirit had dictated that gowns in a maternity hospital be made on such a minuscule scale and decided that reasons of economy had overridden considerations of modesty and even comfort.

'You probably are in labour' the doctor said. 'But there's not much happening yet so we'll send you to the ward for the rest of the night. Is your husband here?'

'He's flying from Tenerife. He should be here by morning.'

'Tenerife?' Obviously the young man associated the name only with holidays and stag parties.

'He's Spanish. We live there.'

He glanced at her name, blushed fiercely. 'Oh I see. Sorry!'

They sent Annie home with Ian. She had nobody. No familiar face.

The ward was half full of women who had been admitted early for one reason or another. She was the only one who was actually in the early stages of labour and they put her in a bed set a little apart, lest she should panic or upset the others. She refused a tablet to make her sleep, but regretted it later when she lay there in the dark, in fear and misery, the pains just acute enough to banish sleep, but not intense enough to give her the hope of a quick culmination. At about four in the morning, she was roused by a midwife putting a hand on her stomach so that she could feel the contractions. They had increased in intensity very gradually but now they were real pains rather than vague twinges.

'I think you might as well go downstairs now, dear.' The woman snapped off her stopwatch and ushered Margaret down in the lift to the delivery suite, carrying her bag for her. Each woman had her own cubicle with the machinery of the technical birth disguised as far as possible. Margaret realised that she had not eaten since the previous lunchtime and that her light-headedness was mainly due to hunger.

'I'd give anything for a cup of tea,' she said. 'Anything.'

'No tea,' they said, severely. 'No anything until after the baby's born.'

'How am I expected to do all this work with nothing to eat or drink?'

They smiled at her but didn't offer her any comfort, or any tea for that matter.

'Is your partner coming?' they asked again. 'Your birthing partner?'

'Yes. My husband. He's on his way. But he's coming all the way from Spain.'

'Does he work there?' They looked at her notes. 'Oh – is your husband Spanish, then? Will he want to be here for the birth?'

He's not a member of a different species, she thought, crossly.

'Yes. He'll manage. He speaks English. He was getting a late flight from the Canaries. He should be here any time now.'

Please God, she thought. Please God and Holy Mother Mary, let him get here soon. Don't leave me alone here without him. She sent a little prayer winging to the Virgin of Candelaria, thinking of the banked flowers and candles in the grotto there.

Afterwards she couldn't remember all that they did to her in preparation. The process itself had already taken possession of her mind and body, but she did remember that the experience was not a pleasant one. Not long after, her waters broke and she felt the fluid leave her body, warm and wet beneath her, felt the pool that had protected her child for so many months trickling inexorably out of her.

'Would you like to sit up?' they said. 'And walk about?'

They had told her earlier that she could give birth swinging from the ceiling if she so desired, but the long, sleepless, foodless night, the fear and pain had taken their toll on her. Now the sudden loss of the watery cushion thrust the baby's head directly against her pelvis and the pain of the next contraction, when it came almost immediately afterwards, would have made her cry out in agony if it had not taken her breath away first.

She sat down on the edge of the bed, feeling her head spinning, feeling the bitter vomit rising to her throat.

'No,' she said. 'No, I think I'd better just stay here.'

She remembered Maria's words, suddenly. 'You do not feel the pain, Margarita. It is you who *are* the pain.'

'You mean,' she said to the young midwife who was preparing to see her through the birth, 'you mean it gets worse than this?'

'Oh yes. Yes, I think so,' said the girl, hesitantly. How could she know? She was too young. She had never given birth. Her job was to keep Margaret cheerful, and keep her working. 'It'll be alright,' she said, comfortingly. 'We can give you something for it, you know.'

All Margaret's resolutions drained out of her with the fluid.

'There's gas and air,' the midwife told her brightly. 'Remember? You can take a breath of this and you'll feel better.'

The next ten hours were, in retrospect, a blur, a moment of time an eternity long. She was always given a choice, but by now she was in no condition to make it. The gas and air did not take away the pain: it simply lifted her mind to one remove from it so that she could see herself undergoing it. They persuaded her to have pethidine which took longer to work. In the end she begged them for it but it only added to her feeling of unreality and did little to relieve the pain.

Whatever they gave her, the pain was ultimately stronger. The pain overrode it all, seizing and shaking her body like some savage dog that would not let go. It was like no pain she had ever known. At some point Luis came in. She heard him say that his flight had been delayed. He had got a cab all the way from the airport. God knows what it must have cost him, she thought, and tried to say it, but he hushed her, bent down and kissed her.

She saw his face, dark and concerned above her, hovering like a face in a dream, saw his brown eyes fixed on hers and felt his cool, familiar hand on her forehead. He sat beside her, encouraging her, wiping her forehead, holding her hand, breathing with her. Although he too must have been exhausted after a night spent in airports and on planes, not to mention the journey from the airport through a strange city, he never once left her side for food or drink. Not while she was conscious, anyway.

She wrestled with the pain and even forgot about the baby, except when once, in the middle of her struggle with the black beast, she heard and instantly recognised tones of worry in their voices. The baby would not come. She was fighting and nothing was happening. She was too tired. She had begun by being tired. Doctors and nurses came and went and she heard Luis's voice raised in anger because he was terrified for their child and for his wife.

'Why are you not doing something?' he said. 'How much longer must she suffer like this?' She heard him at a distance as though none of it had anything much to do with her.

'We will. We will, just as soon as we can,' she heard the midwife say. 'Please calm down, Mr Herrera. We have to get things ready.'

She wanted to tell him to calm down too. 'It's OK,' she wanted to say, but she could hardly speak because her lips were dry and swollen and besides, it was all wrong. She knew that. The pain assaulted her again and wiped her mind clean of all that she had just heard.

Another midwife came into the room: small, fair, kindly. Took her hand, whispered to her, 'It'll be fine. Just hold on for a few more minutes and we'll be ready for you. It will be fine, I promise you.'

When she thought that she could stand no more and that she must just die and that death would be a fine thing, because it would mean no more pain, the experience changed. The child had descended to just precisely the point where she felt the urge to push, but still it could come no further. They ordered her not to push. She panted, restraining herself until she was exhausted. They gave her oxygen and stuck a glucose drip in her arm and again told her not to push. Luis, breathing with her, helped her to control herself but eventually even the breathing failed her and she just gave herself up to the successive convulsions as each contraction racked her lower body.

A doctor came in and seemed to be shouting at her, but perhaps he was just concerned, trying to get to her through the fog of pain and pethidine. She knew, as an animal knows without really understanding the words that are spoken, that they were worried about the child which they were now monitoring with electrodes on its head. 'We have to get this baby out, Mrs Herrera,' the doctor told her loudly and accusingly, as though it were something over which she had any kind of control.

'We're taking you to theatre,' said the fair haired midwife, close to her ear. 'We'll be able to give you an anaesthetic soon. It may have to be a section but the doctor will see if he can get the baby out with forceps if he possibly can. It will be fine. It will.'

She nodded dumbly. Luis was still gripping her hand. She lay flat now but was still racked by the uncontrollable thrusting of her body's efforts to rid itself of its torment. She felt herself being painfully trundled out of the room, into a lift. Green-coated figures surrounded her, loomed over her. Luis had gone. Where was he? She called out his name wildly and a face, strange though not unkindly, peered down at her. It was not her husband. Where was he? She had always been very frightened of anaesthetics but all she could wish for now was blissful unconsciousness. She felt her hands and arms being held still, although she did not feel a needle or a mask, so she could not tell how they anaesthetised her. The pain was too strong and overriding for her to be aware of anything except its sudden cessation. It was curious how the pain actually ceased before she lost consciousness, as though that part of her brain had shut down first. She felt the pain stop and had a second's calm and entirely blissful awareness of its absence before she also felt her breathing cease. She tried to say, 'I can't breathe,' tried to tell them, wondering if there was some mistake, before warm, beautiful blackness enveloped her. That must be what death was like. Not frightening at all.

A short time later she woke up to find Luis gently sponging her face. They were in a quiet room, with one empty bed over the other side. She lay for a while, gathering herself together, letting him tend her, her breathing coming very shallow, or so it seemed to her. Impossible to take a deep breath. She couldn't even try. It was hard to breathe properly although whatever she was doing right now seemed quite adequate to sustain life. After a while, her mind left her breathing.

'Luis?' she said.

'*Mi vida*?' He bent over her and kissed her lightly on the forehead, then sat back and carried on sponging. He looked calmer than he felt. He kept wanting to cry and tried desperately to get a grip on his emotions. It wouldn't do if he were to fall to pieces now. What was there to cry about? All was well.

'The baby. Luis?'

'A boy.'

'A boy?'

'Yes. A *very* big boy.' He could not contain the note of pride that crept into his voice, even though he knew he would have been just as happy with a very small girl. With any living baby safely in his arms.

She felt a vague surprise, nothing more. In her heart she had expected a girl. She didn't mind. The pain had gone. She could scarcely feel her body at all, which seemed a mercy. She was like a head, or rather a skull, placed casually atop some strange pulpy mass of flesh and blood that had very little to do with her.

'A boy?' she said again. Her tongue felt thick, too big for her mouth, an unwieldy organ. 'Is he alright?'

'Yes. Yes, he's fine.'

'Then where is he? Why isn't he here?'

'He's in the special care unit. It was a ...' he paused, trying to think of the words. 'It was with forceps, they said. You understand this? And so he is a little bruised and battered. That's all. They must take him to this unit for one night only to make sure he's fine. You will have him tomorrow. In fact, they said that later today you can go down and feed him if you like. The nurse said they will take you down in a wheelchair. To feed him.'

She found that she could not take all this in at one go. It was too much.

'Is he OK?' she asked again, disbelieving.

He smiled at last. 'Yes, yes. He is fine. I promise. But very big. I think the calculations must have been wrong. He is more than four and a half kilos.'

'Kilos?' she said.

He did some quick calculations. 'I mean – ah, God, what did they say? I mean nine and a half pounds. Why do they weigh Scottish babies in pounds as well?'

'Jesus,' she said. 'That's quite big.'

He took his phone out and showed her a picture. 'Here he is.'

She squinted at the picture, trying to focus her eyes, and saw a screwed-up sleeping face. It was frowning.

'There was a problem. He could not get out because the cord was around his shoulders, they said. Holding him back. And he is so big. That was the reason. That was the problem.'

'But is he OK? Is he?'

'*Si*, Margarita. I would not lie to you. I promise you, he is very well. Everything is fine they say, except that he has a black eye and he is bruised and has a little cut here, on his head. But no big damage. They all say that it will go in a few days and then he will be as beautiful as any baby.'

She looked at the picture again. 'He's already beautiful. But oh God, a black eye. So soon.'

'The world is a hard place.'

'I wish it wasn't.'

He sponged her face and hands again. She felt sensation, though not pain, gradually returning. She was warm and wet below and knew that there was blood down there. She could smell it. He gave her some water.

'Not too much,' he said.

'Tea. I'd give anything for a cup of tea.'

'Soon. Soon.'

They had dragged the baby out of her at four o'clock in the afternoon. Later that evening they sent Luis to the waiting room and washed and changed her, stripping off the bloody gown and sheet. She put on her own nightie, though she felt as though the smell of blood would never leave her.

'You can have a bath tomorrow,' they said. 'Lots of baths. You'll feel much better.'

Then Luis and a nurse wheeled her downstairs, the drip still in her arm, to the quiet, calm warmth of the special care unit where her son lay, huge amid the tiny premature babies, like a cuckoo in a nest. He looked like a diminutive prize fighter after a particularly bad bout and his little face was still screwed up tightly, his forehead creased in a frown. He seemed puzzled and aggrieved at the cruel fate which had so suddenly overtaken him after all his months of comfort. There was blood caked into his hair, since they had been very circumspect and careful in the washing of his battered body.

She was flooded with pity for him, for his bruised face, and she felt tears rush to her eyes as she took him on to her lap. She had expected him to feel fragile but instead she was immediately aware of his strength and warmth, like some enormously compact but powerful machine. She could sense the tremendous will for life, the fight in him, as though he was already eager to start growing.

It was very reassuring.

'He'll be rather drowsy from the anaesthetic,' said the sister, a pleasant middle aged woman. 'He's a big lad, so he'll be hungry too. Don't worry if he doesn't take too much the first time. There's plenty of time. Let him get the taste for it. That's all he needs. And he'll be thirsty. He's had a bad time, just like his poor mum.'

Awkwardly, Margaret exposed her breast to the baby.

'Just hold him gently and touch his cheek with the nipple,' said the sister. 'That's all you need to do. It isn't a bottle. You don't have to put it in his mouth. He'll find it for himself. He doesn't feed from the nipple. He feeds from the breast through the nipple.'

Miraculously, that was what he did, turning towards the nipple with his mouth wide open and fastening on it, his eyes fluttering drowsily, as though he had been waiting for nine long months for it, and then suckling.

'See how he loves it!' said Luis softly in her ear.

Always, afterwards, she remembered not so much the pain and outrage that went before, but this moment, in the calm atmosphere of the special care unit, remembered Luis standing behind her with his hands on her shoulders, watching as their son suckled at the breast for the first time. One side and then the other. Afterwards, he released the breast with a little sigh of repletion and contentment. And always, for as long as she lived, Margaret would remember the first sensation of the tiny, warm, insistent mouth tugging at her, an experience that was not sexual at all, but sensual, exclusively female and deeply satisfying too.

'Have you got a name for him?' the sister asked.

'Eduardo. Edward,' she said, looking up at Luis. They had not discussed it fully, but she knew that Luis loved the name. It was his father's name and he had loved his father very much.

'Eduardito,' said Luis.

Later, he told her that he had been standing close to the theatre entrance when they had wheeled her out. The drip had become detached from her arm and there was blood pouring from it. A nurse had come out to tell him that mother and baby would be fine.

'That is not how I would have described it,' he said. 'I thought you were dead. I thought that I had lost you for ever.'

'Not so easily,' she said. 'Oh no, my love. Not quite so easily as all that.'

CHAPTER FOUR

Sleep little one, because the bogeyman
and the Moorish woman are coming.
They are going from house to house
asking where is the child that is crying?

The love she felt for the child overwhelmed her. Her vulnerability through him was a new and disturbing emotion. Almost at a stroke she understood her own mother better than ever before. So this was what people meant when they said, warningly, 'It'll change your life'. They meant, but seldom said, something deeper and more momentous than the inconvenience of sleepless nights and dirty nappies. They meant the lifelong commitment of loving someone else much more than you loved yourself. Already she saw the lifetime's tightrope walk involved in balancing the loving and the letting go.

It was a terrifying prospect.

The baby's bruises were fast fading but his anxious frown was still there. He seemed very fair, with a fuzz of blonde fluff on top of his head. His eyes had been puffy and bruised at first but now that he could open them they were baby blue.

'They'll probably change,' she said to Luis. 'They'll probably go brown like yours.'

'But they might stay blue, like yours, and that would be good too!'

Because the birth had been so traumatic for mother and baby alike, Margaret spent longer in hospital than the regulation one or two days.

'What a pity,' said Annie, 'That they did away with the old maternity hospitals where they allowed you to recover for a few days. I'm sure it was much better for all concerned, you know. They looked after you.'

Luis hadn't told Margaret immediately, but one of the reasons for his delay in getting to the hospital was that, instead of telling the Border Force official that he was coming on holiday, to visit his wife's relatives, which would have been the sensible thing to do, he had, in his anxiety to get to the hospital as quickly as possible, mentioned her pregnancy and the imminent birth.

'Disaster!' he said. 'They started to question me about the wedding, and what was your nationality, and how long I planned to stay here! They kept telling me that I mustn't work, did I know that I mustn't do any work at all. *Por el amor de dios,* what did they think I wanted to do here other than see you, *los bastardos*?'

He had been almost weeping with frustration and panic, with his English deserting him, until a young female official, one who spoke Spanish, had stepped in, ascertained that his Scottish wife was in a Glasgow maternity unit and in labour at that very moment, stamped his passport and let him go with good wishes for a safe delivery.

A day or so after the birth, a young nurse came and gave the baby a bath, to demonstrate to Margaret how it was done. She was efficient and brisk and Eduardo howled his head off during the entire procedure, his face scarlet with outrage and indignation. Margaret found that she had to clench her fists to stop herself from punching the young nurse and snatching the baby to her breast.

When she told Luis, he said, 'Who is she? Point her out to me and I will go and deal with her!'

She didn't tell him, because in his present, precarious state of mind, he might have done just that. There was such a biological imperative about it all. She had surprised herself by the strength of her own feelings. It was wholly instinctive. She would have killed for this small person.

When she was due to go home, the midwife who had assisted her through most of her labour came in to admire the baby, and to wish her goodbye and good luck. 'You had us worried, I'll admit. We had several emergencies at the same time.'

'What about the other midwife. The one who came in later. Say goodbye to her for me, and thank her for me. She was very kind.'

'What other midwife?' she asked, puzzled. 'There was only me. Until the doctors had to get involved.'

'She was small and fair.'

'I don't think so.'

Afterwards, Margaret wondered whether she had managed to hallucinate a whole other midwife. Pethidine did strange things to your consciousness. Or had it, intriguingly, been a small visitation just when she needed help?

She would never know.

Luis stayed with Annie and they got on well together. He had wondered what she would think of him, wondered if she would be anything like Fiona, but when she hugged him, his heart had fairly gone out to her. She reminded him of his own mother, not least in that she kept two budgies called Joey and Bertie. They lived in a palatial cage, a budgie version of Versailles with plenty of mirrors, and she fussed over them with cuttlefish and millet.

Luis found that her affection for the birds was endearingly similar to that of Maria for her canaries, though he quickly realised that she was much less positive, less decided than his mother. She could be very vague, saying what she thought people wanted to hear rather than the truth. Not to rock the boat, not to cause any trouble, was Annie's chief aim in life, though she failed to notice than sometimes her over-anxiety to please could cause unnecessary complications. She would swither for hours between various courses of action, imagining all possible eventualities and finally begging other people to decide for her. She drank endless cups of tea and expected Luis to do the same. Out of politeness, he was forced to accept, although he longed for strong coffee.

That first evening after the birth of the baby, she took him home and cooked him a huge meal of steak pie and carrots and mashed potatoes, but he found it hard to eat anything at all. His insides were still in an emotional turmoil as he tried to force down a few mouthfuls.

'You're not going to manage all that, are you?' she asked finally, seeing him lay down his fork.

He shook his head, unable to speak for a moment. He struggled to calm himself.

'It's alright, son. All a bit much, eh?' She patted his hand.

He nodded, still speechless. She took the plate away from him, got up and went into the kitchen, bringing back a bottle of malt whisky with an unpronounceable name. She poured him a generous measure and a slightly smaller one for herself and then watched approvingly while he drank.

'Better?'

'Yes. Thank you.'

The whisky on an empty stomach made his head swim, but it was preferable to the feeling of panic, the tears that had threatened to engulf him.

'It isn't very easy to watch somebody else in pain, is it? Somebody you love.'

'Especially not when you are the cause of it.'

'She'll forget it very quickly, you know. Mothers do.'

'I won't forget. I won't forget any of it.'

'No. Well, that's one of the penalties of fatherhood!'

She sat down opposite him, topped up his glass, sipped her own whisky and gazed at him.

'I can't believe you're finally here. I had this picture of you in my mind. You don't really match it.'

'Am I better or worse?'

'Oh much better. But then, I was hearing about you from Fiona.'

'That explains a lot.' He pulled a face. Couldn't help it.

'I know. My daughter-in-law can be a bit difficult. One of my late husband's uncles went off to fight in your Civil War, you know,' she continued, after a pause.

'He did?'

'I never knew him of course. A whole other generation. George was his name. He was the eldest in that family. I was born in Ireland, as you know, but my father was from Glasgow originally. He was working over in Mayo when he met my mother and they married there.'

'I see.' Luis realised that there was a lot he still didn't know about Margaret, not least the intricacies of families that moved around, the way his own had not, had stayed in one beloved place, except for himself, and even he was planning to go back.

'My mother-in-law said George was full of ideas. Full of dreams. She said she went to the station to see him off. She was very fond of him. She was just a wee lass so she got a good telling off from her mammy when she got home. They lived in a tenement just off the Maryhill Road. Her dad worked on the railways. She wasn't even supposed to be out. They had been hunting all over for her.' She shook her head, thinking about her mother-in-law and how daring she had been. But then her own mother had been a formidable woman too. Mayo born but coming, as a young mother, to a Scottish city that was still less than welcoming to Irish Catholics. There were Orange Marches every year even now. Flutes and drums. Thinly veiled hostility disguised as tradition. In some cases, not veiled at all. Woe betide the unwary visitor who attempted to cross in front of the parade.

'What happened to him? Your uncle George?'

'He died. He never came back. He must be buried out there

somewhere. I often thought of going to see, but I never had the money and it was a long way to go. I expect it would have settled itself one way or another whether he'd gone or not. Don't you think so?'

'Eventually,' said Luis. Cousins of his grandfather had died too, in Granada. Many people, relatives and friends, had left his islands for South America. He had a sudden and oppressive sense of the past of his country and, hard on its heels, a wave of homesickness. This was foolish, he thought. He had only just left. And they would be going back quite soon, wouldn't they?

His first glimpse of Glasgow had been from inside a big black taxi on his way to the hospital, with raindrops sliding down the window and his own fatigue humming inside his head. He had left his bags with the hospital porter, too preoccupied to notice the man's bemused expression at the sight of an expectant father clutching a guitar as well as the more normal suitcase. He had borrowed a less valuable guitar from Paco for the journey, reluctant to go anywhere without an instrument, but reluctant to trust his most precious possession to the less-than-tender mercies of baggage handlers. He had left his best guitar with his mother in San Sebastian, happy to do so, as a promise that they would soon return.

When he first stepped outside, the chill dampness of the air had shocked him, but when everything was over and he had seen Margaret and his son settled down for the night, Annie's welcome gave him a sense of relief. Her brick built house with its thick carpets and warm colours was homely and comfortable.

Later that night Ian and Fiona arrived bearing a bottle of Cava, 'to wet the baby's head' they said. But it was an embarrassing party. Ian was diffident, Fiona scarcely addressed two words to him and Annie mediated anxiously between them. He would happily have ignored his in-laws and taken himself off to bed, but he found Annie's discomfort upsetting and mentally cursed Fiona for causing it. He was relieved when they left, wanting only to sleep. He lay beneath the comfortable warmth of a lavender-scented quilt in the guest bedroom, and thought about Margaret and Eduardo for a little while, but within minutes he was fast asleep.

A couple of days later, they brought the baby home. Fiona and Ian had lent them their cot with a new mattress. The weather had turned mild and in the late afternoon, Luis proudly took Eduardo out in his new blue pram, a generous present from Annie, while Margaret sat drinking tea with her mother.

'Well?' said Margaret. 'What do you think?'

'I like him. He's very polite. You've got a good man there, Margaret.'

'I know,' said Margaret. 'And a good man is hard to find!'

She burst into tears. Melancholy engulfed her. All day long there had been visitors bearing gifts of flowers and small garments, fluffy toys and chocolates. They were visitors who, on the whole, had vastly outstayed their welcome. She wished it was just herself and Luis, alone together with the baby. She needed time to get to know her son. To come to terms with the awful responsibility of this small life, suddenly entrusted to her. How could they ever keep him safe?

Annie went over and put her arms around her daughter. 'It'll get better,' she said. 'Don't worry. It's just baby blues, that's all.'

'Are you sure.'

'It's normal. It'll get better. I promise.'

Luis pushed his precious carriage through puddles, leaning over from time to time to make sure that the small cocoon inside was still breathing, or inserting his hand beneath the covers to feel whether Eduardo was warm enough. He noted with a certain amount of dis-satisfaction that the new pram had squeaky wheels. He made a mental note to buy some oil. Or to ask Annie if she had any. The wind, heavy with moisture, made him shiver. The stone houses lowered over him. Children ran past him, teenage boys released from school.

'Ya fuckin' bastard!' shouted one, almost in his ear.

He whirled around, shocked by the violence of the language, but saw that the boy was already racing on, hitting out at his companion with a schoolbag full of books. The insult had been intended for the other boy, not himself.

My son must not grow up in this place, he thought.

He tucked the blanket closer around his baby and turned for home.

Eduardo didn't object to the visitors' handling of him, but that night he objected to going to sleep at all. He wanted to feed or at least suckle at the breast all night long. Nearly blind and dumb with fatigue, she sat on the bed wondering what to do with him, but every time she tentatively edged him from her breast, the unbearable wailing began again.

'Can't we keep him in bed with us?' asked Luis.

'I don't think we're supposed to do that. We might lie on him.'

'You've read too many books. Too many experts who know nothing about babies.'

Maybe she had. Fiona had given her a new baby advice book or sent her a link to a website every week. There was so much to be afraid of. So much she didn't know. So much that she wished she hadn't found out about. Weird genetic diseases that she was fairly sure her mother would have neither known nor cared about.

'Listen. I know about children. Babies. Lots of babies in my family. Neither of us is drunk and he is quite a big boy and I think we would be very much aware of him.'

'I can't risk it. I'm so tired. I *feel* drunk.'

Luis didn't argue, seeing that she was on the verge of tears again. He went back to sleep, snoring a little. She thought it very hard and unfeeling of him, but he was tired and overwrought as well. Somebody needed to sleep if they were to cope with the baby during the day. She put Eduardo back in his crib and he dozed for half an hour or so. But at the end of that time, just as she was falling asleep herself, he woke again with a start and began to cry. Luis woke as well.

'Why didn't he do this in the hospital?' she asked.

'He's hungry.' Luis turned over and yawned.

'But he can't be. He's only been fed half an hour ago.'

'Well he wants more. Or he wants comforting. Or his stomach is sore.'

'But how do we know what he needs?'

'Margarita!' he said, sitting up. 'Listen to me. I can remember watching my sisters with their children. If they had to be fed they just fed them. They did not go by any clocks. I think they feed like this to make you make more milk. Do you understand me?'

'Yes. They said that at the clinic. Bringing in more milk.'

'He's a little animal and he's hungry for your milk or if not that, for the comfort it brings and he wants to be close to you, to the smell of you, your heartbeat. Like any animal. That's what he is. A young animal. Bring him into bed, *por el amor de Cristo!*'

She sat up in her new lacy maternity nightie and stared at him, her face a wretched mask of fatigue. Her obvious distress touched him more than he could say.

'*Querida*, bring him into bed,' he repeated more gently.

At last she gave in and at about four o'clock in the morning she and the child fell fast asleep, propped up together on a mound of pillows, his mouth still at her breast. Luis lay a little apart, watching them, dozing intermittently, always aware of mother and baby beside him, always aware of their safety. When Eduardo finally woke up at seven o'clock, she fed him again and changed him, refreshed even by her few hours of sleep. Luis brought her tea and toast and she realised that she was famished. She still hadn't managed to achieve any sort of routine with the nappies or baby clothes. Nothing was organised and Luis ran about the room, gathering up necessities for her. Superstitiously she had prepared as little as possible beforehand.

'It's a touch of colic,' said her mother. 'It usually comes in the evening if they're going to get it. Luis and I will take him once you've fed him and you can get some proper sleep. He'll be fine during the day.'

'Colic? I read that breastfed babies don't get colic.'

'Perhaps he has not read the books yet,' said Luis, drily.

Margaret managed a faint smile.

'It only goes on for about three or four months,' said Annie, comfortingly. 'Ian had it, I remember. You didn't but he did.'

'Three or four months?' she said, in disbelief. 'My God, that sounds like a whole lifetime.'

CHAPTER FIVE

I leaned against a green pine tree
to see if it would console me
and since the pine tree was green,
it cried when it saw me crying.

Margaret couldn't stop crying. A glance from Luis, the baby's crying, a kind remark from a friend, a sentimental song on the radio, any of these was enough to turn on a waterfall of tears. News stories or even charity adverts about suffering children were the worst. Luis tried to reassure her. It had rained ever since the birth of the baby. Luis sometimes felt as though he were drowning in the indoor and outdoor torrents.

'Never mind,' he said, with an attempt at cheerfulness. 'It'll be much better when we go back to the island. You'll feel much better in the sunshine.'

Margaret gazed at him. 'I suppose so,' she said, tremulously.

On a day when the sun never seemed to rise, and the sky was the same uniform grey, he went out for a trudge through the rainy streets. It had been like this for days. Left alone with her daughter, Annie asked cautiously, 'Don't you want to go back to Tenerife? You would tell me, wouldn't you? If you didn't want to go?'

Margaret shook her head. 'It'll be fine.'

'It's just, when Luis mentions it you seem upset. I wouldn't like you doing anything you don't want to do, just because you think you should.'

'You're a fine one to talk, mum.'

'That's why I know what I'm talking about. I've done too much in my life just to please other people.'

'I don't know,' said Margaret. 'I don't know what I want any more. I'm frightened. I never knew I'd be so frightened *for* the baby. I'm floundering about here. He just assumes we're going back. I want to go. I do. But I feel so ill. My stitches are so sore.'

Annie tried to comfort her but she wasn't sure what to suggest. For lack of any better confidante, she turned to Fiona. The following morning was a Saturday and Annie arranged to meet her daughter-in-law in a suburban cafe where, over the usual flat whites and scones, they had a long and intense conversation.

That night Fiona tackled Ian. She often used the period between getting into bed and falling asleep to browbeat her husband. Ian would be rather tired, longing for silence and feeling oddly vulnerable in his pyjamas and without his glasses. She found that she could usually get him to agree to almost anything in this state.

'It's a sin,' she said, decidedly.

'What is?' Ian asked, clenching his fists under the duvet. He recognised her tone of voice.

'Your sister. Your mother said she's been crying on and off ever since she came home from the hospital.'

'Doesn't that often happen? Baby blues. You had them, didn't you?'

'I wasn't planning to uproot myself and travel to a desert island. That's the difference.'

'If that's what she wants to do there's no way I can stop her. I've tried. Besides, I don't think it's a *desert* island, do you? Quite the opposite, really, from what I've heard.'

'Do you really think she wants to go away?'

Ian turned over onto his back, sighing. Sleep had deserted him. Fiona was sitting up against her pillows, staring into the darkness.

'You don't mean to tell me she's changed her mind?'

'Probably not. But she doesn't want to go just now, that's the point. She needs time with her family. It was a bad birth. She needs time to get over it physically and mentally.'

Ian yawned widely. 'Let them sort it out between them. If she wants to stay on here for a few more weeks, why shouldn't she? I'm sure Luis wouldn't object too much. I don't see where the problem is.'

'She's like your mother. She'll be so afraid of hurting his feelings that she'll never tell him that she doesn't want to go back right away. I think it's up to you.'

Ian felt himself grow hot with fright.

'Me?' he asked, his voice rising a full octave. He couldn't begin to imagine how Luis might react to yet more interference in what he would rightly consider to be his own and his wife's business. 'Do I have to?' he said, plaintively.

'You do,' said Fiona. 'You'll just have to tell him how miserable she is at the moment. After all, you're a man, aren't you?'

'What has that got to do with anything?'

'Don't be daft. You can have a man-to-man talk. We'll take him to the Burrell. Or Kelvingrove. He should see some of our museums anyway.'

With the matter apparently settled to her satisfaction, Fiona turned over and went to sleep. Ian lay awake for hours, wondering what on earth he could say to Luis and exploring possibilities in his mind.

All of them banished sleep.

The truth was that Margaret, full of post-natal melancholy, felt physically and mentally reluctant to contemplate the upheaval of a journey to La Gomera just yet, with all the demands on her that such a change would make. What had, before the birth, seemed an exhilarating prospect, now filled her with gloomy forebodings. After that first apprehension of his strength, she now saw the baby as acutely vulnerable. What if he became ill and she couldn't reach a doctor quickly enough? Glasgow at least offered the reassurance of familiarity. The thought of confiding her doubts to Luis, who would immediately and forcefully try to dispel them, seemed impossible. She knew that he wanted to go home. She knew that he disliked the city, tolerating it only for her sake. She thought that he genuinely liked Annie, but could see from the occasional wry twist of his mouth that the rest of them could go hang as far as he was concerned. She loved him and wanted to please him. She still wanted to be on La Gomera, but to be spirited away there, without all the bother of the journey beforehand. The baby and his endless needs filled her mind to the exclusion of everything else. She wasn't thinking straight at all. She knew it but could do nothing to remedy it. She felt torn between her husband and her son.

On Sunday, Fiona and Ian took Luis to the newly reopened Burrell Collection.

'You can't come all this way and not see anything of our culture,' Fiona remarked, rather patronisingly he thought.

He was reluctant to leave Margaret even for a day, because he was beginning to think that he must go back to Tenerife quite soon, and then to La Gomera to get things ready for her and the baby, leaving her to follow on after. She talked him into the trip. She had a sudden desire to spend a day alone with her mother and son, dozing on the sofa, feeding him when he wanted and eating chocolate, telling herself that it was for the sake of her milk, although she had a strong suspicion that the chocolate kept the baby awake.

'Listen, I think it's a good idea,' she said to him. 'You could do with a break. Go on. You'll enjoy it.'

Luis tried very hard to enjoy it. He was genuinely enthusiastic about the collection of so many varied objects and artworks, but he would rather have come with his wife, rather have enthused and laughed and discussed them with her. Instead he marched along morosely after Fiona and Ian who had very definite ideas about how such things should be viewed. They had, thought Luis, all the right words but none of the right emotions. He began to feel very weary and at last stopped in front of a canvas called The Sisters. A girl stood among grasses and flowers holding a child in her arms. Something in the shape of her face reminded him of his sister Cristina and he was overwhelmed with a feeling of nostalgia for his island and for his family. It was so strong that when Fiona came up beside him he didn't notice her at all until she spoke. She made him jump.

'Such a dreamlike quality about this, don't you think?' she said. 'Matthijs Maris. The Hague school.'

She had attended a lecture here with Margaret, many years ago, and this painting had been mentioned.

'Que?' he asked, unthinkingly.

'Matthijs Maris. The painter.'

'I was thinking of my sister. My younger sister, Cristina.'

'Oh I see.' She seemed rather disappointed, as though she had been anticipating giving him a lecture on Dutch art in general and the Hague school in particular.

If I was at home, thought Luis, I would be able to take the baby and show him to all my family and friends. They would want to come and see him and they'd be delighted, not like this family, so reserved and cautious about physical display. All the children too ... they'd bring presents. I could take Margarita and the baby to see Paco and Carmen. I could play my guitar for him. My best guitar. I miss it so much.

As he thought this, he had a terrible sense of foreboding. Would they ever live there all together? It seemed so far away now, even to Luis, like a place in a dream, a mirage.

They had lunch in the museum cafe where Luis fortified himself with strong coffee, and then walked through the wintry gardens where a thin sunshine filtered down between the naked branches. For once it had stopped raining but it was very cold. Luis watched his own breath, deliberately puffing it out like a child. He caught Ian giving him a bemused sidelong glance, and grinned.

'I'm not used to seeing my breath like this. Well, sometimes up in the mountains. We sometimes have snow on Teide, you know.'

He felt rather foolish and had an inkling of how crushed his wife must feel under the combined weight of common sense of her brother and sister-in-law.

'This hasn't been such a bad winter. Spring's just around the corner now. Almost here. Look – there are snowdrops. And the crocuses are coming out.'

He saw Fiona come up behind Ian and give him a quick, furtive dig in the back, as though to say, 'Get on with it.' Then she turned aside.

'Snowdrops,' she said. 'I want some photographs. Why don't you two just have a seat here for a minute or two. I won't be long.' She gestured at a wooden bench and headed off along the pathway, getting her phone out of her bag as she went.

The two men sat side by side on the damp bench. Piles, thought Ian. This is how you get piles. That's what his Irish grandmother used to say, anyway. Could it be true? He cleared his throat. 'Luis, can I ask you something?'

Luis shrugged, stretched out his long legs. 'Sure. Anything. You're my family now, and you can ask me anything.'

This didn't seem to make Ian any more comfortable with what he had to say, but he persevered.

'Luis, would you consider staying on here for a little while instead of going back to Tenerife immediately?'

Luis had known what was coming. He felt no real surprise. Only renewed misgivings.

'Why? Why should I do that? Margarita will be following on in a few weeks with the baby.'

'But that's the point, Luis. I don't think Margaret is ready to go just yet. And I really don't think she can do without you, you know.'

'Has she said this to you?'

Ian hesitated. 'No. But I think she might have said something to her mum.'

'She has said nothing to me.'

'But she knows that you're so set on going back immediately. I think she doesn't want to mention it to you.'

'Are you saying that she's afraid to speak to me?'

'No. Of course not. That isn't what I mean at all.'

Luis always had that little tremor of insecurity where his wife was concerned, no matter how confident he might appear. He could never quite believe that she told him all that she was thinking and feeling. She was quite capable of hiding the fact that she didn't want to go back to La Gomera. Not so soon, anyway. Doubt, an unfamiliar emotion, invaded his mind. Perhaps he had rushed her into the decision to buy the restaurant. He had simply presented her with his plans and then expected her to fall in with them. He thought despondently that the person he had loved and married back home seemed quite different from the woman who now sat for hours, clutching the baby in her arms, with her face closed and shuttered, save when she gazed down into those tiny features. Where was his Margarita, he wondered, full of innocence and adventure? Was it just the after-effects of an extremely difficult birth, or had the city itself enclosed her, paralysed her with its own peculiar air of Scottish restraint?

'She's settled back in nicely,' Ian was continuing. 'The baby's very young. I'm not saying she won't want to go with you later, because I'm sure she will, but a woman needs her family when she's got a young baby. She doesn't want to be stuck on some wee island where she hardly speaks the language.'

'She's learning the language,' Luis said, defensively.

'But it isn't easy, you'll admit.'

'And what am I supposed to do here?'

Ian was so busy remembering the words Fiona had put into his mouth that the question threw him. They had not thought about what Luis would do. 'Perhaps you could get seasonal work. There are plenty of hotels.'

'Hotels?'

'Well you're a ... a chef, aren't you?'

'I can cook, it's true. But I can't work here, Ian. Do you not understand that?'

Ian looked genuinely astonished. Luis was so exasperated that he wanted to take him by the shoulders and shake him. He sighed. 'Ian, tell me. Did you by any chance vote for your Brexit?'

Ian coloured. 'Well, I did. So did Fiona. We both thought that the EU was assuming too much power. My mother and Maggie were very cross about it. We had to stop discussing it or we'd have had a terrible row. As it was, there was a bit of bad feeling about it.'

'I think there will be more bad feeling now. With me in your family.'

'But surely, Luis, now that you're married, you *would* be able to live and work here. Wouldn't you?'

'No. I wouldn't. That's what this is all about, isn't it Ian?'

'What? I don't understand.'

'You thought I married your sister so that I could get permission to live and work here, didn't you?'

'No. Of course not.'

But that was exactly what Fiona had thought, right from the start. She had said as much. 'I don't trust his motives. He wants to move here. He thinks marriage will make it easier for him. I've seen all those programmes about romance scams.'

Luis sighed, beyond anger now. 'Ian, just how easy do you think it is for a foreigner like me to get the right to live and work here, married or not?'

'Well – easier now that you're married.'

Luis shook his head. 'You don't know what you're talking about. I can come here on holiday for up to six months. No more than that.'

'Six months?'

'That's it. But I can't work. Not really. You should look at your government's website some time. It's deliberately *oscuro*. I could come if I was very rich. Buy my way in. I can come if I want to set up a business. I can do that sort of thing. Meetings, conferences and so on. I've looked. But not ordinary paid work. I can't even do *unpaid* work. *Nada*. Nothing. In case I take one of your precious British jobs.' He couldn't keep the bitterness out of his tone.

'But surely there's such a thing as a spousal visa.'

'There is. But to get one, I have to want to stay here permanently – which I don't. We don't. God forbid that I should be stuck here forever. I have to prove that I'm going to be earning good money. That I have resources. Which I suppose I do, but I'm not about to bring them over here. Why would I? I would have to pay almost £2000 to your government for something that might be turned down, and in any case will last around two years and then I'll have to apply for another one and pay all over again. Oh, and do a language test as well. But I don't want to live here! Fuck that, Ian. And fuck your Brexit while you're at it.'

Ian had never seen him so angry. He didn't know what to say. He had never even considered that Luis might have problems living and working in Scotland, now that he and Margaret were married.

'I didn't know,' was all he could say. 'Are you sure?'

'*Por supuesto! Estoy seguro.* Of course I'm sure Do you think that we haven't talked about all this? Margarita and I? Because we are both EU citizens, it is so much easier, so much better if she comes back with me. There was never any question of us living here, of my working here. I don't think I would ever earn enough to work here.'

'Oh you would if you ran your own business!'

'Can't you understand, Ian? *I don't want to.* What kind of fool would want to live and work here when we have a good business on a beautiful island?'

Fiona came up cheerfully behind them.

'Is that all settled then?' she asked. 'Shall we go back to the car now?'

'Nothing is settled,' said Luis, abruptly. 'Maybe it never will be.'

Ian remained silent. He had a sudden urge to take out his phone, look up rules and regulations. But he would have to wait. Besides, it struck him that Luis must be right.

'Let's go back,' said Luis. 'I want to see my son. And my wife.'

They headed back to the car. Luis drew dark brows into a frown and thrust his hands deep into the pockets of his jacket. Ian hunched his shoulders and rolled his eyes at Fiona. He wished now that she had never persuaded him to speak. Even as he said them, he had doubted not just the wisdom, but the truth of his words. Fiona had been adamant that Margaret wanted to stay in Scotland, but did she? He had never felt that he really understood his sister, and he thought her choice of husbands suspect, to say the least, but he loved her very much indeed and would never willingly have done anything to hurt her. Perhaps he should have left well alone.

Back at the house, Luis managed to corner Annie for a brief moment while Margaret was changing the baby in the bedroom. 'Is this true?' he asked her. 'Is it true that my wife doesn't want to come back to La Gomera with me?'

'Is this Fiona?' she asked.

'No. Ian. But Fiona told him what to say.'

She quailed a little before his gravity. He always seemed such a passionate man. Although she could see that he was gentle too. Just more emotional, more volatile than anyone she had ever known. The way she thought about it was that he had no dimmer switch. He was either very happy or very sad. And now he looked very hurt. Her heart went out to him. What could she say to make it easier?

'I'm not sure,' she said. 'I mean, she definitely does want to go to your island. She clearly loves the place. I think she just might want to take a bit more time about the move. A few more weeks perhaps.

That's all.' She was peeling potatoes in the sink and she bent her head carefully to her task. 'But what do I know? I think you have to talk to her, Luis. All I know is that she's quite sad right now.'

'I can see that.'

'But that's normal after a difficult birth. I really think you have to talk to her about all this yourself. Don't just listen to what other people are saying.'

At dinner, Margaret noticed that Luis seemed unusually subdued but she put it down to a whole day spent with Fiona and Ian. Annie insisted on clearing up, leaving them alone together in the sitting room, with Eduardo kicking on a blanket on the floor.

'Did you enjoy it?' she asked him, with a spark of her natural enthusiasm. 'I like the Chinese pottery best. I find it so soothing for some reason.'

'Yes,' he said, preoccupied. 'Yes, it was very beautiful.' He bent down to Eduardo and touched the small face with a gentle finger. 'How has he been? Our son?'

'He's just lovely. So alert.'

'You've been here before,' one of the nurses had said, smiling down at him.

'And you? What about you, Margarita?'

'I'm fine too. Better, anyway. What are you looking at me like that for?'

'No reason, *querida*.'

He ran his hand gently down her cheek, cupped her chin and turned her face up so that she was looking at him. 'Just so long as you are fine and the baby is well, that's all.'

A few nights later, Mrs Sinclair went out to a Women's Guild meeting and for once they were alone in the house. Luis had discovered that his guitar music, in particular a trio of sweet Venezuelan waltzes, could soothe the baby to sleep. He was glad of his decision to bring an instrument with him, even if it wasn't his most precious guitar. Once Eduardo had settled down, they watched television in silence for a while: an American crime drama. Luis found it hard to follow the convoluted story and the unfamiliar English.

At last he ventured, 'What would you say if I suggested going back home right away? Now. Well, as soon as we can get a flight.'

She stared at him in dismay. 'But we have to wait for the baby to have his check-up. You know that. Three more weeks. And I'm not really fit to travel yet. You don't know how painful it is!'

He saw tears starting in her eyes and knew how a trapped animal must feel, though the bars of his cage were constructed of love: love for his wife, love for his son.

'Don't cry,' he said. 'I can't bear it if you cry. It was just a thought. Nothing more. Would you rather stay on for a while?'

On the television a young man was being ruthlessly gunned down.

'I think I would,' she said. He saw the unmistakable relief in her face and with it his last hope left him.

'Just for a few more weeks,' she said, anxiously. 'You won't go back without me, will you? You have six months!'

'Would you rather I stayed?'

'Of course! In fact to tell you the truth, I can't bear to be without you.'

'Then I won't go back until you're ready. We'll stay on here for a while.'

'It'll only be for a little while. Till I feel better. Till I feel ready to travel. Just a couple of months.' The tears spilled over again.

'You'll soon get over it,' the nurse practitioner had told her, but even that had been the obligatory telephone appointment. Why did it make her feel as though her whole world was falling apart? Luis looked at her helplessly, then put his arms around her, pulling her head down on to his shoulder. What else could he do but go along with whatever she wanted?

Had he pressed the point, she might have told him that no, of course she didn't want to stay in Scotland for good, but that she was fearful of surrendering her precious child not just to his island, but to the overwhelming fondness of his family. Much as she loved Maria and Cristina and the others, Fiona and Ian's cautions had in some small way found their mark. Her present state of mind magnified even small doubts into huge and seemingly insurmountable problems. A sensible part of her knew that she was exaggerating everything, but she seemed powerless to help herself right now.

'Do you still love me?' she asked.

'Mother of God! What can you mean by this?'

'It can't have been very pretty. It was all so violent. So undignified.'

'No, it was not pretty. I never expected it to be pretty. Jesus, Margarita, I thought you were going to die. I thought I would lose you. Both of you. That was all I could care about. I thought that you were going to die!' He held her face between his palms again and looked into her troubled eyes. 'I love you. What more can I say?'

'I shouldn't have had the baby.'

'What are you saying now?'

'I was mad to have the baby.'

She saw the days stretching out before her, an endless sequence of days taken up with the child, an endless sequence of sleepless nights. She could not foresee a time when he would not have colic; when he would not be glued to her breast, suckling there for hours on end; when she would ever be able to read a book or even a newspaper from cover to cover without interruption.

'How could I have done this to you?' she said. 'Oh, God, and it's all my fault.'

She could not foresee a time when the dull misery of the pain where they had cut her deeply would not gnaw into her. The stitches had come adrift and were infected. Sitting and standing were equally painful. She carried a cushion about with her. How could she ever bear to make love again? Nobody had told her it would be like this: this intense fear for her child that seized her so that she would continually rest her hand on his sleeping form to feel the quiet rise and fall of his breathing. The visceral horror of every news item about cruelty to children, starving children, children affected by war. It was like being mother to the whole world. Nothing would ever be the same.

'What is your fault?' he asked, bewildered. 'What have you done?'

'The baby. I just went ahead and had the baby, didn't I?'

'You didn't do it all by yourself, did you? I had something to do with it. Besides, I told you that I wanted children.'

'We never really talked about it properly. We had no time to talk about it. We did everything in such a hurry.'

'You mean we married in a hurry. And you're sorry now?'

'No,' she said. 'I'm not sorry. I love you. I just didn't know about all this, about all these feelings! I don't know what to do with all these feelings!'

He held her close and soothed her as he soothed the baby, patting her back, rocking her backwards and forwards. At last he felt her relax against him and knew that she had fallen asleep. He laid her down with a cushion under her head and a blanket over her, then went and poured himself a large whisky and stood by the window, cradling the glass in his hands, sipping the comforting liquid and staring out into the suburban street, bathed now in the light of tall lamps that seemed to milk all colour from their surroundings, making them one livid yellow. He tried to put himself in his wife's place, seeing the street as she must see it, its very familiarity endearing. All her family and friends were here. All her memories were here. It would be odd if she didn't love the place. It was a love that had lain dormant, hidden beneath her overwhelming passion for himself and his island, only to reassert itself now when she was at her most vulnerable.

To own and run the restaurant has become his great dream, but that had been before he met Margaret, and since their marriage he had entertained his own vague doubts about how she would cope with life on the island. On La Gomera her obvious enthusiasm had enabled him to push any misgivings aside. Now her family had helped to resurrect those doubts. He should never have let her come home to have the baby, he thought, but how could he have stopped her? She was her own woman, after all. How could he dictate what she could and couldn't do? He sighed, refilled his glass, switched on the television again and sat down beside his sleeping wife.

In the end he simply decided to let things ride, to stay on for a while and see how things went. After all, what difference would a few more weeks or even months make? Even if he wasn't allowed to work. He wasn't used to staying at home but there was plenty to do with the baby.

I might as well give it a try, he thought, bleakly. What else can I do? I can't go back and leave her or the baby in this state. I'll just have to give it a try.

CHAPTER SIX

He who plays the guitar
removes strings, replaces strings.
But they are not strings.
They are the ribbons with which
he ties my heart.

March had come in like the proverbial lion and chilly daffodil stalks began to tremble on the suburban verges, lending a spurious cheer to the grey, chewing gum littered streets. It went out like a lion too. The daffodils were looking ragged, but the ornamental cherries were beginning to bloom and the municipal flower beds were full of tulips, shivering in the cold. Just before Easter, they had a call from the elderly owners of the Los Cristianos apartment, asking them if they still wanted the use of it through the coming summer, because if not, their son and daughter-in-law would be interested in staying in it for a few weeks. They were Annie's friends who had retired to Stirling, but had wanted to keep the Tenerife apartment in the family.

'Do we want it, Luis?' Margaret asked him. 'I expect we'll be going straight to La Gomera now, won't we? And they've already been so generous.'

He nodded, still unsure of what she really wanted. 'OK,' he said. 'Whatever suits you best. I'll ask Tina to go over and pack everything up for us.'

'Would she mind? It seems a lot of work for her.'

'I should maybe fly over myself.'

'Should you?' She looked alarmed by the suggestion. 'There isn't much stuff you know.'

'OK,' he said helplessly. 'I'll see what she says.'

It struck Luis that he had already used up a significant part of his six months. Well before the end of August, whether he wanted to or not, he would have to leave and go back to La Gomera. If he overstayed his allotted time, there would be a ten year ban on his ever coming back to the UK. In his present frame of mind, he didn't care whether they banned him from coming back for life, never mind ten years, but he had just enough sense to perceive that it might not suit his Margarita to have to visit her family alone. His chief feeling was exasperation with a country that could so complacently shoot itself in both feet and profess to be content with the outcome. When she pointed out that Scotland had neither voted for, nor agreed to, Brexit, his frustration only increased.

'Then why allow it? Why not take to the streets? You have a parliament here in Scotland, don't you?'

'I don't think it would have made any difference. That's not how it works.'

'Then it doesn't work at all. Don't your politicians know how a union is supposed to work?'

She had to admit that he was right. Westminster had no idea how a real union of equals worked. They just overrode what they pleased to call the other 'home nations' and their wishes by force of numbers and called it democracy. How had they allowed the freedoms they were born with to be so casually removed from them? She had been so lucky that she had other options, but that made no difference to their current problems.

Later, he called Cristina, asking her if she could to go over to Tenerife, pack up their things from the apartment, see if she could fit them into his car that was still parked there, and take them back to La Gomera. He apologised in advance for any mess he had left in the flat and for the trouble he was putting her to.

'I thought I would be coming back almost immediately, you see.'

'It might be better this way, Luis. It's hard with a baby. You're probably better to come straight home to the island when you do come.'

'I'd like to do that, yes. But I could fly back for a week or so if you like. I could get a cheap flight.'

'I don't mind, Lucho. I've already tidied everything up in the apartment. I'll give it a clean as well. They were very kind to let you rent it for so long. I can bring Domingo with me to help with the fetching and carrying.'

'Will he do that?' Domingo was their teenage nephew, his sister Isabel's eldest.

'He will if I ask him. He's always ready for a trip to Los Cristianos, you know that, as long as I treat him to lunch!'

'You're an angel, Tina.'

'Of course I am.' She laughed. 'We'll take some cardboard boxes. To be honest, there isn't a vast amount. I assume most of it belongs to the apartment owners anyway.'

'It does. I think they put a lot of their personal things away in that big cupboard in the bedroom, but I'll get Margarita to make a list of what's ours.'

'What about that place over the restaurant?'

Before he met Margaret, Luis had lodged with friends in an apartment over their restaurant in Los Cristianos. He had worked there as sous chef, during the day, reserving the evenings for his playing and singing.

'There's almost nothing there. Nothing that matters, anyway. I'll be going to see them when I come back, spend a night there, so I can check, but I'd pretty much cleared everything out after we got married.'

It struck him that he had moved around so much in his life so far that he had acquired very little baggage. Until now, when within a surprisingly short space of time, he had acquired a wife and child. He didn't think his wife would take kindly to being thought of as baggage, but it was certainly more responsibility than he had ever had in his life so far.

'Anyway, we could store your stuff here at home till you're ready for it. If Margarita doesn't mind. In fact now I think about it, we could even take some of it to La Manzana if you like. Paco and Carmen will be moving out soon and I've promised to help them too.'

'That would be good. Yes. And you are using the car, aren't you, Tina? I meant to say that ages ago but I kept forgetting. You're on the insurance anyway.'

Cristina had occasionally used the car to visit friends in other parts of the island, or to ferry their mother to hospital appointments.

'Thanks. I will. Well – I have done from time to time.'

'It isn't much of a car really, but it goes.'

'You'll need to get a special seat. For the baby.'

'I will.'

'Don't worry about it. I'll find one for you.'

'Tina, you really are an angel.'

He had left in a great hurry, thinking that he would probably be coming back a week or two before his wife and baby and would have plenty of time to clean up and get ready for them. Then, he had told his family that his wife was still rather unwell and that they had both decided to stay on in Glasgow for a few months.

'But the baby is fine, just fine,' he said, in response to their anxious questions about Eduardo.

He wrote a tactful and apologetic letter to Paco and Carmen, asking them if they might be able to wait a few more weeks at the most. He couldn't begin to imagine giving up on his dream and he didn't really believe he would have to. But he was grimly aware that if they didn't sort things out soon, they might be in financial difficulties. He couldn't work here. He knew that Margaret had her share of the money from the sale of her Glasgow apartment in the bank, and could draw on it as necessary, but they had been planning to use that for renovations to their house and restaurant on La Gomera. He hated the feeling that he was living off his wife's money. It went against all his principles, even though she had tried to persuade him that it was fine, a temporary measure.

'I'm hoping that we can all come over in May or June at the latest,' he wrote to his aunt and uncle. 'But if not, I'll come by myself. Then Margarita and the baby can follow on as soon as possible.'

Eduardo had his six weeks' check-up in April, and was pronounced fit and well. He grew and thrived and, gradually, as his colic began to subside, the rhythms of Margaret's own body began to reassert themselves. But still Luis was reluctant to broach the subject of their return to his island.

'Luis?' Margaret ventured, one afternoon, watching him pace Annie's sitting room like a caged animal. 'I really think it might be best if you went back to La Gomera first, and then we can follow you in a little while.'

He gazed at her, trying to disguise the uncertainty he felt.

'Well I might. Soon. There are things I need to do. And I could get ready for you both.'

'That sounds like a good plan. Doesn't it?'

Why was he so reluctant to leave her here? When he analysed that reluctance, it struck him that he didn't trust her family's influence. Or maybe he just meant Fiona's influence.

The truth was that Luis was beginning to like his brother-in-law. It had begun when they chatted about innocuous topics like the weather and wine and golf and even motorbike racing with all those excellent Spanish riders. Luis knew nothing about golf but he certainly liked the bikes, and it became a point of contact between them. Lately, Ian had begun to take Luis out to one of the local pubs, leaving Annie, Fiona and Margaret to talk about developments with the baby, how he had grown, the state of his tummy, the state of his nappies, the onset of teething. Ian had some fine qualities, such as trustworthiness and loyalty. Luis still thought him impossibly set in his ways, old before his time. But with his Spanish brother-in-law, Ian seemed to relax.

Luis doubted if Fiona would approve.

Luis and Ian made an oddly ill-matched couple, standing together at the glossy bar of the renovated pub, the nearest place to which they could escape. About the only thing they had in common, apart from an interest in MotoGP and its many Spanish riders, was their taste for good wine and malt whisky, the latter, in Luis's case, newly acquired. Luis was much taller than his brother-in-law, and considerably broader in the shoulders. He still habitually wore jeans and tee-shirts but with woolly sweaters and a jacket, as a concession to the rigours of the Scottish climate. Annie had found it in a charity shop, a beautiful, soft, Italian leather garment, and brought it home in triumph. Even now, in April, he still found the weather horribly cold. Within the space of a few weeks after his arrival, Annie, who was never without a pair of needles and a knitting bag, had also made him a creamy Aran jumper.

'My mother taught me,' she told him, when he marvelled at the intricacy of the cables.

'She came from Ireland?'

'That's right.' She had pulled and patted the shoulders. 'Not a bad fit. The trick Is in how you sew them up. It suits you.'

He had retained his Tenerife suntan and looked exotic, compared with the quiet conservatism of Ian who sipped his drink almost primly and cast the occasional surprised glance at Luis as though he still could not quite believe in his existence. They had discovered that they generally got on best by talking as little as possible and concentrating on the whisky, but this evening Ian was looking very pleased with himself.

'Luis, I think I've cracked it,' he said, rubbing his hands together briskly. It was cold outside.

'Cracked what?'

'I think I may have found you a kind of a job.'

Luis's heart sank. 'I can't work here. Not legally. You know that.'

Even if it had been possible, what kind of casual job would Ian have come up with? Waiting at table in the golf club restaurant perhaps? That ubiquitous image of the Spanish waiter had dogged his footsteps since his arrival in the UK. People seemed to imagine that his whole country was populated by men in white jackets carrying food and drinks about.

'Ian,' he said, determined to nip any such suggestion in the bud. 'You know that I can cook and play the guitar. But I'm not a waiter. This is something I haven't done for years, not since I was a very young man in London. And let me tell you, I didn't enjoy it, even then. Besides, I'm not allowed to work. They could throw me out. Deport me.'

Ian looked puzzled, hurt almost. He took out a large white handkerchief and blew his nose. He must be the last man in Glasgow, perhaps the last man in Scotland, thought Luis, still using such large monogrammed handkerchiefs in preference to tissues. I expect he wears pyjamas too, he thought irritably. In fact Ian did wear baggy pyjamas. Luis had seen them in Margaret's apartment, back on Tenerife, when the couple had come to stay. For once, however, he restrained himself from making some sarcastic comment. Instead, he ordered more drinks.

'It isn't a job as a waiter,' said Ian, testily. 'I'd never have thought of getting you a job as a waiter.'

There was a plaintive note in his voice and Luis had the grace to look embarrassed. It occurred to him that Ian was a rather lonely man. Fiona's all-encompassing shadow had apparently discouraged more interesting growths. Ian was drawn to Luis for many of the same reasons that had attracted his sister. There was a spice of fear, of unpredictability in the relationship that had become almost addictive to this man whose life had been so carefully mapped out. You never quite knew what Luis was going to do or say next, and Ian, much against his better judgement, found that stimulating.

'I'm sorry,' said Luis. 'So what's the plan?'

'Well, it's not a job, as such. Not really. That's the point. I know you're not allowed to work. But I have a client called Ricky Mackay. Half Italian, half Scottish. His parents had cafes in a few seaside towns and did rather well out of them. You know, ice cream and coffees.'

'Ice cream?'

'Will you just listen to me while I try to get to the point, Luis.'

'Sorry, sorry.'

'Ricky's done even better for himself. He has a boutique hotel in Edinburgh plus a couple of clubs and a couple of restaurants in Glasgow as well as the cafes. They're gearing up for their summer season. I had a word with him today. He'd like you to do the odd performance in one of his bars. Well, it's a wine bar and restaurant really and they have live music. Only it has to be the right *sort* of music. This is quite a sophisticated audience. Your average bar singer won't do. I thought you might fit the bill. Particularly your playing.'

'I still think it counts as work.'

Ian did too. It was Ricky who had clapped him on the back and said 'For God's sake, Ian. Who would know?'

The public would know, thought Ian. Luis was talented.

'Well he wouldn't pay you.'

'That's fortunate for him. Not so much for me. And I'm not allowed to do unpaid work either.'

'But he said he could pay Maggie a bit. He's actually looking for a property on Tenerife. Genuinely. So that would all be above board. He could consult with her. Just till you decide to go back home. It would be her money. A consultation fee now and then.'

Luis looked at Ian in amazement. 'Are you suggesting I become part of the' – he hesitated. 'La economía sumergida? I don't know what this is in English.'

'The black economy.' Ian blenched.

'And you an accountant too, Ian!'

'Well it isn't quite, is it? Because he really would be consulting Maggie about property. And it would go through the books. All legal and above board. It was Ricky's idea. But the performances would just be casual. A favour for a friend. We thought you might like to do the odd gig, to keep your hand in, so to speak. Nothing regular. You have a guitar with you, after all.'

Luis remembered the government website. No paid or unpaid work. But would any government official here even suspect that playing the guitar and singing counted as work? He doubted it. No government official in Spain or Scotland ever really thought of the arts as paid work although they might pay lip service to it. Bureaucrats always saw it as a hobby at best. Besides, at this point, he found he didn't care. If they deported him, that was fine by him. And if he couldn't come back for ten years, so what? Who would want to? On the other hand, he was really missing playing for the public.

'So what do you think? Will you at least go and see him?'

He shrugged. 'I'll speak to Margarita but – yes. I suppose I could do the odd session for him. Till we go back.'

'You're to go and see him tomorrow. Well, if you want to. He'll even buy you a dinner suit.'

'I have one but I left it at home.'

'Don't look a gift horse in the mouth. This guy's rolling in it, Luis.'

'And I suppose you should know.'

Ian grunted noncommittally.

'I'm an honest accountant. He likes that about me. He says it suits him that the Revenue trusts me not to be fiddling the books. Besides, he makes plenty of money without needing to do any fiddling.'

'But you're still happy with him paying my wife for a made up job, because I'm not allowed to earn it?'

Ian found himself blushing uncomfortably. 'But it isn't a made up job. Not really.'

Luis downed his drink. 'Don't worry about it, Ian. Everyone bends the rules at some point in their lives. Especially when the rules are as fucking stupid as this one. It happens at home too.'

They went back to tell the family.

'Singing?' said Fiona. 'And playing? In a club?'

'Why not?' asked Margaret, defensively. 'It's what he does in Los Cristianos. It's what he plans to do when we have the restaurant.'

'Yes, but won't the audiences here be, well, excuse me, Luis, that bit more sophisticated than you're used to?'

There was a terrible silence while Luis struggled to keep his temper.

'Time we were going home,' said Ian suddenly, handing his wife the car keys. 'You'll have to drive. I've been drinking.'

'Your husband's a bad influence, Mags, ' said Fiona, forcing a smile.

Margaret smiled at her brother. 'Thanks, Ian. '

'Don't mention it. Least I could do. I thought it might cheer him up. He's so talented.'

'He is. And I think we need to get back to where that talent is appreciated.'

'You probably do,' he whispered as he left. Glad that his wife couldn't hear him.

Annie tactfully went to bed and left them alone in the sitting room. Eduardo, nestled in his pram, stirred and twitched briefly, but when Luis rocked him he sighed and slept again without fully waking up. Margaret made tea and they sat and drank it in front of the fire. Luis was beginning to enjoy tea. He supposed that he had drunk so much to please Annie that he was becoming hooked on it.

'It sounds like a good opportunity,' Margaret said tentatively.

'*Si*. It'll do. Just two or three performances, I think. I'm not supposed to do it you know, but hell, I don't care any more. I'll risk it. Although I can't quite believe it'll work out. Not if your brother has set it up for me.'

'That's unfair, Luis.'

'I know. I'm sorry. He's been very helpful. Surprisingly so.'

'He likes you.'

'So it would seem. Well I suppose I like him. But you know you'll have to talk to Ricky about property on Tenerife?'

'I don't mind doing that. So it looks as if we'll be staying for a few more weeks?'

'Looks like it. I only have till August, remember. But I'd like for us to go back long before then.'

'*Por supuesto*,' she said. 'Of course.' Then, 'Luis?'

'What?'

'Do you think we should maybe try to rent a flat, an apartment of some kind – just for ourselves? Just for those few weeks?'

'Does your mother mind us staying here?'

'No. But I mind. I'd like to have the baby to myself now. And I'd like to have you to myself for a bit. Not just the odd half hour like this. I love her very much and I love seeing her, but it does feel like being a teenager again.'

'We'll have to see what we can do then.'

He was dubious. While they were living in Annie's house the whole arrangement had an air of impermanence, but to rent a flat, to set up house here: that seemed a much more definite and inescapable move altogether. On the other hand, Margaret's desire for independence might be an indication that she was getting back to her normal self and that was definitely to be encouraged.

'Just for a few weeks,' she said, as though sensing his unease. Or was it her own? 'Like a holiday let.'

'Could we afford it?'

'Let me pay for it. I have something in mind that won't cost too much, but I'll need to check it out first. I'd really like you to see a bit of Scotland as well, now that you're here.'

'Well that would be nice, yes.'

'We'll never have another chance like this, or not for a long time. And you'll like it better in the summer. I promise you will.'

'I like it now!'

'No you don't. It's so much the opposite of all that you're used to. You don't feel as if you fit in here, I know that.'

'We'll see.'

He watched her face in profile, suddenly wanting to kiss her, not a kiss on the cheek but a passionate embrace, with his lips on hers and his tongue thrusting into her mouth. But he couldn't do it. Not yet.

She put a tentative hand on his knee and he covered it with his own, stroking it with his thumb, but he stayed silent and immobile, watching the dying embers of the fire. There was still some distance between them. The return to Scotland and the birth of the child had only exacerbated the sense of some fearful abyss, with Margaret on one side and Luis on the other. He no longer felt as close to her as he had once been. Their conversations were curiously stilted. He understood suddenly that for her, going back with him had become a more frightening proposition than staying on in Scotland. Giving herself up to him, to his island, his family, all the things she had wanted to do, had become a hurdle.

Back when he had first shown her his island, he had been beset by misgivings. It couldn't possibly work, he had thought, not for two people with such different backgrounds. Then she had persuaded him otherwise. He thought about their short, intense courtship, their speedy marriage and the subsequent struggles of adjustment, followed almost immediately by pregnancy and childbirth. No wonder she was exhausted, her willpower and self-possession all drained away. She needed more time, but he wondered what would be left of their relationship at the end of it. Sometimes he thought it would be better if he just gave up the struggle, packed his bags and went home, leaving her to make up her mind by herself, without any pressure from him. But then her family would step into the breach, exerting their own pressure.

At last she stood up and left him there, climbing slowly and tiredly up to bed. 'Bring the baby with you,' she said, over her shoulder.

He looked up at her with a grin. As always the thought of his son filled him with pleasure and, more than pleasure, with excitement. 'How could I ever forget?' he said.

CHAPTER SEVEN

I slept under a rosebush.
My bed was made of roses.
Rose, I have stripped off your petals.
You are useless now.

The birth of the baby had admitted Margaret into a club, a secret society, the existence of which she had long suspected, but never its extent or scope. It was an exclusive club with a mass of special signs and passwords, a club whose membership was female. It occasionally felt, here at least, like a ghetto. It was as though she had taken a quantum leap in understanding, and when she looked back she saw that the self that had existed before the birth of Eduardo was like a different person entirely from the self that she had almost immediately become.

There was a certain shared understanding between her and other mothers now. She did not doubt that it had been a spiritual experience and one which, for all his empathy and love, Luis had not quite been able to share, or not in the same way, for it had not been his body that was so possessed by the child. No man could ever know it, not fully, however much they might wish it were otherwise.

She spoke about it to Suzie because she knew that Suzie would listen, even if she didn't yet understand.

'You have that enormously self satisfied air of the new parent,' Suzie said, peevishly. 'I knew you would. I knew it would happen to you as well.'

'I try not to overdo it,' said Margaret, apologetically.

'Not very successfully.'

'I'm sorry. It so fills you up that you have to let a little of it spill over.'

'Feel free to spill it in my direction then, if you must,' said Suzie, in resignation.

In the early hours of the morning, sitting with the baby at her breast, listening to him sighing and grunting like a small hedgehog with the pleasure of the warm sweet milk, it had occurred to Margaret that all the male secret societies of the world, all the primitive and not so primitive initiation rites, all the clubs, the freemasonries, the esoteric sects, the ritualised traditions of everything from priestly hierarchies to the House of Commons, were pale, masculine imitations of this momentous rite. Motherhood, through pain and trial, sent the initiate spinning helplessly into a new life. No matter how much people tried to deny it, and they did, the change was monumental. Unimaginable until you had been there. She tried to confide this idea to Suzie but it was no good. Suzie wasn't yet a member of this particular club and although she said she understood, she didn't.

Soon the practical hardships and joys of coping with the child swamped her wilder flights of fancy. She was feeling better physically, though mentally she was still quite fragile. At the baby clinic and in the park, where she walked Eduardo in his buggy, and at the mother and baby groups to which she went on Wednesday afternoons, she sought out other women so that she could talk about babies without feeling embarrassed by her preoccupation. She had always rather despised these kind of conversations before, sitting on the fringes, listening with a mixture of jealousy and indifference, but as with all such groups, once you were on the inside, what had seemed mere jargon now became the stuff of absorbing interest.

There was no doubt about it, the baby put additional pressure on their marriage. Lacking in sleep and with their days more absorbed by the infant than they would have believed possible, they frequently became snappish and cross with one another. But if there were ways in which her relationship with her husband was still under strain, at least they had in common their shared love for the child.

Eduardo was a new and unbreakable bond between them. When, at six weeks, he had smiled, a great big gummy grin, looking from one to the other, they knew that they both felt the same heart-churning sensation of selfless love for him. A couple of weeks later, he followed the smile with a prolonged and infectious chuckle. He was sitting in his baby bouncer. There was a little row of plastic men and women stretched across the front of it and Luis had just flicked them, making them spin around and around. The laugh was a surprise to them both: they had not known he was capable of it, and as they turned to each other they knew that their mutual delight in his achievements would be a source of endless pleasure to them, just as his disappointments would be borne by them with a pain that would never diminish with the passing years. Perhaps Alastair had been right when he had refused to have a child with her because their relationship had never been strong enough to withstand the stresses and strains. They couldn't have done it. He didn't love her enough. But she could see that she hadn't loved him enough either. You needed some special quality between you to add the extra strain of a child or children. She hoped to God that she and Luis had it. She had been sure of it on Tenerife, but was she so sure of it here in Scotland?

On a fine day in early May, Luis went into the centre of Glasgow to meet Ricky Mackay. The bar was in the basement of a large Victorian building, heavy with stone encrustations and very attractive in its own, solid way. Luis had half expected Glasgow to be a grubby, industrial, poverty stricken place. There were areas of the city that were run down and very poor indeed, but today it seemed to him a rather beautiful place with its wide streets, its splendid buildings and friendly people, who showed him the way with a smile. All the same, and in spite of the burgeoning spring, there were too many derelict shops, too many dirty streets.

'Do you burn down all your unwanted historic buildings?' he had once asked Ian, a question that was so close to the awful truth that Ian had no answer.

Nevertheless, Ricky's restaurant was elegant, beautifully designed, with various function rooms. Luis was shown into a chaotic but comfortable office where Ricky sat with his feet up on a leather-topped desk, so big that it almost filled the room. Mackay was big, too: a balding man with a misleadingly genial face. The only indications of his part Italian parentage were his long straight nose, that might at a pinch be called 'Roman' and a certain tendency to use his hands in conversation far more than the average Scot. Luis couldn't decide whether to like him or mistrust him. He swung his feet to the floor, leapt up and sidled round the desk, banging his thighs on the corners, holding out a large hand to Luis in greeting. They shook hands vigorously, stopping just short of a contest that Luis wasn't at all sure he would have won. Not without injuring his fingers anyway.

'Sit down, sit down,' Ricky said. 'Coffee? Tea?'

Luis accepted coffee and a mug of excellent coffee, the best he had had so far here, appeared with magical speed. The chair was comfortable but, Luis noticed, somewhat lower than Ricky's own. Here was a man who liked to feel in control. He noticed Ricky's remarkably well-cut suit, the gleaming shirt and shiny Italian leather shoes. It was all just a bit flash but undeniably expensive. Here too was a man who liked to show off his wealth. They boxed around each other warily, in the manner of most such men at a first meeting, sparring with words.

'So you're Ian's new brother-in-law. Unexpectedly, I gather!' Ricky leaned back in his chair, putting the tips of his fingers together.

'He didn't expect his sister to marry again, no.'

'He speaks very highly of your talents, nevertheless.'

'Does he?' Luis could not resist a raised eyebrow.

'You seem surprised.'

'No. Not really. It's just that he has taken a little time to come to terms with the marriage. My wife and I met and we married quite quickly. I don't think Ian approved.'

Margarita, Luis thought, that's who Ian's doing all this for. Margarita. Not for me. And yet they had been getting on better of late. So perhaps there was a grudging admiration buried somewhere beneath Ian's respectable exterior.

'What do you think of him? Ian, I mean,' asked Ricky suddenly. Luis was immediately wary. Ian was family now and whatever your feelings you didn't discuss family with strangers.

'We get on fine,' he said shortly.

'Bit of an old woman, eh?'

Luis resorted to convenient incomprehension. 'Que?' he said, looking bewildered.

'Under the thumb. Henpecked. You know. Fiona wears the trousers in that house.'

'Well, perhaps Ian likes it that way. Most people seem to end up doing exactly what they want in a marriage, don't they?'

'That's a bit deep, isn't it? Wouldn't do for me. I like women to do what I tell them. I expect you do too. That's the Spanish in you. And the Italian in me. Nothing wrong with it, eh?'

Luis shrugged. He didn't think he was going to like this man very much, but he kept his own counsel and smiled enigmatically. Later, he would realise that Ricky wasn't quite telling the truth. He might like women to do what he told them, but it didn't mean that his wife agreed with him. Or did as he said. Today, though, Luis didn't know what to think.

Ricky misinterpreted the smile as agreement. He rubbed his hands together and sank his chin even further towards his chest.

'Now,' he said. 'To business. I'd like to hear you play if I may, though

I could take Ian's word for it. Honest as the day's long, Ian. Too honest for an accountant but at least HMRC think so as well and that's worth a great deal. Then we'll fix up a few slots for you.'

'You know I'm not allowed to work, don't you? Paid or unpaid.'

'Well if any money is involved, I'll pay your Margaret. A wee fee for a property consultation with me. That's what she was doing, wasn't it?'

'Yes. It was.

'And this won't be regular. Just the occasional gig. Would you mind letting me hear you? It's not an audition. I'd just like to hear what you can do.'

Luis picked up his guitar.

'What about amplification?' asked Ricky. 'Don't you need to plug it in?'

'No!' People often asked him this and it always slightly horrified him. 'This is the real thing. Acoustic. And quite old, although I have an older and even finer one at home. A decent vocal mic will do. Do you have one?'

'I do. Of course. Come through to the bar. There's a wee platform there. I had it set up but I wondered if you might need something more complicated. Clearly not.'

Luis slid the instrument out of its case, as always taking pleasure in the sight and feel of a guitar, any guitar. Wishing that it was his own precious guitar, waiting for his return. Every time he played, he was reminded of Paco, and when he thought of Paco he thought of the house and the restaurant, perched among the flowers and fruits. He desperately wanted to be there, but he wanted Margarita and his son to be with him too.

Ricky looked dubious but when Luis began to play, his face cleared. Luis saw the restaurant manager hovering in the doorway, smiling, giving him a thumbs-up. He played a short, sweet piece by Francisco Tarrega, moved on to a piece of flamenco, full of fierce rhythms, and then finished with a love song from his own island.

Un mujer me pidio
amor, cariño y dinero;
amor, cariño le di,
porque dinera no tengo.

'What do the words mean?'

'A woman asked me for...' He hesitated. 'Love. But it is a strong word. It means passion, maybe? Anyway. Love, affection and money. Love and affection I gave her because I do not have money.'

'You know,' said Ricky, 'this is really authentic stuff. Really authentic.'

It was one of his favourite words and his highest form of praise.

'I suppose it is. It's traditional, anyway.'

'Ian said something about leaving your old guitar behind.'

'I borrowed this one from my uncle, but it's fine.'

'Why did you leave the other one?'

'I didn't trust any airline with it.'

'An old guitar?'

'Some things are very precious. Some things get better, the older they grow. My guitar at home is an antique. Not old and worn out. Old and beautiful. Even this one is not new. Just less valuable than the other one.'

To his surprise, Ricky nodded. 'I think my mother would probably agree with you. And my wife. Anyway – the gig's yours if you want to do it. Do you want it?'

'For a few weeks,' Luis said a little warily. 'Just till we go back?'

'Yes, if that's what you want. We'll see how it goes, eh? Ian said you were planning to go back to the Canaries at some point.'

'I have only six months. I need to be gone by August. But I'd really like to be gone before that.'

'Or I suppose you could apply to live here permanently, now that you're married to Margaret?'

'I suppose I could but I don't want to. And it would be very expensive.'

'Would you think about it?'

Luis shook his head. Surprising himself by his instant revulsion at the idea. Visceral. 'If I'm honest – no. I don't want to live here. I want to be at home. I have a new business to run there.'

'Ian told me. A restaurant. It's a big undertaking. Do you know what you're taking on?'

'I've been planning it for a long time. I have quite a bit of experience.'

Ricky gazed at him as though sizing him up. Luis wondered what else Ian had told him and whether Fiona had had a hand in it. 'Well, let's see how it goes, anyway. As I say, it's just a gig or two. Playing for pleasure, eh? Nothing official or permanent. But I'll make sure your wee Margaret doesn't lose out.'

Luis walked out into the spring sunshine and breathed deeply, trying to rid his nostrils of the smells of spilled wine and last night's pasta sauce. He had arranged to meet his wife in the Botanical Gardens. One of her and Suzie's old university friends was an archaeologist. He was leaving on a field trip to South America and was looking for a reliable house sitter for his flat just off Byres Road for a couple of months. It was a gift. These apartments were 'like gold dust' Suzie had said. She had suggested Luis and Margaret. Did they want to go and see it? The archaeologist, who was taking the place of a sick colleague on the expedition, was in a hurry to fix something up. He remembered Margaret, and would have no objections to the baby. Margaret had warned Luis that the baby would sometimes be a stumbling block in Scotland. Luis viewed this warning with total incomprehension.

'Why?' he asked. 'Animals I could understand. Dogs and cats. They might make a mess of the place. But who could or would object to a baby?'

When she told him just who might and why, adding that cats and dogs would be more acceptable to some people, because they loved their 'fur babies' so much, he simply closed his mind to the idea.

'I can't believe that,' he said. 'Surely it can't be true!'

He threaded through the crowds, holding his guitar close, protecting it like a child from the buffets of passers-by, and finally found his way to the subway as Margaret had instructed him. The station was clean and cool and smelled pleasantly of newly dug potatoes. He leaned against the wall while he waited for the train to arrive, and thought about Ricky Mackay, deciding that he was probably trustworthy and that it wasn't his fault if he managed to be crass at the same time. He doubted if he would ever like the man, but if he, Luis, could keep his mouth shut, then they might rub along together and it would be nice to sing and play in public a few times. The trouble was going to be keeping his temper. Luis had never been one to suffer fools or boors gladly, and he had immediately and impatiently categorized Ricky as the latter, albeit a very clever one. He seldom changed his first opinion, sometimes wilfully disliking someone because of a first unfavourable impression. Ian might just prove to be an exception to that rule, but Luis's dislike of Fiona had, if anything, grown stronger with the passing weeks.

There was a roar and a draught of warm air and a train rattled into the station. He manoeuvred his guitar inside and found a seat. The train was only half full. This was the quieter time of day: too late for office lunch breaks but too early for homegoing. Margaret would have left the baby with her mother and come to meet him.

He got off the train at Hillhead and emerged into a busy shopping street, turning right as he's been instructed and walking towards the Botanical Gardens. He passed a fruit shop with oranges and apples, melons and bananas piled in boxes out on the street. He saw that some of the boxes had 'Espa a' on them and experienced an unreasonable lifting of his heart at the sight of the name. There were tubs of tulips and late narcissi. On impulse he bought a mass of them, four or five bunches, and then had to juggle them with the guitar, feeling foolish and conspicuous in the spring sunshine. He liked this lively, cosmopolitan district and thought that he wouldn't mind staying here for a while, pretending he was on holiday. They would be lucky to be able to secure an apartment here. Ahead of him towered the great Victorian glass and wrought iron edifices that housed the cactuses, the succulents and scented plants that grew in profusion on his island, without need of such protection.

Some distance from the main gate he found Margaret sitting on her jacket on the newly mown grass. Everywhere smelled of hay. 'Don't be fooled by the weather,' Annie had told him. 'It could be pouring down tomorrow. And cold with it.' Margaret wore a dress as a concession to the sunshine and she sat cross legged on the ground with her head bent. She looked young and pretty, much better than she had looked since the birth. He saw that she had picked a little heap of daisies and was busy threading them into a daisy chain. She looks so English, he thought, suddenly, forgetting again that this was Scotland and she was Scottish. All she needed was a straw hat with flowers tucked into it. She looked very much at home here too with her hair gleaming in the pale sunlight. He felt out of place. He wished he were at home. He wished they were both at home, on La Gomera, sitting among the orange and almond trees, drinking wine.

She looked up and saw him, scrambled to her feet, dropped her daisies and said 'Oh damn!' She bent to pick them up.

'Margarita among the margaritas,' he said. He came and helped her, putting down his guitar carefully, and as he bent down she draped the starry crown of flowers around his dark hair.

'I made you a crown, but it's coming apart at the seams. Bit like me really.'

He felt silly, still holding the narcissi, so he thrust them into her hands. She buried her nose in them and came up sneezing. He reached up to take his crown off but she said, 'No, leave it!' so he embraced her instead and kissed her, first on one cheek, then on the other. 'Be careful of my flowers,' she said. 'I love them! How did it go?'

'I'll do a couple of gigs for him. Hope that nobody reports me. He said it would be OK and I suspect he has ways of making it OK.'

'I'm sure he has. And he's getting a professional musician for free!'

'Well not quite. He says he'll pay you.'

'So you do the work and he pays me?'

'Illegal work. I could be deported.'

'Don't!'

'I don't care. And I'm very happy if he pays you. He wants to buy some property in Los Cristianos. He made me play, but he liked it.'

'I think they'll love you. So Ian does have his uses.'

'He does. And it'll be good to perform again.'

'Were you missing it?'

'Very much. I don't think I'd realised how much.'

'It's what you are. What you do.'

She had brought a picnic lunch and began to unpack bread, ripe tomatoes, cut in half, a little bottle of olive oil, as well as fruit and cartons of juice.

'*Pan con tomate!*' he said.

'I know it's Catalan, but I still thought it might remind you of home!'

Tomato rubbed on crusty bread and sprinkled with olive oil. 'The food of the Gods!'

'Well, I think so too.'

'How's Eduardo?' he asked as they ate, sprawled side by side on the grass. 'Did you manage to leave him some milk?' He had left her that morning, struggling to express milk from her breasts with an ugly pump.

She pulled a face. 'Not much. Just a bottle and a half. It's silly really because there's so much milk when he's suckling, but I can only get a few drops at a time with that awful contraption. I got too sore to carry on. Mum will have to give him water instead. He'll be fine.'

'Your mother will be glad to have him to herself for a bit.'

'She was taking him to the park. The granny parade.'

'What is this?'

She chuckled. 'Oh, you know. I'm sure they must do that on La Gomera! They parade their respective grandchildren and compare notes. What colour eyes, how much hair and so on? She'll love it.'

'My mother would love it too.'

A sudden silence fell between them. They had just received a letter from Maria, asking a dozen questions about the baby. Luis had written back and Margaret had added a page or two. They had sent a whole sheaf of photographs, pictures that they had already posted online, but Maria was resistant to computers: Eduardo in the bath, lying on the Shetland shawl Annie had knitted for him, Margaret holding the baby with Luis standing rather awkwardly and formally behind, like one of those Victorian studio portraits. Resentment boiled up inside Luis. He forced it back but it left a bitter taste in his mouth.

'Are you very homesick?' Margaret asked him.

'What do you think?'

She could have said, 'Let's go back now,' but she wasn't able to. Not just yet. The breeze still smelled of green, growing things. The tulips were in blousy bloom. The buzz of traffic was muted and distant.

'We will go back,' she said. 'We will. Just give me a little more time.'

'Isn't that what I am doing?'

'Yes. Yes, you are. And I'm very grateful.' She looked at her watch. 'We're due at the flat in half an hour.'

'I want to see the cactuses,' he said, suddenly stubborn. 'I want to see them first. I like them. They remind me of home.'

' Whatever you want.'

The gardens were almost empty: the office workers who brought their sandwiches here had all gone back to work, and even the students had deserted the place. She was packing up her basket, putting away tinfoil and empty fruit juice cartons.

'Whatever I want?' he said, darkly. 'Do you know what I really want?'

She turned back to him and he saw the blush spread upwards across her face again.

'What?'

She felt suddenly shy of him, shy as if they had just met. He glanced around quickly. Nobody was in sight. Far away across the park an elderly couple walked their dog, proceeding in a sedate fashion while the wire haired terrier snuffled and cocked his leg compulsively on each tree he passed. Luis moved closer to her and kissed her. She felt his tongue in her mouth. He had not kissed her like this since before the baby was born. She had begun to wonder if he would ever kiss her like this again. She immediately felt the answering tremor, but she was afraid of the pain.

He felt her grow tense and whispered, 'Don't worry. It's OK.'

His hand was on the cool cloth of her dress, sliding upwards. He sighed and she felt his finger, finding the edge of her panties, and then very gently inserted between the fabric and her skin. Down it moved, parting her, creeping closer, gently feeling for her and finding her, cautiously, as his tongue just brushed her lips. For a moment she almost surrendered to him feeling the stirring of pleasure in her body, but then she sat up and rolled away from him, glancing around.

'No. Not here, not now, Luis,' she said. 'It's so public!'

'There's nobody about. Nobody can see us.'

'I'm just not quite ready yet.'

'You felt ready to me.' He grinned. He didn't mind. He could wait.

He looked down at her bent head and saw a tiny beetle, crawling through the fine fair strands of her hair, like a creature negotiating some strange meadowland.

'Are you afraid that it will hurt?'

'A little.'

'I can feel where your shape has changed a bit.'

'Can you?' She didn't know how she felt about that. Not exactly anxious. Intrigued perhaps. 'Can you? I'll never be the same again, will I? Do you mind?'

He took her by the shoulders and kissed her on the forehead. 'Why should I mind, Margarita? It doesn't matter to me. I worry *for* you, that's all. Worry that it might be painful. Sometimes I think you don't like yourself very much.'

She was taken aback. 'Of course I like myself.'

'No.' He shook his head, sadly. 'You don't like yourself so much. You wish all the time that you were somebody different, with a different face and a different body.'

'Doesn't everyone?'

'I don't.'

She smiled. 'Well, you wouldn't, would you?'

'It is as if somebody had criticised you, so that at last you believed them. And now, every change that takes place in you, in your body, you see as something – I don't know how to say it. *Algo para luchar.* Something to fight? You still don't believe that I love you as you are, whatever happens to you, however you are. *Como si el amor estuviera condicionado a la juventad y la belleza.* As if love is somehow conditional upon youth and beauty and when that changes, love will change too.'

'But it is. And it does. It does change. You're talking about the experience of so many women, me included. Don't you understand that? Experience teaches us that love is conditional.'

He frowned, not quite understanding, but perhaps understanding enough. 'Not for me. Not conditional for me.'

She was forced to believe him, or at any rate she was forced to believe that he was sincere. He loved her and would go on loving her, seeing love as a conscious decision. If love were a kind of infection, it was possible to wake up cured, much as she and Alastair had done, but if love were a willed declaration, an article of faith to which a couple subscribed through good times and bad, then she could believe that things might be different. She could even believe in happy endings. What had begun by being a passionate attraction could end up as the companionship of a lifetime, but the negotiation of the rocky road to that ultimate goal still frightened the life out of her.

She looked at her watch. 'No time for the cactuses now.'

'No?' He grinned, his bitterness all dissipated. Just touching her had been enough. He felt light-hearted and inexplicably happy. 'Ah well. Another day perhaps.'

'Yes. We could bring Eduardo, couldn't we. Acclimatise him before we take him home to La Gomera!'

'I think we should do that, *si*.'

'But meanwhile, I think we really have to go and see this apartment. And then we have a baby to get back to!'

The flat was on the first floor of a stone tenement building, modernised and sparsely but pleasingly furnished, with venetian blinds at the windows, parquet floors with rugs, pale distempered walls and a large, very shabby three piece suite in the sitting room. There were two bedrooms, one large, with a big bed, and one smaller. Ronald was six foot four and chunky with it. There was plenty of room in the main bedroom for Eduardo's borrowed cot. Besides all this, there was an echoing, old-fashioned bathroom with plumbing to match, including an antique bath with ball and claw feet and a shower cabinet in one corner, its curtain decorated with garish tropical fish. There was a bright yellow kitchen where a new cooker rubbed shoulders with an old and tremendously noisy fridge freezer. Ronald was unmarried and only reasonably house-proud, though he was not averse to the occasional hectic and no doubt muddy affair with whatever woman happened to be working with him at the time.

Margaret remembered parties at his old flat during their university years, and the realisation that what had always seemed a rather glamorous profession was, in fact, one of almost unremitting dust and dirt. Indiana Jones had a lot to answer for. He would turn up from a dig literally brown from head to foot, his jacket, trousers and fingernails caked in mud. He had bought the flat with the help of some money inherited from his paternal grandparents. 'I'd never have afforded the deposit otherwise,' he said. 'Archaeology isn't exactly lucrative.' Now he was off on a field trip to Brazil where, he told them over drinks, he would probably have to contend with spiders as big as soup plates and leeches the size of currant buns. The fantastic quality of his experiences sat incongruously with his quiet Scots voice and gentle bespectacled face. The only drawback that they could see was that they would have to haul the pram up and down stairs, but generations of Glasgow parents had done the same thing for a hundred years.

'You're welcome to use the flat for as long as I'm away,' he said. 'That'll be two or three months and I'd rather have a flat sitter while I'm gone.'

'That will be more than enough for us,' she said. 'We'll be going back to La Gomera before the autumn. Luis only has six months here anyway and he's already used up quite a lot of time.'

'Oh yes. Bloody Brexit. Well, I can't think of any drawbacks to the flat. If the fridge freezer packs up, just buy another and bill me for it. It's already a replacement for a replacement. Complete crap. I don't mind and I know I can trust you, Maggie.'

'What about rent?' she asked, diffidently. 'You could probably get more with holiday lets.'

'I don't want holiday lets.' He shuddered. 'They might wreck the place. In fact I don't want rent at all. You'll be doing me a favour. I should probably pay you. I've packed away any breakables that I'm particularly fond of – archaeological specimens mostly. They're in the big cupboard in one of the spare rooms. And I've put the stuffed owl in there too. I thought that might not go down well with the infant.'

'The stuffed owl,' Margaret said. 'I remember now.'

He had brought it into lectures once or twice, causing great hilarity. Wherever he lived he had always perched it on the back of an easy chair.

'Your grandfather left it to you in his will!' she said, laughing.

'Yes. I got enough to put down a good deposit on this place as long as I looked after the owl.'

They were launched on a flood of shared remembrance, and only when they paused for breath did Margaret realise that Luis had been watching her with a strange expression between pleasure at her enthusiasm and a slight forlornness as though at his own exclusion, not just from her past, but from understanding her past. It was so removed from his own experience. She halted briefly, smiled at him, and then plunged on, reluctant to give up the pleasure of this moment. Again Luis saw a different woman, not his wife, but a girl, laughing, enthusiastic, eyes alight with memory. Perhaps she did belong here after all, he thought, in this big bold city, sharing academic recollections with a friend, not trapped in the dining room of a small restaurant on a quiet island.

'What is this owl?' Luis asked.

'*Buho*,' said Ronald, producing the word triumphantly from some corner of his memory.

'Ah – yes.'

'Like the Latin, I think.'

Margaret remembered that he had always known random facts like this. He got out his phone and they looked the word up and found that he was right. Then Ronald asked Luis if he would play the guitar, so he played a little bit of *Recuerdos de la Alhambra*, but he stopped because he was out of practice and it was so difficult.

'You don't sound at all out of practice to me!' said Ronald. 'I can't even play the recorder.'

They had another glass of wine, Rioja, bought in his honour and then Ronald asked all about the Canaries and the Guanches and was genuinely interested.

'We have to go home,' said Margaret at last. 'Eduardo will be getting very hungry. Mum will be panicking if we don't get back soon.'

Because the apartment was such a bargain, they climbed into a taxi and rode home in style.

'Your friend is a very nice man,' Luis said. 'Unlike Ricky Mackay.'

'Why isn't he a nice man?'

'You won't like him.'

'Why won't I like him.'

He looked across at her anxiously. 'Well, I hope you won't like him.'

'Why?' she repeated, laughing at his sudden seriousness. 'Is he very handsome?'

'No. Not at all.'

'Then why do you hope I won't like him? I should have thought you'd want us to get on.'

'Oh, get on. Get on, yes,' he said, scornfully. 'That is not what I mean. I mean he is not a good man.'

She looked out of the window, wondering at his categorisation of mankind into good and bad. There were no half measures with Luis. She still remembered his reiteration of that phrase '*Soy un buen hombre.*' She supposed that he thought Ricky Mackay '*un mal hombre*', but he would say no more, and she smiled at his virulence and his arrogance. Once more, she found her heart turning over with love for him and knew that she wouldn't have had him any other way. For good or ill, he was her husband; they were together, with the child between, and nothing could change that now.

CHAPTER EIGHT

Give me a single glance
even if it is only a casual one,
to see if in this moment
my soul can be eased.

They moved into Ronald's flat the following week. The baby seemed to enjoy the big bright rooms very much, staring around him with astonished eyes, waving arms and legs enthusiastically in the air. He had discovered his toes and they saw him feeling for them with his eyes tightly shut. Wow, what are these things? Do they belong to me? He showed no signs of becoming any darker. In fact the fuzz on top of his head was growing paler if anything, and his eyes were still bright blue.

'He may have been made in Spain,' said Luis with a slight tinge of regret in his voice, 'But he looks nothing like me.'

'Oh I don't know. He's very handsome. And he's going to be tall. Look at the length of him already.'

Annie visited them. She continued to think her new son-in-law generous, warm-hearted, funny and slightly hyper-active, although she could not help but admire her daughter's courage in marrying him. More used to the comfortable West of Scotland taciturnity of her late husband, she found his volatility disturbing. Margaret's father had been undemonstrative and undemanding: a kindly man of conservative habits with a strong streak of commonsense. Annie still missed him with a nagging sense of loss, a continual feeling of surprise that she couldn't come into the sitting room to find him there in his easy chair, reading his newspaper and drinking sweet tea from a pint mug.

'Would you like some tea?' Luis asked politely. Luis was looking after the baby. Margaret had gone out to the shops in search of new summer clothes, now that her body was resuming its normal proportions.

'I'll make it,' Annie said.

She didn't approve of the way Luis made tea, not heating the pot or allowing the water to boil properly.

She brought a tray through and they sat at the table in the window, watching dusty sparrows playing in the hedge that fringed the square of grass below.

'Margaret seems a lot better,' she remarked. 'Much more like herself.'

'I think she is.'

'Have you spoken to her about going home yet?'

'To La Gomera? Not really, no. I'm waiting for the right moment. I don't want to ... to rock the boat. Isn't that what you say?'

'Well, don't wait too long, will you, son? You know what it's like when you're married to someone. Sometimes you don't talk about things. You just take them for granted. And then after a while you can't talk about things properly, and you're trapped in a situation you never intended. I don't think she wants to stay on here for much longer, Luis.'

'That's just as well, because it would be difficult for me to stay here for good, you know.'

She gazed at him thoughtfully. 'Yes, of course. I always forget. You need to fix a firm date. June or July perhaps if you have this place for two months.'

'It's a good thing Margarita has your Irish ... roots? Is that the word?'

'I suppose it is. Anyway, I think she just needed a bit of a break. Time to recover. Time to come to terms with the baby.'

'Why should she have to come to terms with our baby?'

'Every new mother has to get used to her firstborn. I can remember when Ian was born, thinking, "Oh my God, what have I done?" My mother said, "Well, you can't send him back now." She was right of course, but you do feel like that, just for a few weeks. Then gradually it all falls into place.'

He smiled, liking her very much indeed at that moment.

'You love this Gomera, don't you?' she said, pouring herself a second cup. 'This island of yours.'

'I do. When I'm away from it, I don't feel as if I fit in here very well. Margarita is better at living there than I am at living here.'

'She's always been adaptable, our Margaret. Easy going. I think she'd fit in anywhere. I expect your way of life will suit her well enough.'

'She seemed to be so happy on my island. Sunshine suits her. I wouldn't have asked her to live there if she had not seemed so happy. I thought at first it might not work out, but then she told me she loved the place as much as I do.'

'Tell me about it then, your island and this Golden Apple place.'

'Do you really want to know?'

'I do.'

He told Annie all about La Gomera. He told her about his family and his friends, about the way of life on the island, the countryside and the village festivals and celebrations. He described *La Manzana Dorada*: the long, low building that seemed to be a part of the land upon which it stood, the citrus trees, the almonds and the abundant flowers. He had not had the opportunity of singing his island's praises to a really interested listener for a long time. It was always at the back of his mind, its potency undiminished, singing its siren song of towering rocks, dense forests and blue skies. He took out a book of photographs he had brought with him to remind himself of home.

Annie was impressed. His passion for the place reminded her that, as a girl, she had always yearned to travel, to see more of the world. In the event she had gone no further than back to Ireland for occasional holidays, and a couple of trips to Cornwall. They had run a suburban grocery business so they couldn't get away for long and her husband had always wanted to be close enough to get back home if anything went wrong. He had always worried about the shop.

'People didn't travel so much when we were young,' she said. 'Well, not people like us anyway. Some people got a fortnight in Spain or Portugal but we didn't even seem to get that.'

'Nothing wrong with a fortnight in Spain.' He grinned. 'A month would be better though!'

Annie and her husband had managed to educate their children to a standard higher than that to which they themselves had ever aspired. Ian and Margaret had been the first people in their family to go to university. They had, in some ways, educated their children away from them but they were proud of both of them. Annie would miss her daughter and her grandson, but she would delight in thinking of them somewhere so foreign, to her at least. It would seem like a vicarious pleasure to know that they were leading a life that was so different from her own. She told Luis as much now, surprising him with her enthusiasm.

'Well, there's no reason why it shouldn't be your life too, whenever you want. Perhaps you could come and see us. Spend some time with us. When we are settled in,' he said.

'Do you think so?'

'Of course. Why not? There's plenty of room at the house, you know. And I think you would get on very well with my mother. She keeps saying she would like to meet you.'

'I hope so. But I don't speak Spanish, Luis.'

'She has a little English. And I would translate. And Margarita is getting more fluent too.'

'Do you think,' she said, 'that I should maybe find an evening class in Spanish conversation?'

'Why not? It's not so difficult, you know. And you can do some lessons online, as well. I can show you.'

'Can you?'

'Of course.'

'I might surprise you all yet.'

He thought that she would probably do it. She looked very like his wife for an instant, sitting forward in her chair, her cheeks flushed with excitement at the idea of surprising her family. His heart went out to her.

'I'll speak to Margarita soon,' he said.

'You do that, son, and I'm sure she'll make the right decision for all of you.'

While Luis sought the right moment to speak to his wife about their future, Margaret was beginning to feel much more capable of taking that final plunge. Her growing health and strength had enabled her to see all too clearly that the most she could expect from Luis would be a few weeks' holiday in her native country each year. She had come to the conclusion that it was nothing so simple as dislike on his part. Scotland wasn't good for him. There was too much about the way of life that he couldn't understand. There was also too much about him that the Scots he met seemed to find challenging. They would publicly applaud his occasional performances, but privately, the men in particular would find opportunities to make disparaging remarks about Spain in general and the Canaries in particular. Even Fiona and Ian's friends, who should have known better, seemed to think that Luis's island consisted entirely of high rise hotels interspersed with golf courses. The realisation that he would never fully settle down here, however hard he might try, came to her one day in very early summer when he slouched dejectedly into the flat, too upset to be really angry.

Now that they had a flat of their own, Luis often did the shopping. He cooked a great deal, so it was natural that he should undertake frequent visits to the supermarket, the local greengrocer's, the butcher and the artisan bakery just along the road, happy to find so many small shops in this cosmopolitan area. He was a precise and temperamental shopper, demanding that his vegetables be fresh, prepared to argue over the exact stage of ripeness of an avocado. Margaret, after the first trip, refused to go with him, finding his imperiousness embarrassing, but the woman in the fruit and vegetable shop soon got used to him and gave as good as she got, haranguing him in Glaswegian, only half of which he understood. She even began to look forward to his visits. She was a small, thin woman, full of acid but good natured repartee. Luis, for his part, found her very comforting. Her loud and friendly brusqueness, her cheerful banter, reminded him of home.

'You sell your avocados when they are completely uneatable,' he said. 'This one is so hard it's like a big stone. It won't be ready to eat for a week at least.'

He picked up another fruit, marked down because the green skin was soft and slightly bruised. 'Look! This one is just right and yet you are all ready to throw it away.'

'I never eat the things myself, son,' she replied, vigorously. 'But Kelvinsiders are sold on them. Avocados and sourdough toast. I'd rather have marmalade. And you should shut up about it anyway. You're getting it cheap, aren't you? Are you wanting me to charge you full price for it? Eh?'

'No.' He grinned at her.

'That's better. Nice to see you smiling. Are they nice?' She nodded at the avocados.

'Wonderful. Soft and buttery. If you mash them up with some

lemon and garlic and a little chopped chilli and olive oil ... well, they are even better.'

'Sounds a bit powerful to me.'

'I'll bring you some in if you want to try. Smoked garlic – even better.'

'You do that.'

He was as good as his word, bringing her a plastic box of his own avocado dip.

'Are you a chef or something?'

'Not just now, but I have been, at home in the Canaries. And I hope I will be again some time soon.'

'What brings you here?' The shop was quiet for once. She had made herself a mug of tea and was sitting behind the counter, adding up columns of figures on a calculator and making notes. 'Jeez, but it's hard to make a living these days! Is it the same in Tenerife?'

'Yeah. Worse in some ways.'

'Is that why you're here then?'

'Not really. I married a Scotswoman. We plan to go back quite soon. But we have just had a baby.'

'Good for you. On both counts. What did you have?'

'A boy. A big boy.'

'Smashing. I love wee boys. Girls are great too, but I just love wee lads. Have three of them myself. Mostly grown now.'

'Lucky you.'

'I think so. Here's your avocados. You can come and cook my tea for me any time, son. And you can tell your wife I said so!'

This conversation made him so happy that when, on his way home, he saw a baby in a buggy parked outside a minimarket, he bent down to talk to the child, taking its soft hands in his, clapping them together, speaking gently in Spanish. The child laughed and gurgled and extricated one of its hands to tug at his hair. Then the mother arrived and snatched the child away as if he had been assaulting it, and glared at him as though he ought to have known better. He walked home, his high spirits all dissipated. Gloom descended on him. Again he found himself thinking, my son must not grow up here. My son must not spend his childhood here.

'What's the matter?' asked Margaret, concerned. 'You look terrible.' But when he explained, she shook her head at him in loving exasperation.

'You can't do that here, Luis,' she said. 'I know you can at home, but not here. Not men anyway. Hardly even women these days. Don't you know that we're obsessed with paedophilia here? There have been too many terrible stories. True stories. I know it's awful, but that's just the way it is.'

She felt sick that his gesture of kindness should be so misinterpreted. What could she say to him to make it better? He went and got a beer out of the fridge and sat quietly, drinking it, his head drooping.

She put her arms around him, kissed the top of his head. 'I know how you must be feeling. I know it's all wrong and I agree with you.'

'Do you?' He turned to gaze up at her.

'Oh Luis,' she said. 'Don't look at me like that. I'm not the enemy. I'm on your side. The truth is that if a man shows too much interest in children in this country, it's seen as being faintly sinister. We attribute all kinds of unsavoury motives to him. I suppose we forget that the real villains hide it well.'

She tried to think of a way of explaining the indefensible.

'I remember seeing a little girl sitting on a step in Los Cristianos,' she said at last. 'She was just a tot. A bit like your Marie Carmen. It was those houses in the precinct down by the seashore. You know?'

He nodded.

'Anyway, this man came out of one of the houses. He was about our age. I don't think he was her father but he knew her well. He looked as if he might be her uncle or even just a friend of the family, perhaps.

He bent down and kissed her. On the cheek. And again on the other cheek. He spoke to her very softly and gently, and she smiled up at him and hugged him and then off he went.'

'What is so wrong with that?'

'Nothing. Nothing is wrong with it at all. It's the most natural thing in the world. It was my own reaction to it that was all wrong. Even while I was watching and thinking, how nice, how gentle, another part of my mind was recoiling from it in some way. Not the thing to do. For a man to kiss a little girl like that. And yet it *was* only a kiss on the cheek. Openly and lovingly. And then it struck me that there must be something very wrong with me, not him.'

He nodded sadly.

'And that's when I realised how much we need, how much *I* need, something that you have. Some ability to touch and be physical and show affection that isn't sexual. Women can do it here but not men. And in schools these days, not even women. A small child falls down, the teacher has to think twice about picking them up and comforting them.'

'But that's crazy!'

'It's appalling and it's only getting worse. Every time there's a story in the media about the real thing, about sexual and physical abuse, and my God, there's enough of it, it affects everyone else in their day-to-day interactions with kids. We can't behave normally any more.' She thought of some of the threads she had read on Mumsnet. 'There's too much fear about. The vast majority of people carry on as though they're not even aware of their own deprivation. That's part of why people like you alarm people like Ian so much.'

'Do I? Why?'

'I think he wishes he were more like you, but he's afraid, and so he pretends to disapprove of you. Fiona too. It's their best defence. Do you understand me, Luis? *Me entiendes?*'

'I do,' he said wearily. 'I understand it with my head but not with my heart. I will never understand this way of thinking with my heart.'

Luis never could or would understand the British attitude to children. He had heard Spanish children called the most pampered brats in the world, but if they were, it turned them into human beings: good natured, sociable, outgoing little human beings who accompanied their parents everywhere and stayed up till all hours, falling asleep where they were. And if such treatment gave them an inflated sense of their own importance, what did it matter? Hell, he thought, they *were* important. They were the most important thing in the world, the most important thing in life.

At home on La Gomera if you went out with your children, people congratulated you on having such a blessing. Here they commiserated with you as though children were a species of curse, an affliction, visited upon certain unfortunate people. Except, he thought suddenly, for the woman in the fruit and vegetable shop. She had been happy to admit to loving her sons. And why not? But was she an exception? Or was he mistaken? He hardly knew what to think.

This national attitude was the thing that Luis found most incomprehensible about his wife's country. True, he saw plenty of young fathers spending time with their children, playing with them, talking to them, but occasionally he would also see a young man pushing a pram with one hand and walking alongside it as though it had nothing to do with him at all.

Signs outside hotels saying, 'Children Welcome' threw him into a passion. Margaret found it hard to understand him, until he said, 'In Spain children are welcome everywhere!' and suddenly she saw the world from his perspective and knew that he was right.

'It's like your kids' clubs,' he said to her, once. They had been sitting outside a cafe not far from the apartment with Eduardo fast asleep in his pram.

'What brought that on?'

He looked around. 'I don't know. I was thinking about seeing kids with their parents. You know, the resorts back home all have these kids' clubs.'

'Don't you approve?'

'I don't understand them. Why take a child on holiday with you if you are going to park them with a load of strangers while you go off to lie on the beach?'

'Because sometimes parents need a break? Because the kids like them?'

'How would you know if they liked them?'

She paused. 'Because they would complain.'

He looked at her shrewdly. 'Were you ever bullied at school?'

She thought about it. 'Yes. Yes I was.'

'What happened?'

'It was my primary school. I wasn't even five. Kids start formal schooling here quite young.'

'And?'

'The older girls – we called them the big girls – were supposed to look out for us at break time. And they did. At least, sometimes they sat with us and pretended. But when I think about it, they were awful to us. Nobody would have known, looking at us. It must have looked as though they were being nice wee motherly lassies, looking after the babies.'

He frowned. 'What did they do?'

'Hard to remember, really.' When she thought about it, she could only remember the fear. The overwhelming terror. 'They would pick on us. That's the expression. Have you heard that before?'

He shook his head.

'We sat on this low wall sometimes. Quite safe you'd think. But they would threaten to tip us off it. They didn't like my freckles. Called me 'spotty'. I had long hair. That got pulled a lot.'

'Your hair is beautiful. Maybe they were jealous.'

'Maybe they were. But it made no difference. It was all to do with power, I think. A wee power trip for them.'

He leaned down and stroked the baby's cheek.

'And tell me,' he said. 'Did you ever tell your parents about this?'

'No. Of course not. You don't, do you? I don't think parents know half of what goes on in schools. It makes me afraid for him, sometimes. Eduardo.'

'So you make my point for me. Kids' Clubs. Some people leave their kids there all day long. So many activities, they say. They love it. They just love it. But how would you ever know? Would they tell you if they were unhappy? Unhappy about something they could hardly describe, just as you – even now – can't describe it?'

'But it's not the same as school. Although ...'

'What?'

She started to laugh. 'I did run away from Brownies.'

'What is Brownies? A cake, yes?'

She had to look it up on her phone. '*Guidismo*,' she said. 'Brownie guides. The little version of guides. For wee girls. I hated it so much, Luis. I wasn't bullied or anything. I just didn't like all the organisation and having to do things. Having to join in. Anyway, we were playing this game called Sardines.'

Again he frowned. '*Sardinas*?'

'No. Well – yes, but it's a game. Like Hide and Seek. A horrible game. One person hides and then the others try to find her – but when they do, they join that person, quietly. So eventually, there's just one person left, looking for all the others. And that one person was me.'

'What did you do?'

I was running about, looking for them all. We were in an old church hall with gardens round about. Quite near mum's house. It closed a while ago but it was well attended back then and that's where we had the meetings. I thought they might be somewhere in the garden. They probably were. But then I saw the gate. It was open. And

I ran through it and didn't stop till I got home. It wasn't far, thank goodness.'

He was laughing too now. 'My poor Margarita! What did your parents say?'

'My mum and dad were very surprised. And cross that I was able to do it, of course. They didn't make me go back though. I think one of them must have gone along to explain where I'd gone. God!' She shook her head. 'They'd have been peeing themselves about safeguarding now, wouldn't they?'

'But the fact remains. Most the time, we don't tell our parents everything that happens.'

'No. You're right. We don't. Because sometimes we blame ourselves. But you can't supervise children all the time.'

Even as she said it, she realised how easy it had been to say that about other people's children, and how difficult it would be to practise that where Eduardo was concerned.'

'They must have freedom. But we have to like them as well as love them,' he said. 'I don't understand how people don't like to spend time with their own kids, doing things, seeing things. Doesn't have to involve a lot of money. Everyone can walk, go fishing, make things. Time enough for beach holidays before you have kids.'

'I wasn't that keen on them even then.' She thought about her first husband, stretched out on the beach, refusing to go anywhere. 'Alastair liked that kind of thing.'

'But not you?'

'No. I like seeing things.' She remembered her first visit to Teide, with Luis. Their first date which had turned out to be a near disaster. He was smiling at her. 'Even when I lost my head a bit,' she added.

He leaned over and kissed her. 'It turned out OK in the end though, didn't it?'

CHAPTER NINE

I would like to go back
to the garden of your tender love,
if I could pick the same flower,
three times over.

Rather to Luis's surprise, the couple of gigs in Ricky's restaurant had been a great success. Requests had begun to come in for him to do other one-off performances at this or that hotel or club, requests he had to turn down, explaining that he had only played to oblige a friend. Stressing that it wasn't work. Just a hobby. Hating having to say this, even while he did so.

It was success of a minor kind. There were no enticements to fame and fortune, which was probably just as well in view of his immigration status. Ricky had posted a video of him singing and playing on YouTube and he had started to gain a following, especially among young women, but Luis had persuaded him to take it down, worried about Border Force knocking on the door.

'Not going to happen,' said Ricky, laughing. 'Not in Glasgow. Do you think they'll send you to a prison hulk?'

'*Que*? What is this prison hulk?'

'There's a barge. For illegal immigrants. Like in Great Expectations.'

'You mean the book?'

'I was thinking of the movie.'

Luis thought about prison barges and shuddered. Knowing when he was onto a good thing, Ricky had looked into the possibility of hiring Luis on a Creative Worker Visa. But the constraints were so crazy, the process so ridiculously complicated, that he had said 'oh the bastards can get tae fuck! If anyone enquires, I'll tell them you're my visiting cousin, having a wee practice in my bar. But I wish you'd make up your mind to stay here, Luis. We could really make something of you, you know. I keep imagining all the good gigs I could get for you.'

'I just want to go home!' He was half ashamed of the way it sounded, even to his own ears. Like a miserable child. 'I already am something at home! And I have a business to run.'

'I know you do, son, but it's a crying shame, so it is. I mean look at you. The lassies are so taken with you. You could make yourself some serious *dinero* here.'

'I'm a musician. Not a …' he struggled for the word. '*Lotario.*'

'Is that what you call it?' Ricky chuckled. 'We'd say lothario. Or Casanova. Or gigolo. Take your pick.'

Luis told Margaret all about this conversation, laughing at the thought of himself as a gigolo, but when Margaret incautiously related it to Fiona, her sister-in-law's reaction surprised her.

'You're so innocent, you know,' she said.

'What on earth do you mean?' asked Margaret, irritably.

'Just that you're so trusting. I'd shorten that lead a bit if I were you, Margaret.'

'Luis isn't a dog.'

'You know what I mean. This freedom and trust is all very well, but you know what men are. You should know that more than most. And he's a very attractive man, isn't he? Sometimes you have to fight just to hold onto a man like that.'

There had been a definite change in Fiona's attitude to Luis over the past few weeks. Margaret had first noticed it when they had been visiting the in-laws for Sunday lunch and Fiona had fussed over him, laughing at his jokes, pressing second helpings of pudding on him. It was an indication of a one-sided thaw in the ice between them. Luis maintained an air of distant politeness with his sister-in-law. He still didn't like her very much. Her meddling and her tactlessness and her bossiness irritated him but he remained civil to her if only for his wife's sake.

'She's certainly being very nice to you,' said Margaret, after a particularly trying visit.

'She is, isn't she? She can't seem to get enough of me!'

Fiona had persuaded Ian to take a couple of his clients to the restaurant on one of the rare occasions when Luis happened to be playing. She insisted on introducing him to them afterwards so that he was obliged to sit at their table and have a drink with them.

Sometimes, in passing, she would even lay a casual hand on his arm.

'Perhaps she's noticed your true worth,' said Margaret.

'No. She has a – what is the word? – a crush on me.'

'Perhaps she has.'

'The stupid woman is always fluttering her eyelashes at me and trying to sound sexy whenever she speaks to me.'

'It all sounds very silly to me.'

'It *is* silly. I wish she would stop it.'

Margaret would never have believed it if she hadn't seen the evidence with her own eyes. But he was right. He wasn't imagining or exaggerating. He wasn't the kind of man who thought every woman fancied him, even though many of them did. Fiona had definitely changed her attitude to Luis. It was embarrassing to watch because it was clear that she couldn't help herself. Ian was placid, undemonstrative, self contained, like his father. The children too were quite inhibited when it came to physical displays of affection. Perhaps Fiona was as lonely in her own way as she, Margaret, had been on Tenerife. That was an uncomfortable thought.

'Anyway, she can't have you!'

'*Estoy muy seguro!* I'm sure she can't.'

She became aware that Luis was grinning wickedly.

'What are you doing to do about it?' she asked in some trepidation.

'Nothing. Well, not much, anyway.'

He would say no more and Margaret was forced to leave the matter there, but soon she saw that if he did little to encourage Fiona, he did nothing to discourage her either. Occasionally he would treat her to one of his dazzling, heart-stopping smiles, and Margaret knew just how effective they could be. And once, when the in-laws were visiting the apartment, he played and sang a little love song, looking straight at Fiona while he was singing it. Margaret, ensconced in the most comfortable chair with the baby in her arms, was horrified to see Fiona's features melt into a sort of dreamy fascination.

She felt compelled to raise the subject with Luis again.

'You're flirting. She'll get the wrong impression.'

'Whatever impression she gets, it will be her own fault. Not mine.'

'Oh Luis, you're doing it deliberately!'

'Well of course I am. But only ever in public.'

Luis had been replacing a string on his guitar. Margaret was standing by the window. He finished his task, came over and put his arms around her, pulling her very close. 'As long as *you* don't get the wrong impression. You know who I love, Margarita. I wouldn't have done it if you hadn't been there. You know that, don't you?'

'Yes,' she said. 'I do know.'

'I only love you. *Quiero estar contigo para siempre.* I want to be with you forever.'

'But I'm not sure she understands that! She's a grown woman!'

'Oh – she's not stupid. She'll get over it.'

'I hope so.'

In spite of her misgivings about the wisdom of his behaviour, she thought that she had better leave well alone. Whatever mistakes Fiona might choose to make were her own affair and ultimately her own problem. Whatever casual mischief Luis might choose to get up to, she couldn't stop him. She believed that he was faithful to her, she trusted him implicitly, and that was all that mattered.

In late May, during a settled spell of unusually fine weather, Ricky Mackay gave a barbecue party to which Luis and Margaret were invited, as were Ian and Fiona.

'Bring your guitar,' said Ricky. 'We'd like you to play for us.'

It was, thought Luis resentfully, in the nature of a command performance. It was always happening to musicians. He was tempted to deliberately forget the guitar but Margaret wouldn't let him.

'What about the baby?' Luis asked his boss. 'Can we bring him?'

Ricky pursed his lips. 'Not that kind of party, Luis.'

Somewhat mutinously, Luis agreed to leave Eduardo with Annie and take his guitar to the party instead. Margaret was still feeding him herself, but she was getting better at expressing milk, and the baby loved his nana.

Margaret had not been looking forward to this occasion either. She had gone into town, looking for something appropriate to wear and had found a pretty and stylish cotton dress with a leafy print. She suspected that Ricky's friends and colleagues would be over confident and difficult. Their talk would be of money and golf and the iniquities of taxation. She was right. The house was a large and ostentatious suburban mansion with a heated swimming pool and sauna in the back garden. Every room was swamped by gigantic arrangements of flowers. In the sitting room a life size pottery Dalmatian dog sat on what looked distressingly like a real zebra-skin rug. Margaret caught Luis's eye with something between dismay and hilarity. He grinned, raised his eyebrows.

'*Griferi de oro!*' he said.

'What?'

'Gold bath taps, probably. Dictator chic.'

Ricky's third wife was called Sharon. She was much younger than he was, and very pretty, with a great deal of honey blonde hair, gold jewellery and obviously expensive clothes. Margaret envied the vintage blouse, encrusted with gorgeous antique lace. With it, she wore a soft turquoise leather midi-skirt and matching shoes that looked as though they might have been hand made especially for her. Margaret could only speculate what the outfit must have cost. Sharon was, surprisingly enough, a farmer's daughter. Miss Scotch Lamb of some years previously. To their surprise, Margaret and Luis liked her immediately, found her easy company. She laughed a lot but behind the façade, Margaret thought, there was a keen intellect. Somewhere upstairs, Ricky's youngest child, two year old Ben, was being put to bed by the nanny. His other children, five in all, were grown up and most of them were away from home.

Margaret had met Ricky a couple of times but this was the first occasion on which she had ever done more than pass the time of day with him. He wore a white shirt and tight but well cut jeans, not entirely suitable for a man of his large build. Gold dripped from his wrist in the form of a chunky watch and identity bracelet. He looked rather like an ageing but successful country and western star.

She made polite small talk, but she could see at once that he found her boring. She could think of nothing to say to him that he might find remotely interesting. His eyes drifted away from her face in pursuit of somebody more exciting. She tried asking him about himself, but his answers were monosyllabic. Presently, he excused himself and walked away to greet another group of guests. Ricky was, she saw, the kind of man who could never bring himself to make any real conversation with a woman unless he was attracted to her, but then he would be totally and embarrassingly attentive. She had met such men before and been hurt by their rudeness. Now she was old enough and confident enough to acknowledge that the fault lay with him rather than herself.

She shrugged the encounter off and turned her attention to Luis.

It was one more thing she loved about him. He liked women of all ages, was attentive to them, not in any creepy way, but with a genuine interest, a genuine pleasure in their company. It was probably the result of being brought up in a house with so many strong women. He looked elegant and graceful in a blue linen shirt with the sleeves rolled up, and blue jeans. She had seen Fiona watching him and knew that her sister-in-law thought so too, and the knowledge gave her a perverse satisfaction.

At one end of the lawn stood a couple of large gas barbecues, attended by several of an army of young caterers, where steaks and trout sizzled and steamed deliciously. A trestle table was heavy with salads, cheeses, breads of all kinds, plates, cutlery and napkins. In the breakfast room, where French windows led out on to a paved terrace, was a sumptuous array of glittering bottles and glasses: wines and spirits, beers and soft drinks, the red wine in rows on the table, the bubbles and beer and soft drinks propped up in baths of ice.

'He likes to do things in style,' Ian said to Luis.

'So I see.'

Margaret stayed close to her husband, a little shy of the crowd of braying people, clutching glasses and gossiping with easy familiarity. She was glad of Luis's confident presence. He felt the unaccustomed tenacity of her grasp and put his free hand over hers.

'I don't much like big parties like this,' she said.

'Why not?'

'I don't know anybody.'

'Neither do I.'

Naturally gregarious, Luis liked to circulate, liked to converse, speaking to this or that group, and then coming back to check that all was well with her. A couple arrived late, accompanied by two boisterous dogs, Irish setters. The dogs bounced into the garden, knocking over glasses with their tails and thrusting wet noses into the bowls of cheese dip. Ricky welcomed dogs and owners volubly and impartially.

'Do you see that?' said Luis, emerging so it seemed to Margaret from nowhere, glass in hand.

'What?' She had been looking at the roses. Not a greenfly or a black spot in sight. She supposed there must be a gardener. Or several. Wouldn't it be nice to have money, she thought. It might not be true that money bought happiness, but it certainly brought comfort. She must found out more about gardening. The thought of her own garden, waiting for her on La Gomera, gave her a little thrill of longing to be there.

'Dogs are welcome but not children. Huh!' He was plainly disgusted.

'But I've already told you – we're far more tolerant of our fur babies than of children here.'

'So I see.'

Margaret went away to fill their glasses and when she returned, found her husband at the centre of a small group of guests. One man, a solicitor called Roy, had asked him what part of Spain he came from and when he replied, pulled a face.

'The Canaries?' He pursed his lips.

'What's wrong with the Canaries?'

'I went there once. Like Blackpool with sunshine. Couldn't wait to get home. I expect that's why you've come over here, mm?' He laughed heartily at his own wit.

Margaret caught Luis's enraged eye and winked at him. It was all she could think of to avert the storm. Ever since his arrival, people had been casually denigrating his home to him, asking him if it was true that Tenerife was as awful as the tabloids made out, a concrete jungle littered with drunken or drugged young Brits and local gangsters. Roy's remark was the final straw.

'The next person who says something nasty about *Las Islas Canarias* – I think I will have to punch him on the nose,' said Luis, matter-of-factly. 'I am so tired of telling everyone what a fine place it is. In future, I think I will just have to resort to physical violence.'

The group of admirers melted away. Margaret handed her husband another drink.

'Shut up,' she said. 'Just shut up and smile.'

'I'm sick of smiling. I would rather punch somebody.'

'Be quiet,' she said again. 'Please, Luis. For me.'

'For you then.'

He gulped at his drink and kept very quiet but inside he felt the stirrings of a storm of emotion. The resentment of weeks simmered there.

'Let's eat,' said Margaret. 'Come on. It'll make you feel a whole lot better, I promise. The food smells wonderful.'

After the meal, which did make him feel a bit more mellow, Luis was persuaded to play his guitar, not sure whether he was being treated as an honoured guest or as the hired hand. Always sensitive to nuance, he thought that it was perhaps more of the latter, although Ricky couldn't help being proud of what he considered to be his protégé. Most of the guests listened quietly and applauded very cordially, but there were one or two who carried on drinking and laughing, that peculiarly loud and offensive laugh of a certain kind of over-confident middle aged man. A mobile phone rang in the middle of a tender love song, the comical ringtone shattering the silence. The phone's owner answered it without apology and talked loudly into it until shushed by his neighbours at the same table. By the end of the performance, Luis was practically shaking with suppressed rage. He was used to people chatting while he played. After all, it happened all the time in Los Cristianos. But in this situation, he found it peculiarly offensive.

Margaret was standing beside Fiona, who, tipsy on champagne, clapped loudly after each song. She caught Margaret looking at her, and Margaret saw a red flush that had nothing to do with the evening sunlight spreading up from her sister-in-law's neck to her cheeks. She felt an uncharacteristic desire to shield Fiona from Luis's scorn. She knew how Fiona felt but there was no way of helping her. If she had a crush on Luis – and it was becoming clearer all the time that she did – she would just have to deal with it in her own way.

It grew late and summer twilight descended on the garden. Luis was nowhere to be seen and Margaret found herself beside Roy again. She began to talk to him in a half-hearted attempt to convince him of the beauty of the Canaries. Since his conversation with Luis he had drunk a great deal of whisky and was open to persuasion. He seemed to find Margaret very attractive, though she fancied that he could see two of her in his drunken state. He told her all about his holiday in Las Americas and how his sleep had been disturbed by loud music and then by drunken homeward-going youths at four or five in the morning.

'I expect they were Brits though,' she said mildly. 'The locals seldom drink like that.'

He gazed at her, frowning, as though it had never occurred to him. Like her ex-husband, he had never ventured further than the hotel pool, and so knew very little about the rest of the island. Margaret clutched her glass and nodded and smiled up at him, listening to the drunken wow and flutter of his voice, trying not to breathe in the blasts of fiery whisky coming, dragon-like, from his mouth. She wondered how best to escape. Perhaps she should just abandon him.

To add to her discomfort, she realised that they were alone behind an arbour where a clematis clambered among herbaceous plants. She had only just noticed it, but the rest of the party-goers had moved away. Luis, where are you when I need you? she thought. After his performance, a group of female admirers had gathered around him and she had left him alone to charm them in peace, not noticing that there was an edge to his voice and a sardonic gleam in his eye, even as he accepted their compliments.

She wished that she had stayed close beside him. It would have been better all round. Roy had started to tell her about his own broken marriage, just as she was about to say 'excuse me' and escape. She saw his eyes fill up with alcohol induced tears. He had been divorced the previous year. In an effort to jolly him along, she said, 'Cheer up, Roy. I'm sure you'll find somebody else soon. Just look at me.'

He misunderstood, deliberately so it seemed.

'I am looking at you,' he said. 'You're very beautiful, you know.'

'Oh don't be silly.'

'No. I'm serious. What are you doing married to that guy then?'

'I can't think what you mean,' she said coldly.

'He must be good at something,' Roy screwed up his face, grotesquely. 'Is that what it is, eh?' He laughed, offensively. 'Found yourself a gigolo? Doesn't look as if he has much cash. What was he? A waiter?'

By this time, they were sitting side by side on a bench. She had thought they had better sit down before he fell down but it had been a mistake. She tried to get up again, and his arm shot out. He seized her hand in his own sweaty paw, fumbling at it, trying to scratch her palm with his fat fingers.

'Come on. You can tell me. I want to know. He's very good looking, I'll give you that. All the girls seem to like him. Clucking around him like so many hens. What has he got that I haven't?'

'Well for one thing he's polite and for another he isn't drunk,' she said, trying to pull her hand away. He was surprisingly strong. He pulled her back down beside him and she was shocked to find his free hand fumbling at her breast.

'Oh don't be so stupid!' she said. 'And so offensive!' She stamped down hard on his foot. She was sitting down, and her heels weren't as lethal as Sharon's, but they were sharp enough. His shiny shoes protected him to some extent, but he still slid away from her. 'Ouch! That hurt!'

With a wrench, she was free of him, standing up. Clumsily he rose to remonstrate with her. Then she saw the tall figure of her husband moving past her, his elbow drawn back, his hand clenched into a fist. She had a swift impression of a bowstring drawn taut.

'No!' she said, but it was too late.

'*Cabron!*' said Luis, and punched Roy full on the nose. The hapless solicitor collapsed onto the bench, clutching at his face.

Luis's arm was already drawn back for another blow but she interposed herself between them. Furiously he tried to push her aside.

'*Largate!*' he said, and when she would not move, '*No te metas en esto!*' Don't interfere!

'*Para*,' she said, breaking into Spanish in hopes of getting through his anger. '*No! Es tonto!*' Stop. Don't do it. He's a fool.

Roy was moaning. 'He's broken my nose. He's broken my nose.'

Ricky and Sharon Mackay burst through the bushes. It was, thought Margaret, like a scene from a farce. She had a sudden and unfortunate desire to laugh.

'This man was assaulting my wife,' said Luis dramatically.

Ricky raised his eyebrows in surprise. Sharon covered her mouth with her hand, but not before a splutter of laughter had escaped. Margaret was crimson and almost speechless with embarrassment.

'He tried to make a pass at me,' Margaret said at last, aware that the expression sounded oddly old fashioned. 'He's a bit drunk. Luis saw it. He's very protective.'

She waited, wondering how Ricky would react, but she needn't have worried. Ricky was too proud of his own Italian background.

'Lucky you didn't get a knife in your guts, pal,' was all he said to his unfortunate guest. He put his arm around Luis's shoulders and led him away. 'See to Roy,' he added majestically, speaking to his wife, who still seemed to be trying to suppress another fit of giggles. 'Come and let me get you another drink, pal.'

Blood was still pouring through the hapless Roy's fingers but the nose looked otherwise intact. Sharon helped him to his feet and escorted him to the kitchen. Margaret followed, apologising for her husband, visualising court cases with allegations of grievous bodily harm. Deportation. Roy was a lawyer, after all. Together, she and Sharon mopped his face. The blow seemed to have sobered him.

'My fault,' he kept saying, dolefully. 'All my fault. Forgive me. I should have known better. Give my apologies to your husband. And to Ricky. Do tell Ricky how sorry I am!'

It was clear that upsetting Ricky was a far more serious matter for him than a bloody nose. Sharon was again having difficulty suppressing her laughter. Margaret liked her very much for it.

'I think I should go and find my husband,' she said to her hostess. 'See if he's managed to calm down.'

'I would if I were you. He needs looking after, that one. Mind you, he can look after himself pretty well, can't he?' She went off into peals of laughter again. 'Oh God, Margaret, it's made my day! It's so – I don't know – so operatic!'

Margaret went out into the garden. Word of the fight had spread among the other guests. On the whole their sympathy lay with Luis. They may not exactly have approved of the Spaniard, but Roy was not popular. There was something fascinating about a man fighting for his wife's honour. It matched the stereotype of the hot-blooded Latin. Ian was trying to laugh it off, but she could tell that he was horrified. On the other hand, Fiona was making sounds of extreme disapproval but Margaret could see that she was secretly very excited by the fight. Ricky was not very tactfully soothing Luis's ruffled feathers, and Margaret thought that she had better get her husband away before he burned another bridge and was rude to his host as well. She was relieved to find that he had calmed down and was looking around rather sheepishly for his wife.

He said, '*Lo siento mucho*,' to her – I'm very sorry – in a low voice and allowed himself to be led away.

They took a taxi to their apartment where Annie was babysitting and sent her home in the same cab. They didn't venture to tell her about the fight. Ian and Fiona were still at the party and they would certainly give her all the gory details in the morning. Eduardo slept on and Margaret made a pot of tea but for a little while, the silence of embarrassment hung over them.

At last Margaret said, 'He was very, very drunk, you know. I shouldn't have even spoken to him, but I didn't realise until it was too late. I wasn't encouraging him or anything. I was just trying to be polite. You did overreact though.'

He put his arm around her. 'I know. I'm so sorry. But I lost my temper. It was wrong, but I couldn't help it. I have this impulse to defend you.'

'As you would a piece of property?'

'No. Well, maybe. Not property. But – the person I love. I can't seem to help it. It goes very deep with me. I think you may just have to take me as I am.'

'Actually ...' she said, and stopped.

'What?'

'Actually, it may be wrong of me to say this, but ...'

'What?'

'It's very sexy.'

'Is it?'

'Oh yes. Oh God, yes.'

CHAPTER TEN

Blessed St Anthony,
I ask three things of you:
good health, good luck, and a husband
who doesn't sleep with anyone but me.

A little while later, the baby woke for his feed and went back to sleep again immediately afterwards. The night was warm, with the light already showing in the eastern sky. At this time of the year the nights were only a few hours long. They threw open the windows to let in the fresh air from the communal gardens nearby. The scent of early summer flowers drifted up. Nemesia, she thought. She put the baby back into his cot, then undressed and went through to the bathroom to clean her teeth. Naked, Luis followed her and put his arms around her from behind, across her breasts, over the thin cotton of her nightie, nuzzling into her neck. She felt him grow hard and pressed herself back against him.

'So,' he spoke to her reflection in the mirror. 'What was so sexy about it?'

'You. It isn't the violence. I don't like that. I wish you hadn't hit him. But there's so much energy about you. It's exciting. It excites me.'

He held her tighter, his hands moving over her body.

'Do you want me now?' he demanded, again of her reflection. She saw her face with his own above it, his lips on her hair.

She caught her breath.

'Yes, I want you.'

'Tell me what you want.'

She turned towards him, faintly embarrassed by her reflection, by the arousal in her own eyes.

'Tell me what you want,' he persisted.

'You.'

'Where?' He ran his fingers down her belly, lower, lifting the nightdress.

'Inside me.'

'When?'

'Now.'

'Here?'

'Wherever you want.'

The words excited him as they aroused her. They had never quite got back to normal after the birth of the baby. The times when the baby was asleep and they were awake were few and far between. The times when fatigue had not pole-axed them were also few, and the coincidence of those times with sexual inclination was rare. Besides, she was still half afraid of the pain, the wounds of the birth only just healed, so it seemed to her.

'I'll show you,' he said. 'Come on.'

Luis pulled off her nightie and switched on the shower. Together they climbed inside the curtains and stood close under the soothing stream. Then they soaped each other's bodies, unhurriedly, lovingly, each paying attention to the other. They kissed under the water, and their lips were wet inside and out. He leaned her against the wall and slipped inside her, tantalisingly, very gently, kissing her at the same time with his tongue dipping into her mouth.

They switched off the water and dried each other and listened for the baby, just in case, but no sound came from the cot, except once they heard a little sigh as he changed position in his sleep, and that was reassuring.

As they went to bed, they could hear the sharp notes of the early birds echoing down the street from the city trees, sycamore, laburnum, horse chestnuts, and they knew that they would be exhausted the next day, but they didn't care. Not now. As she lay there, so open to him, dizzy with expectation, she thought of the way he had moved her to one side, to shield her from Roy, not roughly because he was never anything but gentle with her, but firmly all the same.

'*No te metas en esto!*' Don't meddle with this.

The contrast between that and his present abandonment to her was sexy, was a huge turn-on, she thought, half ashamed of herself, wondering why it should be so. She shivered with pleasure, with intense arousal.

Luis, sensing her rising climax, moved round and then pulled her up on top of him, her hands resting on his shoulders. He took her nipple in his mouth just before she came with a cry of satisfaction. He felt her whole body convulse and the sweet, warm milk spouted into his mouth.

'What a thing to do,' she said. 'Taking the food out of the wean's mouth.'

'Wean?'

'Child. *Niño*. Here in the West of Scotland, anyway.'

'I'm not surprised he likes it so much. It's nectar.'

'It's sweet, isn't it? I tasted it when I was expressing it one day.'

He turned her on to her back and she felt him moving gently inside her, a little cautiously for fear of hurting her, his face intent and absorbed, until he too cried out at his own pleasure.

She cuddled up close to him and he cradled her in his arms, one leg over her legs. Outside the light grew stronger.

'Luis,' she said. 'I love you so much. I can't tell you how much I love you. I'm drunk with love for you.'

'And I with you.'

He found her lips again and kissed her, companionably this time, with affection rather than passion. She thought that sometimes this was best of all, this closeness and warmth, this being comfortable afterwards, bodies familiar, fitting together. This not having to dissemble or pretend. Knowing each other so lovingly and intimately.

'Never leave me,' she said, suddenly.

'Why would you think I would ever leave you?'

'I don't know. Luis?'

'What?' He was already half asleep, his face buried in her hair.

'I'll go back to La Gomera with you whenever you like. Just say the word.'

He was surprised into wakefulness.

'What did you say?'

'Let's go back to La Gomera. Let's go back to *La Manzana Dorada*. Soon. I want to be there. I want the garden. Let's not wait any longer.'

'Are you sure?'

'Absolutely.'

They slept, but in a couple of hours the baby woke them with his cries and they staggered out of bed to face the day, fortifying themselves with mugs of coffee and slices of toast.

'Did I dream it?' Luis asked. 'Or did you tell me that you wanted to go back to La Gomera with me?'

'You didn't dream it.'

'It wasn't just the lovemaking?'

She laughed. 'Well, I loved the lovemaking. But I do want to go. Soon. Whenever you like, really.'

By that morning's post, however, came an excited letter from Cristina. She had managed to get some extended leave from the bank, and would be flying over to Glasgow for three weeks.

Luis sighed. 'It means we'll have to stay on for a little while at least. If we're to give her a holiday. Do you mind, now that you've decided?'

'No. Of course I don't. So long as we've made up our minds. Besides, you'll have to contact Paco, sort things out with him. It'll take a few weeks, when you think about it.'

'And I'd like to give Cristina a really good holiday over here before we go back. I think she deserves it. I think it would be good for her.'

Luis telephoned Paco and Carmen later that day.

'Well?' said Paco, 'Are you enjoying being a *guitarrista* in Scotland?'

'Not much. Besides, I play very seldom. It's illegal.'

'How is that?'

'Because I'm a filthy immigrant.'

'Is it really like that?'

'Well – not in Scotland, no. They're fine here. But everything has changed, for sure. Or maybe it was always like that. Who knows? I wonder why anyone would want to come to live and work here. They'd be crazy. If they had other options.'

'That's sad.'

'It is. I want to come home. We both do, now.'

'About time too. I was beginning to think you had changed your mind.'

'Things were a bit difficult after the birth. I think I'm going mad. Living among strangers.'

'But your Margarita was living among strangers too,' Paco observed mildly.

'I know. I have so much respect for her. So much love for her.'

'Well, that's good. But she's ready to come with you?'

'I think she is now. It has taken a while for her to recover.'

'That's what Carmen said. She was right. Carmen and Maria both. Give it time, they said.'

'But now, Cristina wants to come over here for a holiday. We'll have to stay and show her something of Scotland.'

'So I heard. Three weeks?'

'That's what she has. They owed her some holidays. And in any case, we'll need a little longer, just to finalise things here. Pack up this flat. See if we can get flights and so on. I have only six months you know. Which means I must leave here before late August anyway.'

'August would certainly suit us.'

'We could agree to take over the restaurant by the end of that month. But I'll come over well before then. Stay at home with the family. Get things ready. Help with your move too.'

'You don't need to worry about that. We have plenty of help here.'

'I know. But I want to. We could work our way into things and be ready for when the visitors come for some winter sunshine.'

'That would be just fine.'

Paco was very fond of Cristina. 'I'll get the lawyers on to it,' he said. 'Let the girl have a good trip to Scotland, and we'll see you at the end of July.'

'How's the guitar?' asked Luis.

Paco laughed. 'She is just fine. I take her out and play her from time to time.' Paco and Luis both thought of that particular precious instrument as female.'

'Are you sorry you gave her to me?'

'No, of course not. I'm delighted that she has a good home. And a fine musician to play her.'

CHAPTER ELEVEN

Our host told us that there was no means of educating his daughters
on the island. It was a great distress to him that they should be entirely
dependent on him for whatever knowledge they might acquire.
They were exceedingly pleasant girls.

Olivia M Stone, 1887

Just as Luis was longing for home, Cristina was yearning to escape. She loved her family, but ever since Luis had gone off to university and then gone travelling, she had wanted to get away as well. None of her friends had gone very far, except for her schoolfriend Teresa, who had simply packed her bags one day and left without telling anyone, getting a job first in Puerto de la Cruz on Tenerife and then travelling to mainland Spain. She had married on the mainland and now she was settled down with a good career and a family. They spoke occasionally online, sent an infrequent card. But they didn't keep in touch as they once had. Not all of Cristina's female friends had kept their careers as well as their families, unless a couple worked together like Paco and Carmen. For some, the job was simply a stop-gap until they could find a husband, although times had changed and most couples now needed two incomes just to survive.

One by one, all her friends had paired off with young men, either from the island or from Tenerife. Cristina had gone to their weddings and celebrated with them; had been to the christenings of their first and second children. Most of them, unlike her mother's generation, had stopped at two. Cristina had worked in the bank since leaving school and now she was in a position of some seniority and trust. She saw herself in twenty years time, caring for an ailing mother perhaps and still tied to the island and the bank. Much as she loved her mother, the thought horrified her, but she felt powerless to change things, treading water at home.

Luis was always encouraging her to take a job on the mainland or at least on Tenerife. The fault, she thought, lay with her own lack of courage, with the way in which she had allowed the caution of others to influence her, even though they probably had more in common than she realised, both too susceptible to the influence of others.

Now, her brother's marriage had galvanized her into action. Her brother's wife had brought with her something of the keen winds of Scotland. She seemed foreign and fascinating to Cristina, who had immediately and enthusiastically taken to her sister-in-law. When news came that Margaret and Luis had rented an apartment in Scotland for a couple of months, Cristina was secretly delighted, trying to hide her elation from Maria, who looked only for her son's return. Cristina saw that here at last lay an opportunity and an excuse for travel. She must seize it with both hands. She could go and stay with her brother. She could go to Glasgow, if only for a holiday.

She bought a map of Scotland and studied it, repeating the magical place names to herself: Balquidder, Stranraer, Motherwell, Aberarder, Inchnadamph.

Her mother fussed over her.

'You'll take care of yourself? Glasgow is a very big city, Cristina. Even Luis thinks it can be a dangerous place.'

'Not very dangerous. And I'll take care, don't worry. I'm not a child.'

Maria went across to the airport on Tenerife with Juan and Isabel to see Cristina off. Tina's case was full of little gifts for the baby as well as mementos of the island, hints for Luis perhaps including one or two small, carefully wrapped pieces of the pleasing brown pottery of the island for other members of Margaret's family.

Cristina had flown infrequently and then mostly between islands on bank business and a couple of times to Madrid. At the busy airport, the smell of aviation fuel threatened to overwhelm her with a mixture of excitement and anticipation. She had lain awake for many nights worrying about the flight, but when at last she had said her goodbyes and was sitting aboard the plane with her seat belt fastened, nervousness gave way to interest. Her journey passed all too quickly and soon they were descending towards Glasgow airport. The sinking feeling in her stomach was not entirely due to the measure of turbulence as they came down through low cloud. For a few hours she had been suspended in the sky, in a kind of limbo, but now she was seized again by a combination of pleasure and agitation at the thought of stepping out into this foreign place. As she came through the swing doors, she was enveloped in her brother's arms, her head pressed against his shoulder. Behind him she saw Margaret, smiling, holding the baby.

The next few hours were a happy blur. Her impressions of the city, of the apartment, were vivid but disjointed. They took a cab from the airport and joined a motorway that seemed to traverse the city, a dazzling collection of fly-overs and unders, with various bridges crossing the great silver river at the heart of the place. It was all hectic with cars, a slow journey hindered by dozens of sets of traffic lights, and Cristina fell quiet, staring out of the window, stunned by the bustle and urgency.

She was relieved at last to reach the sanctuary of the flat, although the distant buzz of traffic could still be heard. She loved the high, light rooms, full of the scent of baking. Margaret had made scones in her honour. The spare bedroom had been very spartan when they first moved in. Ronald's visitors never minded about their surroundings as long as they had somewhere reasonably comfortable to sleep, but Margaret had borrowed a few small ornaments and a pair of pretty curtains from her mother to make the room welcoming for Cristina. There were flowers and a few books and magazines. Eduardo's cot was in their own bedroom. It was easier when Margaret had to feed him in the night, and the sound of their breathing seemed to soothe him.

'You'll be making a rod for your own back,' said Fiona, smugly.

But Luis didn't mind. 'I love having him beside us,' he said. 'And I don't suppose he'll still be sleeping in our room when he's a teenager!'

'I certainly hope not,' said Fiona, wilfully literal.

'I'll leave you to unpack in peace.' Margaret hugged Cristina. 'Oh, it is nice to have you here. I'll bring you a mug of coffee, and then we can start on the wine. Make yourself at home.'

Cristina sat on the bed and took a deep breath. She was tired and excited at the same time. She got up and methodically began to unpack her bag, hanging jeans and a few tops and a couple of dresses in the wardrobe, arranging underwear neatly in the empty chest of drawers. She had almost finished when Margaret came in bearing an enormous mug of coffee and a plate of buttered scones.

'How do you like your first impression of Glasgow?'

'It's a little overwhelming. After the island.'

'I know. It must seem very hectic. But we'll show you something of the countryside as well while you're here. And it's a beautiful city, once you get used to it.'

'It's all so big. There's so much of it. I thought it would be like Santa Cruz, but there's much more of it. It's wonderful!'

'Do you think so? It's a friendly place, you know. People are very nice here. Very kind.'

'Oh, I'm sure I will get used to it, Margarita.'

In the other room, Eduardo began to cry.

'Hungry boy. He's always hungry.' Margaret stood up. 'Finish your unpacking and then come through, Tina. We'll open a bottle of wine. Luis wants to make some plans. You know what he's like. He wants to show you round immediately. Just make sure you tell him when you've had enough. It took me ages to make him understand that I sometimes wanted to stop for a coffee!'

'Does he like Glasgow so much?'

'Not very much, no. I don't think so, anyway. But he admires it. It's growing on him. It usually does on most people.'

Shabby as it was, these days – and she had been suddenly aware of its shabbiness – there was still an energy about it that became irresistible after a while. Which was a bit like Luis himself. The energy, if not the shabbiness.

'My mother was worried that you might want to stay here for good.'

'Oh no. No. And besides, that would be quite difficult for Luis now.'

'Even though you're married?'

'Even though we're married. I have my precious dual citizenship. But it would be a lot harder for Luis now, even if he wanted to stay here, which he doesn't.'

'And what about you?'

'We're coming back to La Gomera very soon. I can't wait. The sale should finalised any time now.'

'My mother will be so relieved.'

'But you're to have your holiday first. Don't you worry about us. I've been wanting to show Luis something of Scotland before we go back. Somebody's lending us a car.'

That somebody was Ricky, but she suspected it was his wife, Sharon, who had prompted the offer of the vehicle, complete with expensive baby seat.

She went through, plucked Eduardo out of his cot, where he had hauled himself up onto his chubby little feet, and took him into the sitting room. Now that Cristina had finally taken the plunge, she must be encouraged to make the best of the visit. Maybe she would want to stay away longer. Margaret wondered just what Luis would make of such a decision, for all that he himself had joked about it. But when all was said and done, why shouldn't Cristina decide to go to mainland

Spain, or France or Italy, find a job, live a little. She was as footloose as she herself had been when she moved to Tenerife. More so perhaps. Sufficient unto the day, she said to herself as she dandled Eduardo on her knee, while his father busied himself with the meal.

Cristina came through with small parcels and sat down to display her wares: pottery, some jewellery, a couple of books with pictures of La Gomera.

'My mother insisted that I bring this stuff,' she said. 'I could hardly fit it in. She says you are not to forget the island. You are not to forget where your home is.'

'How could I ever do that?'

In truth the things so reminiscent of his home did tug at Luis's heart. For Margaret too, Cristina's very presence seemed to summon La Gomera into her mind and she was back there again, watching Teide floating on a blue sea, in the light that was like no other. During those winter months before the birth of the baby, the Canaries had seemed like a great explosion of sunshine and happiness inside her head, but afterwards and with the advent of summer in Scotland, green, mellow and invariably damp, that perception had begun to recede into the distance. Now it returned with renewed vigour and she was suddenly certain of the rightness of her decision.

CHAPTER TWELVE

I have not seen a better rose
nor a carnation more red
nor a flower more to my liking
than this one that I have at my side.

Margaret's friends and relations, even Fiona, were delighted with Cristina. It was impossible to dislike her. She had the family's good looks and grace, but she seemed softer and more approachable than her brother. As for Cristina herself, she quickly settled down although she was still slightly apprehensive about negotiating the city on her own. Like Luis, she had been largely unprepared for the size of the place and the friendliness of the people. Nor had she been prepared for the shabbiness of so much of it, the chewing gum patches and dog dirt on the pavements, the empty shops, the many derelict buildings in the city centre but she loved the sight of the great silver Clyde winding through the heart of the city.

'I wish you could have seen it earlier,' said Margaret. 'It was better twenty years ago, when I was in my teens, or even fifteen years ago. It was better before the School of Art burned down – twice.'

'You mean the Charles Rennie Mackintosh building?' said Cristina who had followed events with a sense of disbelief. 'How could that happen?'

'That's what we ask ourselves. We had this jewel in our midst, and we threw it away. Well – those who should have been taking care of it did.'

Margaret had gone on a tour of the school not long before it burned down the first time, marvelling at the beauty of it, the wonder of the library, the furniture, the windows. But afterwards, it had struck her that there was so much old wood in the construction. Wood and paper. Tinder dry. She had assumed that there was a sprinkler system. She and Alastair had even donated to the restoration fund the first time round until, unbelievably, the almost-rebuilt gem had burnt down a second time, and now the city was left with a shell, and endless squabbles over money and responsibility. She suspected that sooner or later the ubiquitous student flats that few Scottish students could afford would be built on the site.

'It shames us,' she said. 'Can you imagine if it had happened to the Sagrada Familia? Well, it did happen to Notre Dame, and now it's already been rebuilt.'

'That's so sad!' said Cristina.

'And then austerity followed by Covid has done us no favours. Even I noticed just how shabby the place looks when I came back, and I hadn't been away for very long.'

The reality, she thought sadly, was that it had happened slowly. This once vibrant and still beautiful city – gallus was the Scots word she used in her own mind, meaning bold and daring – seemed to be sliding a little more downhill with every year that passed. All the same, there were still fascinating places to visit. Luis and Margaret took Cristina sightseeing to the Cathedral, the Hunterian gallery, the Kelvingrove Museum. They took the train to Edinburgh, saw the Castle and walked down the Royal Mile to Holyrood Palace.

'You need to see more than just Glasgow and Edinburgh. We'll go to Loch Lomond one day,' said Margaret, thoughtfully. 'It's lovely up there. You can see the proper Highlands. It isn't far from Glasgow. We could take the baby for his first real excursion.'

'What about Loch Ness and the Monster. Might we see that?'

'I don't think so. Well, you can go and see the Loch but I doubt if you'd see the monster,' said Luis.

'People do,' said Margaret. 'From time to time. Well – they see something, anyway. Nessie doesn't pop her head up very often. It's a long way. Scotland is a much bigger country than people imagine. We'd have to stay the night.'

Cristina looked disappointed.

'But there's no reason why we shouldn't go. The four of us could go. You, me, Luis and the baby.'

'Could we?'

Margaret glanced at Luis.

'Why not?' he said. 'You never know. We might see Nessie as well.'

'Why don't I book somewhere for us?' said Margaret. 'We could maybe stay a couple of nights. I'll see what I can find.'

The weather was uncharacteristically fine all the way north, with blue skies and skeins of high white cloud. It was the first reasonably long journey they had taken with the baby, and it amazed the new parents just how much baggage one small scrap of humanity needed.

'Just think how awful it would be if I wasn't feeding him myself!' said Margaret when they were at last under way. 'All this stuff and bottles and sterilisers and powdered milk too. At least my milk is on tap.'

They stopped for a picnic lunch on the way, but it was still a very long drive. Luis and Cristina were impressed by the Highlands, and especially impressed by the loch.

'I can understand now,' said Luis, 'how there might be a monster or two lurking down there. I mean it's big. No – it's massive.'

'And incredibly deep. They say there are underground caves that go a long way back under the mountains. So who knows?'

They had booked two rooms for a couple of nights in a pleasant guest house in Drumnadrochit, a name that Luis said was deliberately designed to trip up unwary foreigners. There was a big double for themselves, and a single room at the very top of the house for Cristina, its tiny size mitigated by a spectacular view of the loch. Luis practised saying the name, tripping over the unfamiliar syllables, laughing at himself. The baby slept intermittently in a travel cot in their room. They ate dinner in a nearby child-friendly Italian restaurant and brought a bottle of wine back with them. Then the three of them, Luis, Margaret and Cristina, sat on the bed together to watch television, buoyed up by pillows and cushions, while the baby slept. He was always happier when people were around him. Noises never woke him, although silence sometimes did.

In the morning, Luis managed to finish a full Scottish breakfast of bacon, egg, sausage, potato scone, baked beans, black pudding and plenty of toast and coffee. Margaret contented herself with a heap of smoked salmon topping a mound of soft, buttery scrambled eggs, while Cristina sampled crispy bacon and eggs, and tasted bits and pieces from her brother's plate.

'That,' said Luis, patting his stomach, 'Was by far the best thing I've eaten in Scotland. Maybe we could serve something like this in *La Manzana Dorada*.'

Margaret laughed. 'And this is the man who keeps going on about authentic local food. There are plenty of places serving English breakfasts on Tenerife. You only need to go to Las Americas. Every second restaurant advertises the full English!'

'Cooked by the full Englishman no doubt. But they don't taste like this. There must be something very special about a Scottish breakfast.'

'There is. It involves tattie scones and square sausage. Or sliced sausage sometimes. Or Lorne sausage. People argue over the name. I don't like it much, but lots of people do. Not sure you can get it in Spain.'

'What's a tattie scone?'

'You've just eaten one. A potato cake. Cooked on a griddle.'

'What is this griddle?'

'A flat pan. I make them in a flat non-stick pan. They're easy.'

'Then you'd better show me how.'

'I will.'

They visited the Loch Ness Centre and heard all about the history of the sightings of the monster. They drove along the side of the loch, but, to Cristina's disappointment, saw nothing except the wake of a boat or two. No monsters. They went to Urquhart Castle where Luis carried his son carefully among the old stones. Eduardo looked about him in happy astonishment at his new surroundings. Everything was a cause for wonder.

'It's a pity we couldn't spend more time in the countryside,' remarked Luis. 'I think I would like it much better than your city.'

'I was thinking the same thing,' said Margaret. 'But if we come back for a holiday, maybe we could have a longer trip around Scotland. Do you think Paco and Carmen would be prepared to look after the business now and then?'

'I'm sure they would, yes. In fact they've said so.'

'If you like this, you'd love the Western Isles.'

'We could take your mother for a trip.'

'I want her to come to La Gomera too.'

'I've been persuading her,' he said. 'And I can be very persuasive when I choose.'

'Oh, I know,' said Margaret. 'I know.'

During the second week of Cristina's holiday, Suzie invited them all to lunch. They took the baby along too, and Eduardo obligingly slept through the watercress soup and salmon mousse. Suzie worked from home most of the time and used cooking as a displacement activity. Laura was away on a business trip. Luis had met Suzie only infrequently and Laura not at all. Suzie had been carefully polite with him. Luis wondered, not for the first time, why she and Margaret were such close friends. Perhaps he sensed that she didn't like him very much.

On this occasion, Suzie had obviously decided to be nice, perhaps in deference to Cristina, perhaps out of consideration for her long friendship with Margaret. Cristina was quiet, listening to the rapid conversation around her, sipping white wine and staring at the rooms crowded with beautiful objects: bentwood furniture, screen-printed cushion covers, woodcarvings from Mexico, thriving house plants, shelves full of books, quilted wall hangings from Chile, and over all the scent of spices, pot pourri and fermenting fruit. Suzie and Laura made their own wine, keeping the demi-johns in the kitchen. Occasionally Cristina glanced across at Suzie in open and ingenuous admiration.

'I just love your house,' she said at last. 'I think it is the most beautiful place I have ever seen.'

'Do you really?' asked Suzie with more kindliness than she ever displayed to Luis. 'Thank-you. We're rather fond of it as well. It's a bit small because we're magpies and collect things all the time. Some people think it's too cluttered.'

'Oh no. No, it is just right.'

'And the Botanics make a great back garden.'

As they sat drinking their coffee after the meal, Suzie looked up and caught Cristina's dark eyes full on her face, the young woman's lips slightly parted as though in disbelief at what she was seeing and feeling. She smiled and Margaret, watching them both, felt as though she were poised for a moment between her friend and her sister-in-law, feeling the sudden confused questioning in Cristina. She glanced over at Luis but he was all unaware and she thought, something important has happened and he doesn't know it. He doesn't even see it. Men think that everything happens in relation to themselves. They so seldom see what's actually going on between people. It's like a whole other dimension and they're blissfully ignorant.

For Cristina the moment stayed and coloured her dreams, although just now she was aware only of an intense admiration. Suzie, casually friendly, showed Cristina the rest of the house and Cristina saw the big double bed in the sunny bedroom and the picture of Laura, fair-haired and smiling, on the bedside table. The spare room was a studio, with a desk and easel and the portfolios of work, with more work stacked around the walls: untidy, enticing, crammed with light and colour. The power of her feelings elated but then all at once saddened Cristina. She was not a part of this world. How could she be? It belonged to Suzie and the unseen Laura. They had forged it together.

All the way home, she was rather quiet.

'Why are you so quiet?' Luis asked. 'What's the matter? Don't you like Margarita's friend?'

Margaret glanced at Cristina. 'Of course she likes her. It's just that Suzie's a bit overwhelming at first. You said that yourself, Luis.'

Cristina, thankfully released from the necessity of replying, bent her head to talk to the baby and hid beneath the dark curtains of her hair.

June had been reasonably warm so far, with not too much rain. Eduardo rolled over, stretched up his neck and began to do press-ups on the carpet. Then he found that he could drag himself along and soon his legs began to work in tune with his arms, and nothing was safe. He was far too heavy now to carry around in the sling and they had to wheel him around in the buggy or carry him.

He had started enthusiastically on real food: mashed potatoes with a little plain yoghurt, carrots, baby rice, but he still preferred breast milk to anything else and was a long way from being weaned.

'I'd get him off that as soon as I could,' said Fiona, somewhat sourly, on one of her visits to the flat.

'Why?'

'Your body isn't your own.'

'Well it isn't really my own yet. It's his at the moment. I don't mind. As long as he doesn't still want it by the time he goes to school.'

'What does Luis think about it?'

'He doesn't say.'

Actually, she thought, he did. He said, 'If I was him I'd get as much as I could, while the milk bar was still open.' He was a man who was supremely comfortable in his own body, and that comfort extended to his whole family.

But she wasn't going to tell Fiona that.

Cristina had been in Glasgow for a couple of weeks when the spell of fine weather broke, and a succession of chilly, rainy days for the last week of her holiday showed her a side to Scotland she had not yet seen.

'This hellish country!' said Luis, coming in with trainers and socks soaked.

'I don't mind it,' said Cristina.

'Don't you?' He seemed quite amazed.

'No. I like it. It makes everything smell so fresh. There's so much greenery. So many flowers. But they're different from the flowers at home. Softer. More delicate.'

Cristina was determined to like everything about Scotland, but the time for her return to La Gomera was looming inexorably on her horizon. A few more days. The thought of returning to the island and the bank, of leaving behind the life of this city, of any city, filled her with dismay. I need to be somewhere with more life about it, she thought.

'When exactly will you be coming back home?' she ventured to ask Luis, wondering if she could delay going back herself.

'Before the end of July. Margaret and Eduardito will follow early in August. But you surely need to get back to work before then?'

She didn't reply. Why did Luis make her feel like a little girl again? They had always been so close. She loved him so much that his disapproval was unbearable to her. What if he didn't agree with her plans?

The schemes she had been formulating in her head? What would she do then?

I'll talk to Margarita first, she thought. She would surely understand.

Margaret did understand and sympathised. Hadn't she herself wanted to get away from the home that, loving as it was, had begun to stifle her? Hadn't she yearned for something new and exciting. And hadn't she found it?

'Luis thinks I ought to go back.'

'I think he just assumes that you will be going back. Do you have other plans?'

Cristina blushed. 'I've been talking to Suzie and Laura. They're trying to find something for me on the mainland. You know? In Spain? They say that have many contacts there.'

'Doing what?' Margaret was intrigued. Suzie hadn't even mentioned this to her, perhaps aware that she would have told Luis, and he might not have approved.

'I'm not sure. Something to do with photography, I think. Suzie mentioned a gallery. Near Barcelona. I have no real experience, but it interests me very much. I have some savings you know. So I wouldn't need to earn a fortune. Not at first, anyway.'

'How exciting!'

'Yes – it *is* exciting. But it's funny too – that I long to get away from the place that you ...'

'Are longing to go back to? Well yes. But for me, it's an adventure you know. One I've dreamed of all my life.'

'Me too, but in a different way.'

'Why don't you stay on here for a couple more weeks?' Margaret suggested. 'That would take you into July. Your ticket wasn't very expensive, was it?'

'Not at all.'

'Well then, we could cancel it. If the job comes off you'll be looking for a flight to Barcelona instead. And if it doesn't, we can just book another flight to Tenerife. Maybe you can go back with Luis.'

'But would he mind?'

'It doesn't matter whether he minds or not. You're your own woman, Cristina. But what about the bank? What about your job? Just in case Suzie and Laura can't find you anything right away. Can you take extra holiday?'

'I can ask. They certainly owe me some time.'

'Contact them and then we'll see about cancelling your flight. No need to tell your brother yet.'

CHAPTER THIRTEEN

What charm that woman has!
I wish I could adorn her with flowers!

Cristina was given permission by the bank to stay on for a further two weeks. They owed her more holiday and didn't want to lose her. Margaret cheerfully presented Luis with a *fait accompli* but he didn't seem to mind.

'And why should he?' she said to Cristina. 'Besides, he's much too busy finalising all the restaurant stuff. He wants to go back before we travel, just to make sure everything's OK for the baby. It'll be lovely to have you here for a couple more weeks.'

Privately, though, she held off from booking Cristina's new return ticket, knowing that when Suzie wanted something, she usually managed to arrange it.

Her instincts were right. A few days later, Suzie came round to the flat with the news that there was a vacancy in a small photographic gallery in the town of Sitges, not far from Barcelona. It was owned by a Catalan friend, Isabella. Her assistant had just left and Isabella was preoccupied with commissions and her own new baby. 'Another one!' said Suzie, with a sigh. The work was not difficult and demanded only a certain amount of efficiency and the patience to deal with the public. Cristina would have to help with organising exhibitions, sit behind a desk, hand out leaflets, take orders, answer the phone and answer questions as best she could. Her command of English as well as her native Spanish was a bonus since many of the gallery's foreign patrons were more familiar with that language. At private views she would be expected to hand round wine and chat to potential customers.

'I'm sure you could do all that no bother at all,' said Suzie. 'The money isn't huge, but it's not bad and you could always look around for something more demanding once you're there. Or use it as a stepping stone to something better. I get the impression that Isabella is looking for somebody she can trust to run the whole place for her. She mostly shows her own work, but she wants to expand and invite other photographers. You might find you get a rapid promotion. '

'Where would I live? I can't afford to stay in a hotel.'

There was a tiny furnished apartment in the building above the gallery, one that Isabella had acquired with the gallery itself. 'Isabella says its just a studio apartment, but quite comfortable, and you can see the sea. It's in one of the old buildings. It will be nice, if I know Isabella. She doesn't stint herself. They need somebody to start at the end of July.'

'Barcelona,' said Cristina. 'I've never been. But I've always wanted to go. Always. I've even tried to learn some Catalan.'

'Even better. You'll like it. And you'll just love Sitges. It's the most beautiful place. A bit stuffed with tourists right enough, but you won't mind that. And it's a short hop on the train to Barcelona. We go there quite often. The best bit about it is that you can work there without worrying about residence or permits, can't you? Unlike dreary old Glasgow.'

'It isn't dreary to me, but I can, yes,' said Cristina. 'What would they say at the bank?'

'Thank-you for all your years of hard work?' said Suzie.

Cristina laughed. 'Well, that's true. Oh Suzie – do you think I could do it?'

'Of course you could do it! Listen, I've arranged a Zoom interview for you here. Tomorrow. Don't tell your brother till you're sure.'

'What about Margarita?'

'Oh you should tell her. But Luis doesn't need to know just yet.'

'Do you think he wouldn't approve?'

'I think he probably worries about you more than he should. You're a grown woman with a life of your own to lead.'

'I hate it when he's upset.'

'Why should he be upset?'

Cristina pulled a face. 'Because he does worry about me, you're right. He knows I'm not very happy at home, but he doesn't know what to do about it. I think he had some idea I might help out with the restaurant. He and Margarita have wonderful plans and I love to hear about them, but that isn't what I want to do. Not at all. I have no interest in hospitality. Or gardening. That's Margarita's passion, not mine.'

'Really? Gardening?' Suzie sounded sceptical. 'I never knew.'

'She never had a proper garden. But I think she has always wanted one.'

'I suppose so. She certainly talked about plants a lot. Always had flowers in the house. I think it was her first husband who couldn't be bothered with a garden. Now I come to think about it. I must ask her about it.'

'Do. She'll tell you all about the gardens at *La Manzana Dorada*.'

'That's the trouble with our loved ones, Cristina, even when they want the best for us. I suppose I'm guilty of it too, sometimes. They can have quite fixed ideas about what is and isn't best without ever really listening to what we want for ourselves.'

'I know that. I think Margarita's brother and sister-in-law were like that.'

'Indeed they were. And still are as far as I know. But this is such an opportunity for you. Isabella is a good friend. I think you'll like her. I think you'll learn from her.'

Cristina took a deep breath. 'OK. I'll come back for the interview tomorrow. I'll speak to your friend. And I'll look up flights.'

'But don't feel under pressure to do anything you don't want to do.'

'No. No – but it's something I've been hoping for. The chance to make a big change. And now it seems to have happened, thanks to you.'

'Serendipity, that's the word.'

'*Serendipia*. We have the same word.'

'She's really desperate for the right person, and I've been singing your praises. You can get a flight from Glasgow or Prestwick. Especially if you're only going one way.'

'What about all my stuff? I hardly brought anything with me.'

'We've thought about all that, Laura and I. First speak to Isabella and see how you get on. She wants somebody to begin quite soon. Why not give it a try and then fly back to Tenerife in a few months and ship whatever else you want. Besides, I'm sure Luis and Margaret would do it for you. But the flat has pretty much everything you'll need for the time being.'

'I have some savings. There wasn't much to spend it on. I'd be fine I think. Once I settled in'

'Exactly,'

'You've worked all this out, haven't you?' asked Cristina.

'Now I feel as though I'm bullying you. Laura always says I'm too fond of organising people, whether they like it or not.'

'No. No you're not doing that. This is something I've been wishing for. But I just didn't see a way of doing it. The only jobs I could find were in hospitality, and I didn't really want to do that. I'd never have thought about this kind of gallery. And yet – I've always been interested in photography – fashion and other kinds of photography. I can't think of anything better! I want to learn.'

'You have flair. That's what I told Isabella. And you certainly have good organisational skills. I think you might blossom there.'

Cristina didn't tell Luis until all the arrangements were made, including her flight to Barcelona from Prestwick, and there was no going back.

'Why do you want such a job?' asked Luis. 'I thought you were going back home soon. What about the bank? What about handing in your notice?'

'I've told the bank. They were disappointed, but Senor Marquez understands. We had a chat on the phone. He said I should seize the opportunity.'

He had gone further than that. 'If you were my daughter, that's what I'd tell you to do,' he had said. He had always liked Cristina as much for her calm efficiency as her sunny nature, but had often thought that she needed to get out into the wide world and find a niche that suited her. Even if, eventually, she came back to the island she loved, she would come back with a broader perspective. It seemed to him that once she flew away, there was small chance of her returning.

Margaret joined in. 'I think it's a great idea. It's owned by a friend of Suzie's. And I think Cristina's old enough to look after herself, don't you?'

Luis frowned, knowing his misgivings were unreasonable. 'Well I suppose it will be OK. Is there somewhere to live? I know this town. Sitges. It is very beautiful. A good place to work. Although there are lots of tourists. As long as you're safe and it's a proper job.'

'Oh it's a proper job, Lucho!' Cristina's eyes were sparkling. 'And there's somewhere to live too. A nice little apartment. I'll send you photographs.'

'Then I'm sure it will be fine.'

'Suzie has an exhibition opening. She's asked me to go along and help with the private view. Just for the experience, you know?'

'And are you going?'

'Oh yes. I want to. Just to help out. See how things work, you know? I can't tell you how much I'm looking forward to it!'

'What is all this?' Luis asked Margaret when Cristina had gone to bed. 'Where did all this come from? And why did nobody tell me?'

'It'll be good for her. A bit of independence. Don't you go spoiling it by objecting.'

'Why would I do that? I'm happy for her, just as long as she's sure about it.'

'She deserves some excitement and freedom, doesn't she? And you needn't look so sceptical.' She hugged him. 'I've told you, you're a real Gomero at heart, Luis. You like to hold on to your family. And Cristina really cares about what you think. She could never be happy without your blessing, so you'd better agree with a good grace.'

'Or you'll what? What will you do?'

'Oh, I'll think of something.' She moved closer and kissed him. 'Something to persuade you.'

'You don't need to persuade me.'

'But I enjoy it!'

The truth was that they were happier at that moment than at any time since the birth of the baby, happier perhaps than at any time since their marriage. Luis was delighted at the prospect of going home with or without his sister. Margaret was relaxed and contented with him and with the baby. Physically they were very close too. He had the sense, sometimes, that she might be managing him, not allowing his temperament to get him into unnecessary trouble, but he didn't mind. He enjoyed this feeling of being subject to a new confidence and capability in his wife. It seemed motherhood had given her more than enough and to spare. They had become a conspiracy of equals. It reassured him, gave him a sense of being very much loved.

'Be nice about it,' she murmured, still close to him.

'Aren't I always nice?'

'Not always. No. Good, but not always nice.'

'Alright,' he said. He would have agreed to anything at that moment. 'I'll be nice. How can I be anything else?'

CHAPTER FOURTEEN

All these islands are
daughters of the giant
Teide with snow on his face
and fire in his heart.

Margaret sought out Suzie. She had taken Eduardo out for an afternoon walk and headed in the direction of her friends' little house at the back of the Botanics.

'Come in,' said Suzie. 'The kettle's on.'

'It always is, isn't it?'

Margaret sat down, bouncing Eduardo on her knee.

'What will he have?' asked Suzie, a bit suspiciously.

'Probably me.'

'Still?'

'Yeah. Why not? He's only a wee chap.'

'He looks quite big to me.'

'Well he's certainly growing. And eating. Can't keep up to him in clothes. He's no sooner grown into them than he's grown out of them, if you know what I mean.'

'I suppose so.'

'Your lack of enthusiasm is obvious!' Margaret laughed. 'I've got his cup somewhere.' She fumbled in her bag. 'He quite likes water. The trouble with babies is that you have to carry so much stuff around: nappies, tissues, cups, changes of clothes. If you forget something, you're in trouble. It helps to have the milk on tap so to speak.'

'We might get round to it one of these days.' Suzie coloured up. 'You know. The baby thing.'

'Might you? That would be great!'

'Do you really think so?'

'Yes but I'm prejudiced.'

'Laura's starting to get very broody. She's just waiting for me to catch up with her, I think.'

'And have you? Caught up, I mean?'

'Well ... ' Suzie gazed at Eduardo and he gazed back at her with big blue eyes. Then he gave her a gummy grin. His teeth were just coming in but the smile was still mostly gum and very engaging. 'Now that I see your wee boy ... We've got a friend, a good friend who's prepared to do the needful. And be involved as well. Be a dad. We've talked. I think we could make it work. But we have to be sure. When you're messing about with somebody else's life, another small person, you have to be sure, don't you?'

'You do. But I think lots of us just get taken by surprise. And who's to say that isn't the right way after all? I used to overthink everything. Now I wonder if it isn't better just to jump in with both feet. Luis taught me that. And now this little lad.'

'Maybe you're right. We'll see. Laura likes to be organised. Likes to cover all her bases. Anyway, how's Cristina liking the idea of Sitges? She's offered to lend a hand with my private view. I don't suppose it counts as work, so long as it's for a friend.'

'She's liking it very much indeed. Actually, I wanted to talk to you about Cristina.'

'What about her?'

She bent over Eduardo. 'Cristina's blossomed while she's been here. More than that, I'm sure you've noticed that she's blossomed in your company. You and Laura. I've often wondered if Cristina might be ...'

'You don't need to spell it out. But wouldn't she know that for herself? It's not hard to figure out, is it?'

'I don't know. No. Maybe. I honestly don't think it occurred to her until now. There isn't anyone else for her to confide in. Well, no other woman over here that she feels so close to. The island is very self contained you know. Not a million miles from small islands over here. All small, self contained communities are a bit precarious. So many secrets. So many checks and balances that are taken for granted, and no way of being anonymous the way you are in a city.'

'That's true. You remember, I had a fellowship on Skye for a while. It's not even a small island, it's huge, but I know what you mean. Easy to upset the balance. There was a new landlady who took over the local pub while I was there. She was slagging people off without any idea that they might be related to one another – and they often were. Cousins with different surnames. She didn't last long.'

'That's it exactly. And Cristina's family is more self contained than most.

'Do you want me to speak to her?'

'What on earth would you say?'

'Probably nothing. I don't want to put ideas into her head. But maybe the ideas are already there. What about your Luis?'

'What about him?'

'How would he react?'

'I've never known him to be anything but positive about his family.'

'He might surprise you where his sister is concerned. I wouldn't raise the subject if I were you. Let's face it – she's going to be living somewhere else. This is absolutely none of his business. I'm not ashamed of anything about the way I live, Margaret. I love Laura and she loves me. But we don't confide the details of our private life to all and sundry either. Do you?'

'No. I certainly don't.'

'What Cristina wants and hopes and feels is entirely down to her.

I'm sure her brother does love her as you say. If he does, he'll understand. He may be a bit surprised. He'll get over it.'

'You're right.'

'Poor Margaret. Trying to please everyone as usual. Making sure nobody gets hurt. Why don't you cross that bridge when you come to it? I think all Cristina needs is a safe place to roost, and if she wants to spread her wings and fly then that'll be good too. She's coming along to help with my opening, anyway. But I'm not going to force things, Margaret. It's all down to her.'

Luis was playing and singing in Ricky's restaurant more often than he had intended, secure in the knowledge that he would soon have left the country. The gigs were by no means regular, nor were they much publicised, and he wasn't on the payroll. As far as Ricky's staff were concerned, he was just doing a favour for a friend. Instead, an occasional generous payment in Margaret's name would arrive in the bank account, marked for 'property consultation'. Ricky and his wife were genuinely thinking of buying a villa on Tenerife, and it would be true to say that they had discussed the market there with Margaret.

'For God's sake, don't suggest La Gomera to him' said Luis. 'We might finish up as neighbours.'

'You needn't worry. I don't think our island is Ricky's idea of fun at all. I think Las Americas or Los Cristianos is more his line.'

He noticed her use of 'our island' and was touched by it.

'He'll probably finish up with a chain of casinos,' said Luis, gloomily.

'Well it won't affect us, will it?'

'No. I don't suppose it will. I just don't trust him.'

'Me neither. But I do trust Sharon. Still, it makes me uneasy.'

'What does?'

'You working when you're not allowed to.'

'I know. But what can they do?'

'I don't know. Deport you?'

'I'm going in a few weeks anyway. Ricky says it's a grey area. He'd be in much more trouble than me if I really was working for him. I looked up the regulations. They don't make sense. It says I can work for up to six months. But then I can't work paid or unpaid for a UK company. So what do they mean? I have no idea!'

'Typical government website.'

'Our bureaucracy is just as bad if not worse. Anyway, I just play and sing for a bit and then I go.' He kissed her hand.

'Talking of which, you'll need to be off soon. You promised to give Cristina a lift to her exhibition thing. I'll go and hurry her along.'

Cristina was in her bedroom, trying to decide what to wear. Trying to decide if she had anything stylish enough. She was surrounded by such clothes as she had brought with her and a couple of dresses she had acquired since arriving.

'I've no idea what it will be like.'

'Cristina, whatever you wear, you always look lovely. In fact you'd look pretty in a bin bag. But I'll tell you something. It won't be just as dressy as you think it will be. This is Glasgow. People like to be smart but do it on a shoestring.'

She picked up a black cotton dress with cutwork embroidery around neck, sleeves and hem that Cristina had bought in Primark earlier that week.

'Wear this.'

'It cost very little. But I do like it.'

'It doesn't matter what it cost. It's so stylish. Put it on. Have you got heels?'

'Just one pair. Well, sandals really. But they have heels.'

'Gold. Good.' Margaret went away and rummaged on her dressing table, finding a chunky gilt and black necklace and several bangles. 'It's just costume jewellery but it'll look great with that dress. Let me brush your hair.'

She stood back and gazed at Cristina. 'You look fabulous. They'll be asking you where you got your designer dress from!'

'I won't tell them!'

'No. Leave them guessing.'

'Wow!' said Luis, when he saw his little sister emerging from her bedroom. 'How beautiful you look!'

Cristina blushed. 'Do you think so?'

The baby stirred and started to whimper.

'Isn't she gorgeous?' Margaret pushed her towards the door. 'You'd better be on your way. The milk bar's open.'

Luis dropped his sister off at the gallery on his way to play at Ricky's bar. Margaret had been invited to the private view but had decided to stay at home with Eduardo, thinking that Cristina might be better off on her own, without any supervision from family members, however well-meaning. Cristina had promised to get a taxi home. Laura and Suzie were already there, Suzie pacing about with pre-exhibition nerves and Laura doing her best to remain calm.

The gallery was small – two rooms only, and a tiny kitchen through the back. There were originals of many of Suzie's book illustrations, several pieces of digital art, some delicate watercolours and a series of beautifully executed charcoal sketches of Laura at home, reading, writing in a notebook and frowning in concentration, curled up in a chair gazing at the television, standing at the kitchen table with a mug in her hand – images that were nicely executed but striking mostly because of the loving perspective of the artist.

'This'll be a good experience for you before you go to Sitges,' said Suzie. 'That's the extra wine over there and there's more white in the fridge through the back. And orange juice. Just make sure everyone gets well tanked up. That way I may sell something!'

'You'll sell plenty anyway,' said Laura, reassuringly, 'You know you always do.' She turned to Cristina. 'She always gets in a tizz before an exhibition. She'll be alright once people start to arrive. Won't you, Suze?'

Luis was lingering by the door.

'Are you sure you don't want me to pick you up on my way back?' he asked Cristina again.

'I'll be fine. Besides, we can't be sure exactly when it'll finish.'

'No,' added Suzie. 'We have no idea when the last guest will finally be persuaded to leave the building. Usually it's when the wine runs out. Then we go to the pub.'

She was busily piling crisps and nuts, as well as a variety of olives into dishes and arranging them on a table, well away from the pictures.

'I could always pick you up from Suzie's apartment if you like.'

'You don't have to worry about me.'

'We'll make sure she gets home safely. Don't worry,' Laura told Luis, patiently.

I'm not a child, Cristina wanted to say, but she kissed her brother on the cheek meekly enough, and he left.

'You look lovely!' said Suzie, impulsively. 'So elegant. Did you bring that dress with you?'

Cristina blushed. 'No. I bought it here. You'd be surprised where I found it.'

'Wherever you got it, it suits you.'

Cristina polished glasses and then poured out Rioja and Pinot Grigio. Suzie and Laura had set up folding tables, leaving the desk free for potential sales to be processed. Guests began to arrive and the wine and snacks began to disappear. There was a lot of kissing, Cristina noticed. These people seemed as much at home with kissing as her fellow islanders. It surprised her.

The two rooms filled up quickly. Lots of people seemed to have come as much for the free wine and the social occasion as for the pictures. There were art school lecturers and other artists, as well as a couple of actors holding court in a corner with their backs firmly to the work on display. There were two journalists and an 'influencer'. There was a drunken poet who had arrived in that state and was doing his best to maintain it with Suzie's wine, while at the same time discussing the contents of his latest collection with an elderly and rather pretty woman who turned out to be a Scottish novelist of some distinction. His voice could be heard droning on and on throughout the small space. Later on, when she could extricate herself from his alcohol-scented proximity, she bought two of Suzie's sketches of Laura.

'The Byres Road mafia are out in force tonight, I see,' Laura muttered to Cristina.

'Mafia?' said Cristina, surprised.

'Just a joke. The literati. They like to think everyone's listening when they speak. Very few people actually are.'

'I see.' But she didn't quite understand, only that Laura was being quietly sarcastic, and including her in the joke, which was nice of her.

Cristina had seen very little real drunkenness in her own family. It was uncommon on the island and even then mostly involved foreign visitors, stag and hen parties in a state of advanced inebriation, and they tended to stay on Tenerife where there was more night life. She had seen plenty of drunks in her few weeks in Glasgow and not only stag parties. She had talked about it to Luis and they had put it down to a combination of weather and temperament. Sometimes, the Scots seemed to drink only with the aim of getting drunk, while the Spanish, on the whole, drank for the pleasure it gave them. Cristina would never understand why so many men seemed to find it a sign of manliness to vomit in the streets, while to the Spanish it was a sign of weakness. They might drink, but they considered it a matter of shame to appear drunk. And mostly, they ate at the same time. Other than the poet, most of the visitors to the exhibition opening seemed sober enough, although the wine disappeared with astonishing speed. The younger visitors drank the least.

In Ricky's bar, that night, Luis was surprised to see Fiona with a group of women friends, sitting at one of the tables quite close to the little stage that had been set up for himself and the other musical performances. There was a small but expensive digital piano on which a musician from the Conservatoire regularly played popular classics as background music, and there was a jazz singer with a significant body of fans, who performed in the bar at least once a month, unless she was away on tour. Luis had heard her once or twice and liked her voice very much. His own performances were the occasional treat, even though Ricky would have preferred to give him a regular slot. All the same, he too had begun to build up a following of his own. Word had got about, as it so often did in the city.

Tonight, he was preparing to sing as well as play a Latin American set that included *Besame Mucho*, a song that Ricky always requested, and the strange, sad and sexy *Sombras*, about shadows and passion and the pain induced by intense and probably hopeless love. The Scots, the Irish and the Spaniards had that much in common, that so many of their songs were about doomed love. In between, there would be a handful of cheerful Canarian melodies.

On the whole, he loved to play for his wife. Tonight, more than ever, he wished she were here. Fiona's unexpected presence made him feel uncomfortable, especially when – in the middle of a particularly affecting passage – he caught her gazing up at him, her hands folded under her chin. Once, he saw one of her friends giving her a distinct nudge, at which she laughed, shifted position, shook her head.

When he took a break, he felt compelled to go over and speak to them. Anything else would look rude. She introduced the others, three of them, as a party of her fellow lecturers, out for a birthday treat for one of them. They had eaten in the restaurant and then come through to the bar for his performance.

'Oh we've heard all about you from Fiona,' said the youngest of the trio. 'I must say you live up to expectations.'

Fiona giggled. 'I just said you were a very good musician.'

'Aye right,' said the friend.

He was embarrassed, an uncharacteristic emotion for him.

'We just love your music!' That was the eldest and the most sober among them. 'Especially that one about ... shadows, was it? I've been trying to learn Spanish for years.'

'*Sombras. Si.*'

'It sounded so sexy!' said the forthright friend, pointedly.

'Ah – it is just a song. In fact it is an Ecuadorian *pasillo*' he added, hoping to inject a more serious note into the conversation. '*Pasillo* is little step. It is a kind of dance. As well as a song.'

'How fascinating,' said the sober friend. The other women looked suitably grave. Fiona, he noticed, was frowning as though – what was the expression Margarita had taught him? – as though the others were stealing her thunder. Worse and worse.

'You must excuse me,' he said. 'I need to get some water before I play again.'

'Of course. But would you join us later? For a drink? We'd love to hear more about your music, wouldn't we, girls?'

That was the third friend, a pretty woman, albeit heavily made up, with overly botoxed lips. They reminded briefly him of the fishes he and his father had caught, when he was a boy. He was seized with a sudden desire to laugh.

Fiona was nodding. 'Oh please do,' she said. 'It would be such a treat for us all!'

He shook his head. 'I'm so sorry, but I have the car and I need to get home. We have a new baby as Fiona knows. I don't like to be out too long at night.'

'We understand!' That was the sober friend. He was relieved that she was there. But what on earth was Fiona doing, bringing her friends here when she knew that he would be performing? His wife must be right. She had clearly changed her mind about him to such an extent that she had a crush on him? And he had encouraged it, out of sheer devilry. Or at least done nothing to discourage it. It was an uncomfortable thought. He would have to put a stop to it, but how on earth was he going to do that? Ignoring her seemed to make no difference.

He went back onto the stage and played again, studiously avoiding even glancing at Fiona's table. He finished with the heartrending *Malaguena Salerosa*, in which a man tells a woman how much he loves her, but she despises him because he's too poor. Luis was always wary of playing it when his wife was in the audience, remembering one of their first dates, her first visit to his island, when he had so seriously misjudged her opinion of his family, and thought he had lost her for good. But this evening, he had played it deliberately, wanting to bring back the memories for himself. He thought about that time now and all that had come after and how very much he loved her and his baby son. But perhaps it had been a mistake to play it tonight. When he had finished, he put his guitar carefully into its case, raised his hand in a casual salute to his sister-in-law and her party, and took the opportunity of slipping out of one of the side doors of the restaurant, a staff entrance that led out into a narrow close. He felt faintly ridiculous as he drove home. How had he allowed this situation to arise? Had it been his fault? And what on earth could he do about it now? He thought it better to say nothing to his wife about it for the present.

In the gallery, Cristina was gradually able to put a few of the red 'sold' stickers on to the pictures – mostly framed originals of various book or magazine illustrations – and was glad for Suzie's sake. When the last guest had been ushered through the door, Cristina was left amid the debris with Laura and Suzie. They worked together in near silence for a while, clearing up, washing glasses, hoovering up crisp crumbs.

Outside, Suzie, who had been entrusted with the keys by the gallery owner, set the burglar alarm and locked up.

'We really should go to the pub,' said Laura doubtfully. 'People expect it.' A small group of guests had headed off half an hour earlier, leaving the trio to clear up.

'I can't be bothered. They're only going to get pissed or more pissed. Somebody will start crying or quarrel and I don't want to do that tonight. I'm already buzzing.'

'Alright. Let's go home. Are you coming, Cristina?'

'Yes. She's coming for coffee,' said Suzie.

'Come on then. The car's over here.'

It was dark, the pale darkness of a northern summer. The air smelled of petrol, grimy trees and dust.

Laura, who had been drinking only mineral water, drove home and Cristina sat in the back. Suzie leaned over the back of the seat to talk to her.

'Your brother isn't expecting you home early is he?'

'No. He won't be in until later tonight. He's playing.'

'He's a wonderful musician, isn't he?' Laura had been to the restaurant to listen. 'Well I thought so, anyway. I love Spanish guitar. I'd like to talk to him about it.'

'He's very good, yes. And I'm sure he'd be delighted to talk about it. Not many people do seem to ask him about it. Not here, anyway.'

'But not an easy brother, perhaps?' Suzie ventured.

The remark was misjudged and Cristina immediately leapt to his defence. 'I love him very much. He has always been very good to me. I don't want to hurt him. That's the last thing I want to do.'

'Sometimes people hurt themselves whether we want them to or not.'

'That's what Margarita said.'

'Then she's very wise.'

'I'm glad she married my brother. I'm very glad he has her. She's so good for him.'

'Well, I used to wonder, but now I'm inclined to agree with you. Still, I'm not sure if he's all that good for her.'

'Suzie doesn't think any man is good enough for any woman,' said Laura, laughing.

'But you don't feel like that, do you, Laura?'

'Of course not. I have brothers. Two of them. I love them to bits. And we both have lots of men friends. She just likes to play devil's advocate sometimes. Don't you, sweetheart?'

'Sometimes.'

In the apartment, Suzie switched on the lamps and Laura made coffee. She brought out a bottle of cognac and a platter of cheese and biscuits. Cristina felt the smooth strength of the spirit sliding down her throat, warming her. The two women were easy listeners, easy companions. She told them about her childhood, about the pleasures of her friendship with Teresa, about the increasing feeling of alienation as she grew older. She had gone out with young men, and tried to feel the sensations so obviously felt by her friends, but all she had known had been a vague disappointment.

'Did you ever make love?' asked Suzie, softly.

Cristina shook her head. 'No. I couldn't. I couldn't go so far. Partly because of who I am and where I live. My background. But other girls did it anyway. For me it wasn't hard to say no. I didn't want to. One of them told me I was cold.'

'Harsh.'

'Not really. I was cold where he was concerned. I didn't want him. Didn't want anything he could give me except friendship. But that wasn't enough for him. I've always known I was different but I've never known why.'

'Until you met Laura and me?'

'Not even then.'

'Not even now, perhaps?' said Laura.

'I don't know. I love the way you live. I love what you have together. This house. Your lives. I think women are so much nicer than men.' She blushed, fiercely. 'I just don't know. I don't even know what you do.'

Suzie spluttered with sudden laughter. 'We do what everyone does only longer and better.'

'Suzie!' said Laura, reprovingly.

'Well it's true. And it's no big deal. It's maybe the least important thing. Or one of them, anyway.'

Laura frowned. 'It's true that affection matters more. Loyalty. Love. But not much help to Cristina.'

'No. I can see that. And I'm sorry. Cristina, you just have to find out what you really feel in your head and your heart. There's no hurry. No pressure. Or there shouldn't be. And if anyone tries to persuade you otherwise, they don't have your best interests at heart. If you meet the right person, male or female, you'll know. But I think getting away from home, getting away from your family, without ever falling out with them – well, that's a good way of giving yourself the freedom to explore.'

'I think you're right,' said Cristina.

Laura patted her hand. 'But you can't force these things. Nobody should ever try to dictate to you how you should and shouldn't feel. It's personal. Nobody's business but yours. Moving away will be an adventure. One you're more than ready for. After that, what will be, will be.'

They put her in a taxi before midnight. 'Off you go, Cinderella,' said Suzie. Back at the apartment, sleep evaded her for some time. She lay staring into the gloom, hearing the soft night-time noises of the old building: the rattle in the water pipes, the contracting creaks and groans of timber as the air cooled down, the little whine and sob of Eduardo as he stirred in his sleep and woke, and the quiet tones of Margaret feeding him and shushing him down again. Singing to him.

The singing soothed Cristina too. I must do what is best for me, in the best way I can, she thought. In Sitges. Then she turned over and promptly fell fast asleep.

A few days later, Luis and Margaret took Cristina to Prestwick Airport, leaving Eduardo with Annie for a few hours. Knowing that they would soon be leaving themselves, Annie was taking every opportunity to spend time with her grandson. They went on the train and made sure that her suitcase was safely checked in, that her cabin baggage was the proper size and weight, and that the flight was on time. They managed a quick cup of coffee before seeing her through security. The flight would arrive very late in the evening, but Isabella had promised to meet her at the airport and drive her to Sitges, where she would see her safely installed in her new apartment. Even so, Cristina had pre-travel nerves. She had infected her brother and Margaret too, both anxious on her behalf, although they were trying very hard not to show it. At the gate, Luis hugged and kissed her, reluctant to let her go.

'Look after yourself, Tina. We'll miss you.'

Seeing his anxious expression, Cristina summoned her courage. 'I'll be fine. You're not to worry about me.'

'If you have any problems at all, just get in touch. Message us. We're only a short flight away,' added Margaret. 'And send photographs!'

'Yes I'll do that.'

'It's all so exciting.'

'Almost too exciting.'

'I know. But that was how I felt when I went to Tenerife, and look what happened to me!'

'Well, I think that was my brother's good luck that he found *you*, don't you?'

'Oh *por supuesto*. Certainly!'

Luis gave his sister a gentle push towards the gate. 'Off you go, sweetheart. Enjoy yourself.'

'I will. And don't let Eduardito forget his best aunty, will you.'

She passed through, turned and waved and then was gone.

Margaret took her husband's hand. 'She'll have the time of her life.'

'I hope so.'

'Come on. Let's go home. We have our own journey to make soon and we're not half ready.'

CHAPTER FIFTEEN

When I was a baby in my cradle
everyone gave me gifts.
Now that I'm older,
no-one gives me anything.

Sometimes it seemed to Fiona as though she and her husband were drifting further and further apart. What will we do when the kids have grown up, she thought, and her own lack of response terrified her.

'Is this all there is?' she said aloud, not intending for anyone to hear her. 'Is this it, then? Is this what all that planning and dreaming was for? Did we go wrong somewhere? It was meant to be better than this.'

It was early morning and she was sitting in the kitchen in her dressing gown. Ian came in, fastening his tie. 'First sign of insanity, you know,' he said cheerfully.

'What is?'

'Talking to yourself. Any breakfast on the go, Fee?'

She looked at him with something approaching loathing. 'I haven't made it yet.'

He raised his eyebrows in surprise but he knew better than to remonstrate when Fiona was in this mood. He wondered just how much she had had to drink on her night out with the girls. It wasn't like her to have a hangover, but there was a first time for everything.

He was quite happy to get his own breakfast, but she didn't like him disturbing her kitchen. He had once made the terrible mistake of clearing out one of the kitchen cupboards and reorganising things while she was out for the day with the children. She had never let him forget it and had spent the evening restoring order.

'How about you get it yourself, this morning?' she said. He noticed that she hadn't showered or dressed yet. Or even taken off last night's mascara. Panda eyes, he thought, but didn't say. He heard the kids shouting at each other in the hall.

'That's not fair,' Rory screamed at his sister over some minor dispute. It was never fair. Life wasn't fair.

'I'm going for my shower.' Fiona got to her feet, ignoring the rumpus.

'I'll go and sort them out. Then I'll make the toast.' Ian tried to inject a note of injured endurance into his voice but Fiona ignored that too and went into the bathroom. She took her time about the shower. She was going to be late for work but she didn't care. As she dressed slowly and carefully, and then sat down to dry her hair, she heard Ian shepherding the children into the hall.

'We're off then!'

She opened the door a fraction so that she could shout through.

'You know you're going to Grandma's straight from school,' she called to the children. 'She'll probably give you your tea but if not, you can get a takeaway. Dad'll pick you up from there on his way home. You can get a pizza if you like.'

'Why? Where are you going?'

'To Aunty Margaret's, I told you. I'm taking that pullover I knitted for Teddy.' This was her own name for the baby, nobody else's. In fact if anything, Luis was fond of lengthening the name to Eduardito. Little Edward. Although 'Lalo' was another affectionate version of the name.

'I thought I might as well go straight from school.'

She came out of the bedroom. 'Did you hear all that, Ian?'

'Fine, fine. No problem at all. You smell nice.'

'You bought me the stuff. You don't usually notice it.'

Ian left the house with Rory and Lottie, feeling desolate, not quite knowing why. Living with Fiona had always been rather like living with a capricious and unpredictable minor goddess. You never quite knew when some innocuous action on your part might be misinterpreted and then there would be hell to pay. Ian had spent much of his married life trying to get it right, trying to do what Fiona wanted in order to keep the peace. He had begun by wanting to please her because he loved her. Now, he tried to please her because of some vague, ill-defined, but powerful sense of fear. When he thought it through, logically and unemotionally, he could not imagine why he felt like this. What on earth could Fiona do if for once he didn't try to placate her, but instead insisted on having things his own way now and then? Nothing, he thought. It was like when he used to count for the kids. One... two... two and a half ... and they had never questioned just what would happen if he ever got to the magic number three. The impetus to obey was now so deeply ingrained in him that rebellion seemed not just inadvisable but downright impossible.

Later that day, Fiona arrived at the apartment, reeking of scent and bearing a bunch of slightly wilted garden flowers for Margaret and a knitted fair isle cardigan for Eduardo. She was a neat knitter and the garment was nicely done, just big enough for him to grow into. Luis was in on his own when she arrived, busy in the kitchen. Margaret had taken Eduardo to the baby clinic and had obviously had to wait. Luis, when he and Fiona were alone, was always friendly but slightly distant. His calculated and mischievous flirtations had all been reserved for more public occasions when he knew Margaret could keep an eye on things, but recently, he had even put a stop to those.

'I'm cooking,' he said abruptly. 'Margarita will be here soon. I thought she'd be back by now.'

He poured her a glass of wine and deliberately left her in the sitting room, but presently she drifted into the kitchen as she talked to him. He was making *gazpacho*, chopping up tomatoes and cucumber, peppers and garlic, and processing the vegetables in small quantities in a blender with water, vinegar, and olive oil. She watched in silence the way he worked, very quickly, with a chef's slightly manic air of absorption, coupled with intense focus. She took a big gulp of wine. The kitchen seemed suddenly very stuffy. His physical presence was overpowering.

'I see you use breadcrumbs,' she said in the sudden silence as the blender stopped.

He swung around, too close to her in the small room, the knife brandished in his hand, and she stepped backwards involuntarily, clutching at her glass.

'What?' he asked. He had been totally engrossed in his work, thinking that he would put his own *gazpacho* on the menu at *La Manzana Dorada*.

He glanced down at the knife. 'Oh sorry,' he said, smiling. 'I didn't mean to menace you.' He put it on the chopping board.

'It's a nice knife though.'

'Yes it is. I got it on Byres Road. There's a cook shop. It's Japanese. Beautiful, isn't it?' I'll have to remember to put it in my hold baggage when we fly home.'

'You don't want to be arrested.'

'Margarita said she shouldn't buy it for me because it's unlucky to buy somebody a knife, unless they pay you, so I had to give her some money for it.'

'Yes. I've heard that superstition too. It cuts your friendship. Cuts it right in two. But I only meant I noticed you used breadcrumbs.' She gestured at the heap of wholemeal breadcrumbs in a dish on the work surface.

'Oh yes, yes. I put in breadcrumbs.'

'That's a very cheffy thing to do.'

He shrugged. 'I am a chef. So?'

'It all smells lovely.'

'It *is* lovely. Why don't you go and sit down through there? Put the television on if you wish. Have some more wine. My wife will be back very soon.'

She was wearing too much perfume, he thought. It was a strong, sophisticated scent, a scent for winter nights, not for *gazpacho* with the in-laws on a summer evening. It made him feel a bit sick. He noticed that she had on lipstick and blusher. She was so close to him beside the work surface, uncomfortably close, that he could see fragments of face powder clinging to her nose and her cheeks. Her eyes were pale blue and the roots of her hair were coming in dark beneath the blonde. She seemed to have dressed up for the occasion.

He thought, bitterly, she is such a busybody. At first she wanted to be rid of me. Hoped that I would eventually go back alone and leave Margarita behind with the baby. But why would she want that? Now she seems to have changed her mind about me, but not in a good way. She wants me for herself. This sudden perception horrified him. Can it be true? How could she even imagine that? He thought she must be a little mad.

He had a sudden fear of a situation that he didn't know how to manage. He hoped Margarita would come back soon. He examined the pale eyes and saw that they were gazing up at him with desperation and desire. He knew that it had all gone much too far and he hadn't noticed. He had done nothing in his own eyes but a little light flirtation, always in his wife's presence. The kind of thing he could safely indulge in when he was playing back home. But he shouldn't have done it at all. Margarita was right. It had been a silly thing to do. All the same, he felt a certain sympathy for Fiona, his natural good nature reasserting itself. He set down his knife and tried to push past her into the sitting room, wiping his hands on a cloth. To his horror, she misinterpreted the gesture and came even closer to him, gazing up into his face.

'Oh, Luis ...' she began. 'We mustn't.'

He gazed at her in horror. 'Mustn't what?'

'Well, this. The way we are with each other. You know? The songs you sing for me. The way you look at me. But we mustn't. It would be too hurtful for too many people ...'

'Enough! *Callarse!*'

He stepped away from her into the sitting room. He couldn't let her go on.

'Don't be silly, Fiona,' he said, as though he were speaking to a child that had gone too far in some fantasy. 'There's nothing between us. Nothing. Never has been and never will be. Only in your imagination.' He spread his hands, but it had the effect of pushing her away. He poured himself a glass of wine and offered to fill hers, but she shook her head dumbly, her gaze fixed on him, on his lips.

'Oh Luis!' she said. 'Don't be like that!'

'Like what? What am I like?'

'Well, you know? It's obvious, isn't it? I used to think you didn't like me, but now you've changed your mind. You like me. You really like me!'

'Fiona, this is crazy! You know nothing about me. There's some dream going on in your head, but it has nothing to do with me at all.'

'I don't know what you mean.'

'Look, I'm sorry if you got the wrong impression. The truth is that I sometimes flirt a bit when I'm playing. It's part of the performance. Margarita often tells me not to do it, that I'm – what does she say? Walking on thin ice. But most people don't mind it. It's all words, nothing more. Just words and looks. Never touch. Never. And it's true. I like women. Women of all ages. Sometimes I think women are so much nicer than men. But that's as far as it goes. No further. Never. Not now.'

He saw that she was blushing, the red spreading up from her neck to her cheeks.

'I have no idea what you mean,' she said again.

'Margarita said I was behaving badly and as usual she was right. She's right about most things.' He was speaking half to himself. He turned to her again. 'It was unkind of me, even though I did nothing. Well, maybe I was nicer to you than I should have been. But it meant nothing. Do you understand? It was just a silly game.'

'I don't believe you.'

He was suddenly exasperated. *'Ay dios mio*, I don't even like you very much. And I love my wife. Nothing will change that. Ever. Do you understand me? I'm very sorry if you're unhappy, but that's not my fault. Now. Let's be ordinary. Like brother and sister. Let's talk about something else, eh?'

She thought for a moment that she was going to break down and cry with the embarrassment of it all. She knew what he meant but couldn't admit that she knew it. He *had* been flirting with her. He'd admitted it, but it meant nothing. She had known all along that it meant nothing. Even while she was telling herself stories about him, every night, before she went to sleep. Stories in which he suddenly turned to her. Realised how much she meant to him. How Maggie meant nothing. Of course they were fantasies. Nothing more. But still, it was hurtful to know just how far they were from the truth. How much he – the word itself cut through her like his fancy chef's knife – disliked her. He *disliked* her. She gulped down her drink, held out her glass and he refilled it. Then he went back into the kitchen to finish making his *gazpacho* while she sat in silence staring into the empty fireplace. By the time Margaret came home with the baby, she had recovered her composure sufficiently to be able to take Eduardo onto her lap and talk to him, while Margaret went through and helped Luis to finish the meal. In the kitchen, Margaret raised her eyebrows, aware that something had gone wrong, that there was an atmosphere in the room, but Luis just shrugged and carried on cooking, feigning innocence.

Fiona stayed on for a couple of hours. Anything else would have looked strange and besides, why shouldn't she? She had done nothing wrong. Nothing at all had been done on either side. That was how stupid it all was. Except that Luis had behaved badly. Very badly. It was unforgiveable to make her believe that he ... but there, her imagination failed her. She cringed before her own humiliation.

Margaret served the soup with crusty bread and cheese followed by fruit, and Fiona even managed to eat some of it, although she thought it would choke her. After the meal, Luis took himself off to the bedroom with the baby and his guitar. Eduardo liked to fall asleep to his soft playing. They could hear it now with the occasional gentle song.

'Thank God for that guitar,' said Margaret. 'It's like magic. I sometimes wonder if it's because he could hear his dad playing and singing before he was born.'

'Do you think so?'

'I do.'

Fiona had been trying to think of something to say that didn't involve Luis.

'How's Cristina?'

'Fine,' said Margaret. 'She seems to have settled into her new job quite quickly. She and Isabella hit it off right away. We miss her. It was lovely having her around the place. She's such a sunny young woman.'

'Did your friend Suzie find her the job?'

'That's right. It was very kind of them. She was looking for a fresh start. An adventure. And I gather Sitges is a beautiful place. I quite envy her.'

'But you're going back to a beautiful place yourself.'

'So I am. I can't wait.'

'She became good friends with this Laura and Suzie, didn't she? Cristina.'

'I suppose so. They're nice people.'

'They've been together for a long time, haven't they?'

'Oh yes. They've been a couple for a long time. They're in a civil partnership you know. Now they're thinking about marriage and a baby.'

'That would be a big step. Let's hope they know what they're letting themselves in for.'

'It's a big step for anyone, isn't it?'

It struck Margaret that there was nothing that she or anyone could say that Fiona wouldn't manage to find fault with. Her default mode was to find the negative side of everything, to be worried, to be offended, to criticise. The glass of her life would always be half empty. Margaret gazed at her and saw that tonight there was something sad and raw about her, something that made her even more prone to criticise than usual. She suspected that it had to do with her husband. He had been flirting again. He did it thoughtlessly, just by paying attention, making people feel special. Men as well as women. It didn't matter. He could be so charming. Irresistibly so. He had done it to her from the start, that day in Los Cristianos, when they hardly knew each other, when he had rescued her from a group drunken 'stags' and taken her for a drink afterwards. But then there had been a genuine and immediate mutual attraction. The lightning strike of love at first sight, and how often did that ever happen? Almost never. She felt sorry for Fiona and guilty on behalf of her husband, even though she knew he had done nothing much at all except encourage an unwise infatuation out of some misplaced sense of mischief.

'And what about Cristina? Does she have a man in her life.'

'I don't think she does. I haven't really talked to her about it, but she was happy enough to move away from the island.'

'A man or a woman?' Fiona was fishing.

Margaret sighed. 'I don't know. And to be honest with you, I don't think she knows either. It's up to her to decide what she wants.'

'Does Luis know?'

'There isn't anything for him *to* know, is there? I don't really want to talk about this, not behind her back. Don't you go mentioning it to him, Fiona. I think she's just never found the right person yet.'

'No,' Fiona said with a touch of spite in her voice. 'I can't imagine he'd be very pleased.'

'I don't see why not. He's not a dinosaur.'

'No, but he's quite traditional in some ways, isn't he? He likes to be the boss in his own house.'

Margaret was suddenly indignant. 'That isn't the way he is at all.' A strained silence fell between them. 'I don't think you know the first thing about him.'

'I know that he's very foreign.'

It seemed to be the ultimate insult. Margaret wanted to laugh, but couldn't.

The songs and the music had stopped.

'That's our Eduardito out for the count,' said Margaret.

When Luis came through and offered to make coffee, Fiona shook her head.

'No thanks. I won't sleep. And I must be going. I promised to help Rory with his school project. You know how it is.'

'Well come again soon,' said Margaret, warmly. She sensed an atmosphere, sensed that something was wrong, and her impulse was always to try to diffuse it with kindness. 'The cardie's gorgeous and the flowers are lovely. Thank-you so much.'

'Oh, just from the garden, you know.'

As Fiona walked back to her car, she was ashamed to find that there was a lump in her throat. Tears threatened. She took a deep breath but a torrent of unwelcome emotions flooded through her: anger, mortification and a profound jealousy of Margaret. It wasn't fair. She had got so used to pitying Margaret, to assuming that her personal life was and always would be somewhat chaotic and unsatisfactory. There had been something obscurely comforting about it. Well, at least I'm better off than poor Margaret, she had thought. Now, all that had changed. Margaret was the lucky one, with a handsome and undoubtedly loving husband, a new baby and a beautiful home to go back to – the kind of home and business you read about in the Sunday supplements. How had that happened? It was not what she had expected at all. She had predicted disaster, and it hadn't happened. How could she have been so wrong? Instead, Margaret seemed contented with her lot. It wouldn't do for me, she thought, stoutly, but she knew that she was lying to herself.

'She was very quiet,' said Margaret, when Fiona had gone.

'I know.'

'And she wouldn't stay long, either. What happened?'

'Nothing happened.' He hesitated. 'Well, I told her I felt nothing for her, that's all. Beyond what is right and proper. I confessed to being a – a flirt.'

'You actually *told* her that?' Margaret was dismayed. She felt herself grow hot with vicarious embarrassment. Poor Fiona.

'Oh I couldn't stand it any more. She had me cornered in the kitchen while I was trying to make *gazpacho*, if you must know.'

Margaret couldn't help but laugh, it was so ridiculous.

'Cornered in the kitchen? Oh Luis!'

'Well. It was so stupid. There she was with her scent and her make-up. I suddenly saw it for what it was. It was ridiculous. *Ella era tan estúpida!* So stupid! She began to speak as though ...*no se, no se!*' Briefly his English deserted him.

'As though what? Tell me!

'As though we were in some kind of relationship. As though I fancied her or something.'

'I told you so!' Margaret was exasperated. 'Didn't I warn you what was happening? I could see the way she was looking at you!'

'Well, you were right,' he said, sheepishly, starting to stack the dinner dishes. Anything to avoid confronting his own stupidity. 'I was in here and she was right up close to me and she started to say such silly things.'

'What things?'

'I hardly remember. How we must be careful not to hurt other people. It was nonsense.'

'I told you. I said she had a big crush on you.'

'And she did. I can't think how it happened.'

'Of course you can think how it happened. You were deliberately charming her. It's what you do. To *everyone*, when you have mind to do it.'

'Not very seriously. Nobody in their right mind would have fallen for it.'

'Well she fell for it. Because she wanted to. And now she'll hate you for it. I suppose you know that.'

He looked disconcerted. 'I don't think so. She'll get over it. People do.'

'Not so easily as all that. Not when she feels humiliated. *Humillada*.'

'I don't really want to have to think about Fiona at all. She's so silly that she makes me angry. Do we have to talk about her?'

'Then we won't talk about her,' Margaret agreed, although she worried about it a good deal. Perhaps it was just as well that they were going back to La Gomera very soon. She could imagine that any family gatherings would be uncomfortable to say the least for the next few months but perhaps given time the whole thing would settle down.

Oh well, she thought, at last, ever the optimist. I don't expect it'll do any harm. Surely not even Fiona would spread gossip about Luis. Surely she wouldn't take it seriously.

CHAPTER SIXTEEN

Who had a golden beak
and the throat of a rooster,
the ears of a woodpecker and
the music of a canary?

Luis and Margaret were now the official owners of *La Manzana Dorada*. They would use Margaret's divorce settlement money to develop the restaurant and its surrounding plantation. They would be able to renew the orange and lemon groves where needed and sort out the irrigation. Margaret was hoping to make the gardens into as much of an attraction as the restaurant itself, with Carmen's enthusiastic help.

The old building, beautiful as it was, needed sensitive and reasonably expensive renovation, and Luis had a yearning to use the land to its full capacity so that he could begin to supply even more of his own produce for the restaurant. He suspected that the way of the past could also, with some modifications, be the way of the future. Besides, modern farming methods were so recent on La Gomera as to be innovations; and many of their more extreme manifestations were impractical because of the difficult geography of the island. He thought that it should be possible to combine the best of the old ways with the best of the new. He had never wanted to be tied down to his father's smallholding, but *La Manzana Dorada* gave him an opportunity to combine all of his interests in one. The prospect excited him and the thought of sharing all this with his wife and son filled him with joyful anticipation. He was all set to go back, with Margaret and the baby following in August, by which time he was hoping to have everything ready for them, especially for their growing son. He was planning to toddler proof the place as much as was feasible.

He had finally admitted to himself just how homesick he had been. He hadn't felt this way for years, not since his time working in London, skivvying in a restaurant kitchen with a *loco* chef shouting and swearing at them. Then, his longing for his island had been acute and unmistakeable. He had forgotten about it until now, when it crept up on him and he finally saw it for what it was. It wasn't that he disliked the city. He could see its good side, see the friendliness of its people. In many ways they reminded him of home. His desire for home came to him in the night, like an illness. The word was *nostalgico* in his own tongue, but the English word seemed more accurate. It was a sickness, deep inside him. The only cure was to go home. Only then, he would worry about his Margarita. Because what would happen to them if she felt the same? How would they manage then?

His uncle and aunt, Paco and Carmen, had left some of their furniture behind at *La Manzana Dorada*, good wooden pieces mostly: a couple of antique Spanish chests like treasure chests with decorative bronze fittings, a heavily carved and inlaid walnut cabinet that managed to look robust and delicate at the same time, and a couple of sturdy fruitwood chairs, all of which were probably as old as the house. The couple didn't have room for them in their new house and Margaret had already said she would be delighted to have them, since they seemed to be a part of the history of the place. Luis wanted to give the rooms a coat of paint, buy new mattresses and install a good shower, as well as a new computer, given that the old one had been failing for some time. The kitchen was fine, as was to be expected, and he knew that his uncle and aunt would have left the house clean and fresh, but there were also things to be bought for the baby. Cristina and his mother had already selected what they thought might be a suitable room for a nursery, and decorated it, installing the wooden crib that Margaret's office colleagues in Los Cristianos had bought for them before she left to have the baby.

He knew that they would probably move it into their bedroom for the time being, until Eduardo was a little older, given that he always slept more peacefully when they were in the room with him. Luis would need to buy a cot because he was already growing, and perhaps a nice single bed, and a baby bath to fit inside the huge old enamel bath that filled half the bathroom. They had already had to buy one for the Glasgow apartment, but it didn't seem worth their while shipping it all the way to La Gomera. There would be a lot of enjoyment in organising the house to suit themselves, but he still wanted everything to be nice for their arrival.

Nothing was said about Fiona's humiliation until Ian invited Margaret out for lunch a few days later. He was so guarded about arranging it that she thought it was going to be a last-ditch attempt to try to persuade her that she was making a big mistake in going back to the island with such a young child. They were in a child-friendly Italian restaurant with Eduardo, who had been fed, dozing in his buggy between them.

'So you're finally going,' said Ian. 'I suppose I knew you would, sooner or later. He's the kind of man who likes to get his own way.'

Margaret was forced to smile at this assertion, knowing where it came from. If anyone was fond of getting their own way it was Fiona.

'You make it sound as if he's bullying me into it. Nothing could be further from the truth. I want to go. I really want to go. I've always wanted to go back. I just couldn't make up my mind when.'

'I do know that.'

'The birth was very difficult. It's taken me a long time to get over it. Longer than I thought, anyway. But I certainly don't want to spend another winter here when I can be on La Gomera in the sunshine.

Besides, Luis's family are desperate to see their new grandson. It isn't fair on them to keep him here.'

'What about mum? It isn't very fair to her to leave her here, is it?'

'You know mum approves. She's had a long time with him and she's planning to visit us. Just after Christmas we thought. It's so dreich here then and the sunshine would be good for her. We'll pretty much have things sorted out by then. She can stay for a few weeks if she wants. There's plenty of room. We'll get the restaurant up and running first, but there's a spare room for mum. There's even an *azotea*!'

'What's an *azotea*?'

'A traditional platform. On the roof. The views are wonderful. The house is long and low but the views from the *azotea* are to die for.'

'It does sound wonderful. Can we come and visit you?'

'Would you want to?'

'I would.'

'And Fiona?'

He hesitated, fiddling about with his napkin. 'I never know what Fiona's thinking these days.'

'Well we'll be back for holidays. It isn't the other side of the world. It isn't far, whatever you think. His family are very kind, you know. Kinder to me than you lot ever were to Luis.'

'I think we've been very nice to him,' Ian protested. He attacked his plate of lasagne enthusiastically. Nothing ever kept Ian off his food.

'You've tolerated him. All except Mum. She loves him and she shows it.'

'Well, it's true that the better I knew Luis the more I thought I liked him. No. Like's the wrong word. Admire. I admire him. I began to regret persuading him to stay after a while. He seemed so unhappy here.'

'You noticed?'

'Oh yes. He's never fitted in. Never been really happy here. Even I could see that and I don't think I'm very touchy feely, am I?'

'No. You're not at all touchy feely, Ian. But I love you anyway.'

'So it'll be good for you to go back, I think.'

'We should have talked about it more,' she said. 'But I was feeling so ill after the birth. It's one of the problems of being married to somebody who thinks in a different language.'

'Luis's English is very good.'

'It is, but there are nuances. Oh it's hard to explain. Sometimes, I think that even though we might be using the same words, the ideas behind them are so different that we'll never quite reach each other. And at other times, I think that we're so completely in tune that none of this matters.'

'Do you?'

'I do. I wouldn't have married him otherwise.'

'You don't have to come from different countries to speak different languages,' said Ian fervently. 'Sometimes I feel as if Fiona is from another planet.'

Margaret laughed. 'Maybe I make too much of it. We're still adjusting to each other.'

'And you really want to spend the rest of your life there?'

'The rest of my life is a long time I hope. But I think so. And right now, I can't wait.'

'Then I hope it all goes well for you. I really do.'

She knew him very well. There was something wrong. She wondered how to approach it. At last, when they had finished eating, and were drinking coffee, she patted his hand across the table.

'Ian, is there something you're trying to tell me?'

He looked into his coffee cup, shrugged. Sighed. 'I don't know.'

'Just spit it out!'

'Well, it's Fiona.'

She supressed a groan. It would be. And she thought she knew what was coming.

'She says ...'

'What does she say?'

'She says Luis made a pass at her.'

The old fashioned expression almost made her laugh. Except that it wasn't funny. Not funny at all.

'When was this?'

'When she was round at yours. You were out with the baby. She said he was in the kitchen and she went in to fill her wine glass and he – made a pass at her. You know. Touched her. Inappropriately.'

'Oh for fuck's sake, Ian!' She spoke so loudly that nearby diners looked round at them, frowning. 'Sorry, sorry.' She lowered her voice. 'Do you believe her?'

'I don't know what to believe. He can be very … flirtatious. Can't he?'

'But not physically. You know that.'

'He was pretty physical with that lawyer at Ricky's party.'

'Yes. When he was defending me. From what amounted to a sexual assault. The bastard grabbed my boobs, Ian!' Again, nearby diners looked around.

'Shush!' Ian looked aghast. 'You'll have us thrown out in a minute.'

Margaret had suddenly realised that she was in a cleft stick of Fiona's making. But she had to defend her husband against what amounted to a dangerous allegation.

'I already know about this.'

'Do you?' He seemed surprised.

'Luis told me about it that night, when she'd gone. It was Fiona that cornered him in the kitchen. She – well yes. She made a pass of sorts at *him*. He was horrified. She thought he fancied her. And I'll admit, it *was* partly his fault. Because he'd noticed that she had a bit of a crush on him, and the fool encouraged it.'

'How?' Ian raised his eyebrows.

'Oh when he was singing. You know those devastating little love songs he's so good at. And he's a good looking guy. When he turns on the charm, and you feel the full blast of it, it's hard to resist. I know that all too well. But it means nothing. Well, it usually means nothing. And there's never any touching. Never anything physical at all. Well, except with me of course. But that didn't happen immediately. He was quite shy, if anything.'

'Except with you?'

'He was scrupulously polite at first. And it wasn't casual charm. He meant it with me, and then he almost lost me. But that wasn't anything he did, not really. He just misunderstood my first reaction to his family.' She sighed, remembering that first terrible quarrel. 'It was so silly. He thought that I suspected that he was after my money. That was it in a nutshell. And you know he wasn't after my money. I never once thought he was, even though you and Fiona did.'

'No. He wasn't, was he?'

'He was wrong to treat Fiona like that, but it was sheer mischief. Do you really believe he made a pass at her? Tried to kiss her? Groped her? Luis? '

Ian sighed. 'Not really. But she's so convincing.'

'How?'

'Oh there's been weeping and wailing. You should see her. It's as though she's playing a part. Red nose and all. She says she's traumatised.'

'Traumatised by rejection more like. He's a good man, Ian. What is she going to do about it?' She had a sudden chilling thought. What if Fiona went to the police? Accused Luis of assault?

Ian shook his head. 'Oh, nothing. Don't worry. She's making a meal of it right now but she'll do nothing. It'll blow over.'

'How do you know?'

'Because I know my wife. She's in the drama of the moment. Oh but you do believe me, don't you?'

He looked at her solemnly. 'I think I believe *him*. I wondered if he had told you about it.'

'Of course he did.'

'He's what you'd call an honourable man. But it was a damn silly thing to do. I wish he'd just ignored her. It was a crush. She's had them before.'

'Has she? Who?' Intrigued, Margaret couldn't resist the question.

'Oh nobody you'd know. Well, Ricky for a few months.'

'Ricky!' She was truly astonished.

'Aye. I know. He just laughed at her. You see, I'm not enough for her.' He looked sad, suddenly.

'Oh Ian, no. It's not that. It's that we all need a bit of excitement in our lives. Especially when we're heading for middle age. And to be fair, we should believe women when they accuse men of these things.'

'We should. But just occasionally women don't tell the truth either. It doesn't do anybody any favours, does it? Don't worry about it. I'll speak to her. It'll be fine.'

The baby woke and was carried off by the big bosomed Italian grandmother who ran the restaurant to show to the staff. He seemed very happy with the novelty of it, leaning his head against her and smiling. They ordered more coffee and for the rest of the meal, they spoke about things that didn't matter, the baby's teeth, Annie's garden, television programmes. But at last, Ian looked at his watch and stood up. 'I'll have to get back. Got a client coming in at half two. I'll pay for these. And listen, I'll run you to the airport when you go. Luis is going quite soon, isn't he?'

'Yes, he is. But are you sure.'

'Of course. I wouldn't have suggested it otherwise.'

Eduardo fell asleep again, exhausted by socialising. Margaret walked slowly through the city. Fiona's feelings for Luis and her husband's unwise encouragement of what had turned out to be a serious crush were preying on her mind, but it was hard to worry too much on such a day. Sunshine and showers had alternated all morning and there had been rainbows. In Woodlands Road a man was pushing a barrow full of yellow melons from his van into a shop. A woman in a blue sari was steadying them for him but one broke free and rolled away. Margaret fielded it neatly and handed it back to her. 'Thank-you,' she said, smiling, glancing down at the baby. All would be well, thought Margaret. Surely, now, all would be well. Margaret pushed the buggy with its slumbering burden homeward, allowing her mind to dwell contentedly on their future together. Whatever might befall them, at least their mutual love was assured.

CHAPTER SEVENTEEN

Goodbye, dear dove!
I'm leaving you now.
I will not torment you any more,
nor will I love you in this lifetime.

Afterwards, she couldn't remember how the row had begun. The baby was asleep, which was a mercy. Normally, they would have deliberately woken him at this time, afraid that he would be awake half the night. They had not shouted at each other. They had been too conscious of him and his needs, so they had conducted the quarrel *sotto voce*, and that, somehow, made it worse, because shouting might have released some of the pent up emotions for both of them.

He had mentioned Fiona, scathingly. Tired and stressed, she had related Fiona's side of the encounter, baldly, without qualification.

'She told Ian you made a pass at her. Touched her inappropriately. Now see what a mess you've got us into!'

He was at first shocked and dismayed, but all too quickly, dismay had turned to anger. 'She's lying! I never touched her. I couldn't even get past her to get out of the kitchen!'

'Are you sure?'

Why on earth had she said that? She trusted him. Even Ian trusted him. He had behaved unwisely, rather than inappropriately. She knew that there was no way on God's earth that he would have made a pass at Fiona. But the question had just popped out, thoughtlessly. The way these things do, when both people are tired, sleep deprived and in the middle of moving house and, in her case, moving country.

'You think I'm unfaithful to you. You still believe that I'm unfaithful to you!'

He had said this once before, when they were first married, when the Sirocco had come to Los Cristianos and in the terrible heat of the wind that blew from Africa, they had quarrelled over the girls that always eyed him up in the bars where he played, bought drinks for him, tried to get his attention. He had become very angry then, gone out, drunk a bit too much and been full of remorse in the morning. She had been unjust. He had done nothing wrong. She knew in her heart that she was unjust now. She blamed him for his folly, perhaps for his self love. He simply couldn't resist responding to the flattery of a woman, any woman, who fancied herself in love with him. He would never be physically unfaithful. Nor even mentally unfaithful. He had made that choice, that decision when he married her. But like a cat with a mouse, he couldn't resist playing, and for a moment or two, she hated that in him, hated the cruelty of it. The image that came into her mind, suddenly and surprisingly, was of a bullfighter, taunting a wounded bull. How ridiculously dramatic. And how can I ever cope with him, she thought, suddenly. When he's so alien? How can we ever understand each other? The notion frightened her.

'How would I know?' she said. 'How would I know what you are?'

He had been standing with his back to her, his arm resting on the fireplace. Now, he whirled around and stared at her, frowning, as though she too was a stranger to him.

'What did you say? What did you just say to me?'

'I don't know you.'

'Then you've never known me. And you still don't trust me.'

She lost patience suddenly. 'Oh go to hell.'

'*Seguro que si.*' For sure I will, he said, and walked out of the room.

She closed her eyes briefly. When she opened them again he had gone. She heard the slam of the apartment door and his footsteps tattooing sharply down the stone stairs.

She sat down, too shocked to cry, too shocked to do anything but stare into space. She felt cold, so she turned on the gas fire, poured herself a glass of wine and sat on in the living room, cradling the glass in her hands. When Eduardo awoke, she went through to the bedroom, noticing that Luis had taken his jacket from its peg in the hallway. Numbly, trying not to think about what had just passed between herself and her husband, she woke the baby up, fed and changed him, and then played with him. She thought she had managed to behave normally with him, but after his bath, he was fretful and sad and he was reluctant to sleep. He wanted his father to play for him. At last, she found some of Luis's guitar music on her phone, and that soothed him.

The moment he was asleep, reaction set in. She was shivering, although the room was warm. She made herself a cheese sandwich and ate it without tasting it. She drank several cups of tea, put on the dishwasher, and then crept into bed, expecting every moment to hear Luis returning to the apartment, not knowing how to react to him, wanting to cry but determined not to.

He did not come.

At last, she fell into a miserably restless doze. When Eduardo woke in the night Luis was still absent. She fed her son and then lay on her back, angry and disappointed in her husband. How could he do this to her? How could such a small thing become so momentous? As though her marriage was a giant house of cards. One incautious movement and it had all come tumbling down. When sleep came, it seemed heavy and dark and full of unpleasant dreams. She had lost her way in some vast alien city. The streets were impossible to navigate, consisting mainly of crumbling stairs and tunnels. She was looking for the airport, but when she got there, she found that she had somebody else's passport. She must go back. But how? She woke again at six o'clock in the morning. The bed beside her was empty. It had been empty all night. She got up and went through to the kitchen, mechanically putting on the kettle. Luis had never come back to the flat. She wondered, in dread and anxiety, just where he had been and what he had been doing.

Luis spent the rest of the night walking the streets of Glasgow, angry and frustrated. He didn't know what to do with himself. Couldn't cope with his feelings. But what were his feelings? He knew in his heart that his wife trusted him. Knew that this was largely his own fault. He saw old and young homeless people propped in doorways and under bridges, trying to sleep beneath an assortment of blankets, sleeping bags, quilts, cardboard. An old man asked him for a cigarette. He shook his head, but felt in his pocket and handed the man the loose change he found there: four or five pound coins. It would not buy cigarettes, but it might stretch to a hot drink and maybe a bacon roll in the morning. Once he was stopped by a policeman. The car had cruised past him and stopped just ahead of him.

'Where are you off to at this time of night, sir?'

'Just walking.'

'Where do you live?'

Luis gave his address politely enough. He had had enough antagonism for one night without arousing official wrath as well.

'You're a long way from home.' The officer looked suspicious.

'To tell you the truth, I have had a quarrel with my wife. I left the house and I'm just walking. I'll go home now. Maybe.'

The policeman looked at him in the gloom, the street lamps draining the colour from both their faces. 'Off you go then. And try and make it up, eh?'

'Make what up?' The expression confused him.

'The quarrel, son. You can't spend your nights walking about the city. Too many folk doing that who don't have a home to go to without you adding to them.'

He nodded, quickened his pace but he didn't go home.

Morning came. The dark space of the Clyde turned silver. The city was all pink and grey. He found his way to Central Station, washed in the public lavatories there and breakfasted in a coffee bar on a triple espresso and cake. Fortunately his wallet and phone had been in his jacket pocket when he had snatched it up on his way out of the flat. He drew a little money out of their joint account. He went into an internet cafe, where he managed to book a flight to Tenerife, using his credit card. He got two seats: one for himself and one for his guitar. He couldn't put it in the hold even though it was only his second best guitar. It cost him a small fortune but he didn't care. Them, he thought. It cost them. He was overcome by recklessness. What did any of it matter? Then he walked up the hill to Buchanan Street and got on a subway train crowded with university students heading for afternoon lectures. He got out with them all at Hillhead and went back home.

Earlier that morning, Suzie had come round to the flat where she had found Margaret upset and anxious. She had spent some time comforting her friend, trying not very successfully to advise her about a situation that was totally outside her own experience. She was desperately sorry for her while at the same time feeling that she had only herself to blame for having married such an impossible man. But she couldn't say this. She loved Margaret too well to say what was in her mind and could only hug her.

'He'll turn up today, don't worry. He'll probably be very contrite. But if you don't mind, I'd rather not be here when he does come. I'd probably say the wrong thing. Oh, Mags!' Suzie shook her head in exasperation. 'Why on earth do you love him so much?'

'Because he's a good man and now he's feeling hurt. He thinks I've betrayed him by not believing him.'

'But that's so stupid. So over the top. I mean ... Fiona! '

'Maybe so, but isn't that what happens when women aren't believed? You'd be the first to say that.'

'I would. I know. But he's always struck me as an honest man. Believe me, I know a creep when I see one, and he's never come across like that. He irritates me with all this macho stuff. I'll never understand it. But he loves you to bits. You and the baby. That's clear.'

'I've never seen him like that before. He looked terrible.'

'He's never seemed very kind to me but I don't think he'd lie to you. I do believe that Fiona had a serious crush on him though. I believe that.'

'She had started talking about him a lot. You know the way people do. When they fancy somebody?'

'I do indeed. I used to talk about Laura all the time to anyone who would listen. Still do, I suppose. And it's the way you talk about *him*. Look, is there anyone I can phone?' Suzie asked helplessly. 'Annie?'

Margaret shook her head. 'She'd probably tell Fiona. No. Just let it be. He'll be home soon, I'm sure. You're right. I'll wait for him. We'll wait for him. He'll be desperate to see Eduardo. He'll be home soon enough.'

Somewhat reluctantly Suzie left her friend but there seemed to be nothing else she could do. She certainly didn't want to meet Luis again in his present frame of mind.

Luis arrived home early that afternoon. Margaret looked very pale, with dark circles under her eyes but she had waited long enough for worry to have turned to anger again.

'So you've decided to come home at last?'

His characteristic shrug. 'My things are here.'

'Do you include me and Eduardo among your things, Luis?'

He frowned but didn't reply.

'Where have you been?'

'Just out. Why? Did you think I had another woman?'

'Oh don't be so stupid. Of course I didn't.'

'I could have been with somebody else. How would you know?'

'I do know. If you can't see how much I love you and trust you, you're a fool. I've married a fool.'

'That can be remedied,' he said, in a very low voice, as though half ashamed of himself, which indeed he was.

'What did you say?'

'That can be remedied.' Louder. 'You've got rid of one husband, so why not another?'

He might as well have struck her. It was like a physical pain. The deliberate attempt to hurt.

'Oh yes, I've done it once so why not again. Why not another divorce?'

She was crying now, the tears running down her cheeks, but she stood before him, defiant and unapologetic, her patience all gone. It had happened once too often for her sensible Scottish self. Eduardo watched them and began to cry too, sensing unhappiness and anger. She picked him up and shushed him and took him into the spare bedroom, kicking the door shut behind her with her foot. Anything to get away from her husband. She lay on the bed, so recently vacated by Cristina, with the baby in her arms, singing to him, soothing her grief with the small, warm body. The baby was used to having an afternoon nap and his eyelids drooped. Luis went into their own bedroom, pulled a suitcase from under the bed and began to pack it with necessities. It didn't take him long. Somebody, he couldn't remember who, had given them a soft toy, a small blue elephant, as a present for Eduardo. There was something about it, about the shape of it from behind, that reminded Luis irresistibly of his son. At the last moment, he tucked it into the suitcase, under the jeans and shirts. He couldn't fit the Aran sweater in, so he left it folded carefully on a shelf. He was fastening his guitar into its case when Margaret finally came through. Eduardo had fallen asleep and she had left him in there on his back, on the bed, with pillows on either side of him to stop him rolling off if he woke.

They argued passionately, again in whispers to save waking him. There was something very foolish about it but they had gone too far for laughter. She saw the suitcase all packed and ready, and misgiving made her heart lurch.

'What's that?'

'I told you. I came for my things.'

She shook her head in disbelief and dread. 'Where are you going? Where will you stay?'

'I'm going home.'

'Yes, I know. You're going back to La Gomera next week and I'm joining you at the end of the month.'

'No. I'm going tomorrow. I've got a flight to Tenerife. From Glasgow airport, tomorrow morning.'

He saw her frown, her lip trembling, then she pulled herself together with an effort.

'What about me?'

'It's a flight for me. Not for you. I'll stay at the airport tonight.'

A thousand questions and remonstrances flooded her mind but she rejected all of them. She was very tired. Too tired to argue with him. To angry with him. What was the point?'

'You're leaving us?'

Us, he thought. That struck home. Deliberately he ignored the plea implicit in the pronoun. Sheer mulish obstinacy overtook him. Let her suffer. He suffered, didn't he? He had suffered for months, here in this alien land, where they treated their dogs, their fur babies, better than their children.

'I never want to see you again,' he said simply. 'We're too different. I should have known. I was right that day on La Gomera. That first day on La Gomera. You should not have come looking for me, Margarita. We are quite different. It's better if I go.'

He looked angry, tousled and very handsome. Incongruously she felt the warm blast of his sensuality, even while she knew that she had no way of reaching him. Overcome by emotion, she moved to stand in front of him, forcing him to look at her, reaching out to him.

'No,' she said. 'No, you can't do this, Luis! You can't just leave me alone like this. Please. You can't leave us. *Don't do this to us!*'

She felt as though the words had been torn out of her in her panic to make him understand how foolish this was. How could he not hear and understand? Where had all the love gone? If it could be so suddenly withdrawn, had it been real at all? Had it been a lie, then? Had she been deceived all over again?

He shrugged her off, as though her touch was repellent to him, his face serious and cruel. '*Vete al diablo!*' Go to hell.

Humiliation flooded through her. This was how Fiona had felt, only a million times worse. She wouldn't try again. She stepped back and watched him, utterly speechless. She felt dizzily as though some fissure had opened up in the ground beneath her feet and she was falling into it. Wounded and bleeding. The one being taunted. She shook her head, pushed the empty air away from her in a gesture of denial, and ran back into the spare bedroom, lying beside the baby, hiding her face in the pillow. Luis picked up his case and his guitar and walked out of the flat again, more slowly, but still in anger.

He was miles away in the airport before the thought struck him that he hadn't even kissed his child. He remembered the sensation of the little fingers clutching at his, of the petal soft cheek against his lips, and had to bite them to stop himself from crying aloud. He was light-headed by now from lack of sleep. He drank more coffee, ate a soggy burger that tasted rancid. Read a newspaper. Then he dozed fitfully on an airport seat. His phone vibrated a couple of times. She had texted him. He ignored the messages and switched the phone off. In the early morning he washed and changed into clean clothes from his bag, waiting to be called for his flight. They didn't like the idea of allowing him to bring the guitar on board, but since he'd paid for two seats, there wasn't much they could do but take it out of its case and inspect it very carefully. He supposed they were looking for weapons, wanted to point out that he was not a *mariachi*, like in the movies, although he wasn't foolish enough to say so. It surprised him that in the middle of this tragedy, he was capable of making a joke.

He tried to think of nothing at all but even on the plane, regret came seeping into his mind like cooling water. His temper was gone, his anger quite abated. By the time he came fully to his senses, by the time he realised that he was an impulsive fool who seemed doggedly set on destroying that which was most dear to his heart, he was on Tenerife again and back on the ferry to La Gomera. He had brought his guitar but left his beloved wife and child in Glasgow. He had frightened and insulted her, told her that he never wanted to see her again. That had been a lie. He had known it almost as soon as the words had come spilling out of his mouth. When she begged him to stay, he had walked out, seized with the drama of the moment. It had almost killed him to do it. He had wanted to see her again, to hold her and kiss her, almost as soon as he was through the door, but out of perversity and pride he had persisted. He thought, I've gone too far. She'll never forgive me. This time, I've really gone too far.

CHAPTER EIGHTEEN

Goodbye lover of my soul!
Not of the soul — that is a lie.
How can two loves that forget each other
be part of the same soul?

Luis's family received him with guarded enthusiasm. They were always delighted to see him, but they had expected him to arrive the following week and were surprised by his sudden appearance. Maria especially was puzzled and disappointed when she enquired after her daughter-in-law and Eduardo, and Luis would only say, 'They can't come yet,' refusing to be drawn on the issue, refusing to explain. Something was very wrong, she knew that immediately, but when would he tell her what it was all about?

Paco and Carmen had already moved into their little house in Vallehermoso, taking as much furniture as they would need. Luis went from room to room at *La Manzana Dorada*, touching the familiar pieces, thinking how much his wife would have loved it all, had loved it when first she had seen it. He tried to think about her and Eduardo as little as possible, but it wasn't easy. She was always in his mind. He couldn't exclude her. The pain of separation grew worse rather than better with the passage of time. He wouldn't phone or even text or message her for fear of rejection and after those first few attempts when he was still in the airport, she hadn't messaged him. He waited to hear from her. He waited, blaming signals, broadband, the mobile, the post, until he could blame none of these things any longer, but still no communication came.

It was as though Margaret, so Scottish and practical and loving, had been drawn into a battle of pride and feigned indifference that seemed very Spanish. At first she found it hard to believe that he really would fly off and leave them, but when she was sure that Luis had gone, when she was certain that he was already back on the island, she allowed her tears to fall freely. The sense of personal humiliation, of betrayal, confounded her. She had pleaded with him to stay but he had rejected her. He had told her that he would never leave her, but in the end he had gone back on his word. She woke each morning to a sensation of utter wretchedness. Only sleep brought some relief.

For several days she stayed in the flat with the baby, tending to his needs and playing with him, sleeping when he slept. She hadn't known that there could be so many tears, so much salt water inside her as she had shed during those days. Was it worth it? Was he worth it? She had begun to doubt it. Better to feel nothing at all. The only good thing to come out of all this, she thought, was Eduardo. She couldn't wish him away. At last, she felt tinder dry and brittle as a skeleton leaf, as though all the love had leached out of her with the weeping. Only then did she leave the flat, visiting her mother and telling her briefly that Luis had gone back to La Gomera but declining to answer any more questions.

She refused to have anything to do with Fiona at all.

'Tell her I don't want to see her,' she said to Annie. 'Tell her she's caused enough trouble in my life. I don't care if I never see her or speak to her again.'

'You haven't fallen out?' asked Cristina, sadly, when they spoke on Messenger. 'Say it isn't true!'

'I don't know what's true and what's false any more. Yes, we've fallen out. I'm not going into it here, Cristina, but he was determined to be angry about something. I suspect he blamed me for a lot of things. He wasn't ever happy here.'

'But you weren't expecting him to live in Glasgow, were you?'

'I wasn't, no. Anyway, he'll be fine now, won't he? He's gone back home. He'll be living the dream.'

'But without you? And Eduardito? I can't believe it!'

'You'd better believe it because that's what he's done.'

'How could he do such a thing?' Cristina said, despairingly. 'I thought he loved you.'

'So did I. It seems I was mistaken.'

Margaret's apparent coolness hid an emotional maelstrom. She didn't want to speak to anyone, but Cristina knew Luis better than almost anyone else.

'He is his own worst enemy, sometimes,' she said. And then, tentatively, 'What did you quarrel about? Can you tell me?'

'He thought I didn't trust him.'

'Oh that's so silly.'

'I don't know. I said something I didn't mean. Something and nothing. My sister-in-law Fiona – she had a crush on him. You know what that is?'

'Of course. But lots of people have had crushes on Luis. He's good looking and charming and he plays like a dream. But it means nothing. Not now, anyway.'

'She said he felt the same.'

'Oh nonsense. He didn't even like her very much. He told me so.'

'I know that. She sort of made advances to him, and he rejected her, and she got cross.'

'Well surely you believed him.'

'I did. I do. But he has this tendency to imagine that I don't trust him. I do trust him.'

'He loves you very much.'

'Perhaps that's not enough. I can't bear jealousy. It ruins everything.'

'Then he has to learn to control it.'

'I thought he had. Oh, Cristina! I'm just tired of giving in to him. Tired of feeling like this.'

'Give him a little time. I think you haven't had enough time to get used to each other. But why did he go? What happened?'

'We had a row and he stormed out. I thought it would all be fine when he came back but it wasn't. It just got worse. He was colder. More determined. It was horrible.'

'Ah the fool. What a poor fool he is. He will be at home on La Gomera now and so sorry for what he has done. But hasn't he contacted you? Or you him?'

'He would have phoned or written or messaged if he was sorry.'

'Margarita, he will. Just now, his mind will be full of knives.'

Margaret shrugged. 'Then I hope they kill him.'

'You don't mean that.'

'Don't I?'

'You must go after him,' said Cristina. 'You must fly to Tenerife and then go straight to La Gomera.'

'And what if he still doesn't want me? Why should I do that when it's his fault? No. I'm not going. I have Eduardo to think of now. He's more important. Luis just doesn't want me any more. It's finished, Cristina. Another marriage down the drain.'

Cristina hesitated. She knew her brother all too well. What she had not expected, however, was for Margaret to be infected with the same mulishness. She had seen these kind of quarrels at home: all hot air and drama. If nobody backed down, if nobody gave in, they were quite capable of lasting down the generations, capable of blighting lives.

'He didn't mean it, I'm sure.'

'You didn't see his face. He meant it.'

'Look, he has fallen out with me as well from time to time. I just ignore it and by the next day, he hardly even remembers what it was about. Will you at least write to him, even if you won't phone him?'

'If he's sorry, let him contact me. I'm damned if I'll phone him again. If he wants to, he can always message me. I don't want to talk to him any more.'

Margaret was tired to the bone and quite unshakable. If he wouldn't contact her she wouldn't even write to him. On La Gomera, Luis too was adamant. If she wouldn't write to him with at least a word of encouragement, how could he bring himself to speak to her on the phone or online? What could he say? 'I'm sorry,' seemed altogether too feeble a phrase in their present situation, and so each remained locked into his or her own intransigence.

Luis spent all his days at the restaurant now. He had taken the opportunity of whitewashing the walls of the dining area. The floor was of ancient stone flags and he and Margaret had planned to soften them with colourful striped mats and decorate the walls with whatever examples they could find of the craftwork of the island: winnowing forks, baskets, old wooden utensils. He had already begged a few items from Antonio's mill. One morning, Luis set off from his mother's house carrying Pedro's old astia, and when he had hung it on one of the newly whitewashed walls, he felt, in spite of all his overshadowing gloom, that the place really belonged to him. There was a small platform area and he had envisaged himself performing there occasionally.

There was still so much to do. During the last few years Paco and Carmen, with the best will in the world, had found it difficult to maintain the building. Some of the red roof tiles needed replacing, walls wanted whitewash, doors and shutters were peeling and needed painting. The building had flaking green double doors with an ancient knocker in the shape of a hand. Luis had always loved it. This led into a cool passageway off which, on one side, was the main dining room of the restaurant. On the other side was a storeroom, but he and Margaret had thought about converting it into a craft workshop – perhaps a lacemaking studio where craftswomen could make and sell the fine drawn-thread work of the islands. On the outside wall of the restaurant area were more double doors, leading to a terraced area with a vine clambering over a rickety pergola, a few tables and umbrellas. Margaret had talked about putting a few tables out there and selling plants.

Beyond the restaurant was the kitchen, which was clean and well maintained. Carmen had been scrupulous about her kitchen, and it needed only a modicum of new equipment. At the end of the flagged passageway were simple but well maintained customer toilets, before another door led into a courtyard, bright with potted geraniums and hibiscus, showy with bougainvillaea. This climber went rioting about the rooftop *azotea*, a platform accessed from a worn stone staircase, and edged with a stone wall topped by a wooden rail. On either side of the courtyard were comfortable living quarters: a sitting room, bedrooms and a bathroom. They had decided that the big bathroom needed work, had planned to tackle it first of all, installing a walk-in shower, but keeping the cast iron bath, which was good quality. There were some striking old tiles in there that Paco said had come from Seville, and they would certainly be treasured. There was a reasonable lavatory and a tiny shower room on the opposite side of the courtyard, conveniently placed between a couple of bedrooms, but the family bathroom looked a little shabby. The flush on the lavatory was erratic. You had to pounce on it when it wasn't looking.

He thought, I must choose a new shower and a new toilet as well. Check the central heating and hot water. I need to get a plumber in, need to find out how much it will cost. But if Margarita and Eduardo aren't coming, perhaps the old stuff will do for now. All the same, he asked his friend Antonio for the name of a reliable plumber and went down into San Sebastian to order some new items. Ones that Margarita would like.

He bought a few pieces of furniture as well, though not much. Paco and Carmen had left enough for him to get by. They had even, he saw with a lump in his throat, set up the nursery. The room was fresh and clean, with rugs on the floor and pretty muslin curtains. Cristina had brought the cot across from the Los Cristianos apartment. He found out later that Antonio had gone with her in his van, specifically to bring it back, and they had set it up together before she left for Scotland. His first thought was that he ought to move the cot into the main bedroom before his family arrived because they had planned for Eduardo to sleep with them for a while longer. Time enough for him to have his own room when he was a little older. But would his son come? Would he ever sleep in any of these rooms, so lovingly prepared?

Before she moved out, Carmen had left a pile of small pressed sheets and baby blankets in the linen cupboard. The sight of it all made his heart ache. He was briefly tempted to put them out into one of the many sheds, but couldn't bring himself to do it. Instead he dragged the cot into the master bedroom and made it up with some of the bedding, taking the blue elephant that he had brought from Scotland out of his bag and sitting it at one end. Then he rested his forehead on the warm wooden rail and burst into tears. There was nobody about. Nobody saw him. He cried as though his heart would break, then dried his eyes, left the room, and feverishly set about his work again.

He was trying desperately to submerge his misery, his desolation without her, in his work. He and Margaret had planned to replace some of the pottery in the restaurant with the rich red-brown clay vessels of the island as far as they could. Luis had a little cash in hand and so he placed an order for a few pieces of the primitive but intensely satisfying pottery, a token gesture only. Perhaps they would be impractical. Margaret had some idea of using Tenerife lace tablecloths, but that would have to wait. For what, he thought? He had been counting on his wife's money to help with the renovations, that much was true, and now so much that they had planned wouldn't be possible. What could he do?

To hell with her, he thought defiantly. I'll do it anyway. I'll do it without her if I must.

Then he painted and whitewashed and cleaned and mended as far as he could, with a natural energy that left him drained, exhausted at the end of each day.

Maria was worried about him. She was worried about his silence on the subject of his wife and son, worried about the hurt and anger that she saw in his eyes, fretted about the glooms that descended on him, like clouds on the top of Benchihigua. She saw that he occasionally snapped at Isabel's youngest children, or that he was impatient with Domingo. He refused to let his nephew help out with the work at the restaurant, wanting only to be alone each day, working like a dervish, drowning his thoughts in a tide of physical effort.

One night, she waited for him at the end of the track that led up to her smallholding. He generally left his car there when he came home. Infrequently now. Mostly he slept at *La Manzana Dorada*, where he was working, renovating, but just occasionally she could persuade him to come back to San Sebastian to eat and sleep. Today she had pestered him until he agreed. She suspected that he did little of either eating or sleeping when he was alone. It was growing dark and she stepped out of the shadows to greet him, placing her hand on his arm, making him jump.

'*Madre de dios*,' he said. 'You nearly gave me heart failure.'

'I want to talk to you, Luis.'

'Oh yes?' He sighed. He had known that sooner or later his mother would corner him and he would have to tell her the whole story. It had only been a question of time.

'Luis, you have to tell me what has happened. Me at least. You'll speak to no one else. I've asked Paco and Carmen and they are as puzzled as the rest of us. Cristina will tell me very little, even when I call her. Where's Margarita? Why is she not with you? When will she and the baby be coming to join you?'

He sat down on a crumbling stone wall at the side of the track. His mother joined him. It was a warm night, full of the sound of the cicadas celebrating the heat.

'I don't think she'll be coming at all.'

'Not coming?'

'We had a terrible quarrel.'

'It must have been very terrible then. What did you do? What was it about?'

'Why do you think any of it was my fault?'

'It's usually the man who's at fault.'

'That's outrageous. It was about Margarita's sister-in-law.'

'Fiona? You spoke of her. You weren't very fond of her.'

It helped that he didn't need to look at her face as he spoke.

'I wasn't. But she took a fancy to me. She tried to – tried to kiss me. In the kitchen. I was making *gazpacho*.'

He heard a little noise. It was his mother, not very successfully smothering her laughter.

'It wasn't funny!'

'Holy Mother Mary! Is that it? Is that what you and Margarita quarrelled about? Like – like a pair of teenagers?'

'Fiona told her husband it was me. That *I* had tried to kiss *her*.'

'And did you?'

It came out as a wail of aggrieved denial. 'No. Of course not. I couldn't stand her. But she had a bit of crush on me and I didn't discourage her.'

'Ah. I see. You were flattered, weren't you, son?'

'I suppose I was.'

'You fool.'

'But Margarita, she didn't believe me. She asked me if I had kissed her. If it was true.'

'Oh, I think she believed you well enough. You don't have it in you to be unfaithful to her. But you like the admiration. You always have. She was just giving you a hard time. Good for her.'

The truth of this brought him up short. The wisdom of it. 'And you utter fool, look what you've done now. There are more things in this world to worry about than a silly little flirtation.'

Maria's grandmother had, as a girl, been in domestic service to a rich landowner in the north of the island. The almost feudal system of *caciquismo* dominated all their lives. The local *caciques* or bosses decided who worked, who ate and who starved. Young unmarried girls often had to work as servants and were seduced by the men for whom they were forced to work. Maria remembered being told about one of her great aunts to whom this had happened and how the fifteen year old pregnant girl had thrown herself from one of the high island cliffs. Amalia, Maria's grandmother, had been more fortunate. The work was hard but her employer was a harshly religious man who shunned all the pleasures of the flesh. Amalia was glad that this was so, although it had meant her courtship and marriage had been a clandestine affair.

Things had been a bit better for Lucia, Maria's mother, but not much. Lucia had married young, a love match. Maria's father had died of tuberculosis while still in his thirties, leaving her mother alone with four young children. After that life had been a relentless struggle until they had all gone to live on the smallholding of a widower to help him and his own surviving children. But then there had been such gossip about the relationship between her mother and this man that eventually they had been forced to marry, even though it was against their inclination. The priest had come to see them and a wedding had been arranged. They got on well enough from day to day, but it was significant, thought Maria, that there had been no more children, only his two and her mother's four. A big enough family to provide for anyway. Maria remembered her stepfather, Mateo, as a grave and rather humourless man, who spoke little, but she thought that he had probably grown to love her mother, because he had been inconsolable when she died and had survived only a few months after her.

Maria's own husband, Eduardo, had been a good, kindly man, and handsome too. Luis was very like him. He had a little land of his own, and when he found her working hard on her stepfather's farm he had taken her to his heart. His songs had all been of love. He had taught her the virtue of tolerance and she, who had seen the effects of intolerance, had been a willing pupil. Besides that, good manners and generosity were the foundation of everything for Eduardo. They had tried to pass their shared beliefs on to their son but now she wondered if they had really succeeded.

'Has Margarita mentioned any of this?' he asked. She must have said something.'

'No, sadly, Margarita has not even written to me. Cristina and I have spoken, but she hasn't actually said very much. At least *she's* very happy where she is.'

'Is she?' It struck him that he had been so preoccupied with his own feelings that he had barely messaged his sister, let alone spoken to her. Besides, what would he say?

'It was a relief to me, in a way, when she went away, although I still miss her very much. For a while everyone seemed to be flying away. Now her letters from Sitges are so full of happiness. She writes and speaks to me very lovingly of her work and her new friends.'

'She must have written about Margarita and me!'

'No. She only said that there was some kind of separation. She said you must explain yourself. But you avoid being alone with me, don't you? So I thought I should take it into my own hands and make you speak.'

'I often wish my papa were still here, don't you?'

'Every day.'

'I wish I could talk to him.'

'Then speak to him. You know how he would answer you!'

'But I can't hear him say it. I try to recollect his face and I can't. Not properly.'

'You were his favourite, Lucho. If he ever had favourites. This – you and Margarita and the baby – this would have broken his heart. It's breaking mine.'

He said nothing, glad of the darkness.

She sat beside him in silence for a while, then said gently, 'So you quarrelled with Margarita over nothing, and now nothing will mend it.'

'Yes.'

'And yet, you can't see that love comes and goes like the wind and there is little we can do to help or hinder it. We bend or we break.'

She bent down and peered at his face in the twilight. 'Lucho, my darling, if you are not very careful, you will snap like a brittle twig.'

'I thought I understood her, but I didn't.'

'Then you didn't speak to her enough.'

'We don't have the words. Our tongues are separate and our minds are separate.'

'Then you must invent a whole new language. Just for the two of you.'

'Oh.' He laughed now, shaking his head ruefully. 'That's not so easy.'

'Whoever promised you it would be easy? Not me, for sure!'

'It's too late. She would have phoned me or written. If she still felt anything for me she would have messaged me.'

'What did you do to her?'

'I was very angry. I think I frightened her.'

'You didn't strike her? Tell me you didn't.'

'No. No, I didn't.'

She shook her head. 'For all that we often quarrelled, your father never once raised his hand to me. Never. You never saw that happen, Luis.'

'No. And I didn't do it. But I lost my temper. I said things I didn't mean. Even when I was saying them. I can't pretend I didn't do that.

I was ashamed of myself afterwards. I didn't know that I had such feelings.'

'You love her too much, maybe.'

'How can you love someone too much?'

'Quite easily. Sometimes you love someone comfortably. But sometimes the feeling is so strong that it consumes you. Especially at the beginning. And if you break away from the person, you leave bits of yourself behind. You are never the same. Never whole again.'

'If I get her back, if she comes back, I'll never be so angry with her again.'

'I'm sure you will!'

'I don't promise never to lose my temper. But I would promise never to reject her again.'

'You should promise *her*, not me. Things will improve once you know each other better. Will you not phone her, or email her? You can swallow your pride, surely. Ask her to come here. If she comes, you can talk. She loves you, I know.'

'I can't do it.'

'Of course you can. Don't be so pig-headed. Will you ruin your whole life for the sake of your own stupid pride?'

'And if she won't come?'

'She will come.'

He shook his head, but later that evening, he took out his phone and tried to call the flat in Glasgow. Margaret wasn't there. She had gone to see her mother, taking the baby with her, and had decided to stay the night. There was no answering machine. He let the phone ring for a long time, picturing it sounding out in the empty apartment, letting it ring for far longer than was necessary. When she came back to the flat, she did the usual '1471' but somebody else had phoned in the meantime, somebody selling insulation, and the fact that he had tried to contact her didn't register. He thought he would try her mobile, but only dialled half the number and then gave up. He could email her when the new broadband was set up, but what would he say? He felt desolate. He had left it too long. He had arranged to meet Antonio and they drank far too much and Antonio came up to Maria's house to spend the night because he couldn't drive home without risking life and limb as well as prosecution.

'She was out,' said Luis shortly, in response to his mother's enquiring gaze.

'Then you must try again.'

After that, he stayed at *La Manzana Dorada*. The mobile signal was poor there, although there was a landline in the dining room. Some nights he would sit and stare at the phone in the eerily empty room, but he could never bring himself to dial the number again. Besides, they might have left the flat now and moved back in with her mother. He didn't know. He had that number too, but he didn't use it. Annie might answer and he wouldn't know what to say to her. Obscurely he thought that if his wife rejected him, his last hope would be gone. The telephone was, in his mind, a last thread, tenuously connecting him to Margarita, but he was afraid of its fragility, afraid of breaking it once and for all. So he didn't phone her and disguised his reasons even to himself as wounded pride.

CHAPTER NINETEEN

We meet a man with a long pole, one of the climbing or leaping poles used throughout the archipelago by the peasants. The natives are particularly active and leap immense distances when following their goats. These poles are a Guanche legacy, the leaping being spoken of particularly by the first rediscoverers of the islands as a noticeable custom of the islanders and one in which the people of Gomera especially excelled.

Olivia M Stone, 1887

In September, he was able to open the restaurant for four days a week. He employed a young man from Agulo as part time waiter and to help with some preparation in the kitchen and a woman from a nearby smallholding, who kept the place clean for him, working an hour or two, a few times a week. He restricted his menu to a few local dishes he knew how to cook really well and he advertised the reopened restaurant locally as well as further afield on Tenerife. He did a little public relations work himself, visiting all his old acquaintances on the island, having a leaflet printed and distributing it everywhere, even setting up a Facebook page and commissioning a very basic website from a young web developer in San Sebastian. Slowly but surely, he began to get advance bookings for meals as well as casual tourists dropping in. The coach parties for whom Paco and Carmen had catered came back to the restaurant and told him they liked his cooking. He knew that Paco had been spreading the word as well.

He was good at all this and if Margaret had been there he knew he would have enjoyed it, but in his present circumstances it was a one-sided kind of existence. He was far too busy to play at the moment and in any case, all the music seemed to have gone out of him. Paco visited and tried to encourage him, but his much loved guitar stayed silent in its case. All his music reminded him of his absent wife and child.

Soon, he might have to employ extra help. He needed time to talk to his clientele, to give his restaurant a personal touch, to start playing again. He would emerge from the kitchen to converse in his good English, in his limited German and even managed to wish good day to a party from Finland who had found their way to this remote spot. But he longed for Margaret to be there. This had been planned as a partnership. He wondered if he was going to be able to manage the business all by himself. Then, childishly, he vowed that he would make a success of it, if only to show her that he didn't need her.

Although he closed the restaurant for three days a week, he carried on working, clearing outbuildings, looking over the citrus plantations, making plans for growing beans and tomatoes, avocados and other salad stuff. Paco came to help and brought with him a young cousin called Salvador, the three of them working companionably together. Luis found the work among the trees and plants therapeutic and soothing. When he was out there he managed to exclude his family from his thoughts for a short while. Instead he thought about his hands on hoe or spade or fork, about the smell of the earth, and the clean new smell of the water as they built irrigation channels. There were several wells on the property and he was planning to make full use of them to improve the land's productivity.

He was working so intensively now that he found it surprisingly hard to sleep at nights. He was just too tired, tired beyond sleep. The house was too empty, and his bed like a desolation. When she visited him, his mother noticed him growing thinner, noticed the lines of fatigue about eyes and mouth.

'Like a thin branch,' she repeated to herself, thinking about the stupidity of it. 'If he does not bend soon, he will break.'

But she didn't know what else she could do or how she could persuade him to change his mind, contact his wife, start things moving again.

One day, when the restaurant was closed, Luis had finished his work early, and gone to San Sebastian to his mother's house. He had eaten there and then lingered until evening, talking to Juan about different crops and fertilizers and drinking strong coffee. 'Why not stay?' Maria asked, but he refused and set off to drive back to the restaurant before it got completely dark. On the road out of the village, he passed a woman walking slowly along, hand in hand with a toddler, a little boy dressed in yellow shorts and a red tee-shirt. He was carefully scrutinizing every pebble on the pathway beneath his feet. There was something familiar about the woman and he slowed his car as he went past to look at her. Across twenty years he recognised the familiar, neat features of Teresa: still dark and pretty, though childbearing had broadened the slenderness of her youth and the small breasts had grown full and round. She glanced up at him suspiciously, pulling the child closer to her, then her face lit up with a smile of delighted recognition.

'Lucho Hererra. Is it really you?'

'Teresita!'

He stopped the car, got out, went over to her and shook her hand; then after a moment's hesitation bent and kissed her cheek.

'What are you doing back here?'

'We're on holiday,' she said. 'My parents hadn't seen this latest little one for a long time and he's growing so quickly.'

'How many now?'

'Four,' she said. 'Two boys, two girls. The eldest is fifteen already. This is Carlos. He's only two.'

'Are they all with you? And your husband?'

'No, no. Just Carlitos. José is working and the older children are with their other grandparents in Madrid. My husband, thought that I needed a break. He said I was looking peaky, so he sent me over here for a couple of weeks for a rest.'

'Do you often come? Tina never mentioned seeing you.'

'Not really. I used to have a job until I was expecting this last one, so I couldn't come very often. I'm just taking a break.'

'I didn't used to come very often either.'

'They said you were working on Tenerife. Or was it abroad?'

'I've been everywhere.'

'I remember now. You're married. To an English lady.'

'Scottish.' He could hear Margarita correcting the error, could hear her voice in his head.

'And Cristina – she's in Barcelona now, isn't she? I was asking about her in the town.'

'Well, she's in Sitges. Not far away from the city. That's right.'

'So where's your wife?'

'Not here, yet. She's still in Scotland, with our little boy.'

'I see,' she said, though she didn't see. He was being too noncommittal, evasive almost. There had been gossip in the town, though Maria never contributed to it and nobody would dare to ask her outright. Nobody knew for sure what had happened, but Luis had come back minus wife and child, and was now working all the hours that God sent in Paco's old restaurant. All Maria would say was that Margarita, the Scottish wife, would be coming when everything was ready, but surely any wife worth her salt would want to help with such a task? At the mention of his wife, however, Luis looked so grim that Teresa decided to leave well alone. The child was growing bored, tugging at his mother's skirt and whining. He wanted to go home.

'We were just out for a little walk, before bed.' She gestured at the infant. 'If I tire him out he sleeps better. We must go. It was nice to meet you.'

'When are you going home?' he asked.

'Next week.'

'You should come to the restaurant for a meal. As my guest, of course. We could talk about old times. Do you have a car?'

'I could borrow one from my brother,' she said simply. 'I may do that.'

Her face, without make-up, still looked young and fresh, though with fine laughter lines around the eyes. She wore a plain cotton sundress in pale yellow that reminded him irresistibly of that other lemon dress, in the ruined house, all those years before, when he had kissed her but nothing more. Her hair, which reached to her shoulders, was tied back from her face. It was still dark but with a few streaks of grey. She picked up the child and sat him on her hip. Luis tickled him. He regarded Luis very seriously, with large eyes, his mother's eyes, and stuck a finger in his mouth. Then he suddenly thrust his head against her breast, up and under her chin, cuddling in with a gesture of trust that gave Luis a sharp pain in his heart. He wished he had Eduardo in his arms: wished that he could hold his own fair son so close and feel the little head tucked under his chin. Abruptly he got back into the car.

'I'll maybe see you, then,' he said.

'Perhaps.'

She waved to him cheerfully and took the child home to bed.

The following week, not long before she was due to return home, Teresa borrowed her brother's car and drove out to the restaurant. It was an impulsive gesture and one which she was not entirely sure was sensible. Her marriage to José was happy enough, though she knew that he had had the odd fling. It was nothing serious: just that he liked to think of her as a good mother to his children, but occasionally he found himself attracted to another kind of woman altogether. She had heard him say to his male friends that three wives was polygamy, two was bigamy, and one was monotony. She didn't like it but she tolerated it. For how much longer, she wasn't sure. Until the birth of this last child she had managed to hold down a good job in the human resources department of a large tech company in Madrid, where they lived now. They had even paid for help in the house, but the birth of Carlos had so tired her that she had decided she must take a break, if only until he went to school, and José had gone along with that too. In most ways, he was easy-going.

She supposed she should be happy to have such an obliging husband, to have children who, in spite of the odd crisis, were very little trouble to her, being on the whole a good natured bunch, but she realised in her heart that she was feeling restless and discontented. Perhaps she had married too young. Perhaps she had been married for too long. Perhaps she craved some excitement. At any rate, her first sight of Luis, looking even more attractive than she remembered, albeit in a rather haggard way, had aroused in her a feeling of physical anticipation that she thought she had lost for good. For some days she managed to quash it but at last, when she was almost due to return home, she drove out to *La Manzana Dorada*, promising herself that she was only going for a meal.

The restaurant was not busy that evening and the half dozen customers had almost finished before Teresa arrived. She had dressed carefully in a silk dress and smart shoes, with her hair piled up on top of her head, but very little jewellery or make-up. Her parents looked at her askance but she ignored their disapproval.

'I'm off to see an old school friend,' she said vaguely. 'They're throwing a small party. For me. Well, I don't come home too often, do I?'

She ate fresh prawns and salad and drank mineral water. Luis, at last, came and sat at her table, bringing a bottle of wine and two glasses, but she refused.

'I'm driving. But you have a drink. You look as though you need it.'

The waiter cleared up around them and he sent the young man home.

'I'll clear this one myself,' he said.

'Will he gossip?' she asked. 'Leaving us alone here.'

'Maybe.' He shrugged. 'But I don't think he cares. It doesn't matter, does it?'

'I don't know. Does it?'

'We are just two old friends talking about old times. Who gives a damn what anybody else thinks about it?'

He made fresh coffee and poured two cups, bringing it back to the table. In the warm, dim light she looked quite beautiful. He imagined himself reaching out and touching the full breast, running his finger over the nipple. He imagined kissing her as he had kissed her once before, his tongue in her mouth. Briefly this thought crossed his mind but he felt nothing. There was no desire at all. He only felt very tired and very miserable. She was watching him curiously. He put his elbows on the table. His brown arms were criss-crossed with scratches from the tree pruning.

'Luis,' she said at last, 'Forgive me if you don't want to talk about this. But why don't you tell me what's wrong with you?'

'Is it very obvious.'

'Yes, it is. And you've known me for a long time even if we don't see much of each other. Can't you tell me about it?'

'My wife and son are in Glasgow. I'm here. We don't speak on the phone, and we don't write. I don't know if she'll ever come here. And I don't know what to do.'

'Doesn't she like it here?'

'I think she loves it. Loved it, anyway. When she loved me.'

'So you had a quarrel?'

'Yes.'

'Quarrels can be made up. People do it all the time. You should hear me and José going at it hammer and tongs from time to time. But then we calm down. Make up.'

'Not this one. Not this quarrel.'

'Was it so very bad?'

He paused. 'The silly thing is, it wasn't. Or it shouldn't have been. Not really. No. But we are very different.'

'Of course you are. Completely different backgrounds. And languages.'

'That's what her family thought.'

'Isn't that what makes it interesting? I mean – you'll never be bored, will you?'

'I suppose so.'

'Then you must mean you're too proud to make the first move.'

'I'm afraid. If the truth be told, I'm scared.'

'Ah. Afraid she might turn her back on you?'

'Yes. Yes, I suppose so.'

'Do you still love her?'

'I'm going crazy with loving her.'

Lucky woman, she thought, and knew that if he had given any indication of wanting her she would have gone along with it. Lust. Unfinished business. She had always wanted him. Or perhaps it would only have been a small and rather mean revenge on her husband. Back to the matter in hand, she thought. He was still her friend, even if he would never be her lover.

'Your wife and Cristina – they like each other?'

'Very much.'

'Then why not write to Cristina? Or message her. Ask her to act as go-between. I'm sure she would. She's always loved you to bits. You must know that.'

He didn't explain that his sister was exasperated with him. Besides, it suddenly seemed to him like a good idea. He would contact

Tina. Perhaps Margaret would see it for the gesture of reconciliation it most certainly was.

He said 'It's very kind of you to listen to me like this, Teresita. I've tried talking to my mother but it's easier when it isn't a member of the family.'

She got up suddenly. 'You were very kind to me to once, Lucho. Remember?'

'I remember.'

'It's the least I can do to repay you. I've always thought well of you, you know. I don't like to see you so unhappy.'

'And what about you?' he said, at the door. 'We never talked about you. Are you happy? With José?'

'Me?' She laughed lightly. 'Oh, I'm happy. You needn't worry about me.'

He reached down and kissed her on the cheek, but as he did so she moved her face and kissed him full on the lips, pushing her tongue into his mouth, tasting him. She felt him draw back in surprise, then allow himself to be kissed for a moment, then pull away again. He shook his head.

'I know,' she said. 'I remember. You don't love me. I was just getting my own back, that's all. You needn't worry.'

She installed herself in the car, leaned out of the window and blew him a kiss. Again he thought she looked brave as a little soldier.

'I hope you get back together again with your wife,' she said. 'I think you still love her very much, whatever this quarrel was about. She's a lucky woman. Does she know she's a lucky woman?'

'I was a very lucky man.'

'It'll be alright, you know.'

'Will it?'

'Oh, yes. I feel it in my blood.'

She drove carefully home to her parents' house, went in and sat looking down at her sleeping child, stroking the fine hair away from his skin, damp with evening perspiration. His eyes were hers, but when he was asleep like this, he had his father's unmistakable features. She lay down beside him and fell fast asleep.

At *La Manzana Dorada*, Luis went and found pen and paper and sat down to compose an apologetic and loving letter to his sister. It took him half the night and many versions, and the kitchen rubbish bin was stuffed full of discarded drafts, but at last it was completed to his satisfaction. It didn't seem like the kind of thing for an email. His heart was lighter than it had been for some time as he put it in an envelope, addressed it and, the following morning, took it into Agulo to post it.

CHAPTER TWENTY

Look through your window
and ease the pain of my love!
Look through your window —
the sweet air of morning is coming!

Margaret had taken to calling Eduardo 'Edward' simply because everybody else did and she didn't have the strength to argue. She had never felt quite so alone in all her life, not even after the divorce from Alastair, but she struggled on, if only for the child's sake. He was going to be tall, like his father, but he was very fair, with blue eyes, still very much her son. Only his long face with well shaped lips and high cheekbones, already showing through the baby plumpness, betrayed his Canarian parentage.

He was beginning also, she thought, to have some knowledge of speech. One day, while she was talking to him, she saw it happen. It was as though, at a stroke, he realised that words were not simply sounds: that they actually had meanings. He was not capable of reproducing them yet in any meaningful way, but she saw his face change, saw the swift dawning of comprehension there. Fascinated, she had come to understand that the advances of babyhood are not gradual at all. Her son's growing was a series of plateaux intersected by giant leaps in comprehension, in mobility, in size.

He could grow out of his clothes within a week. One day he couldn't crawl, the next day he could and then within an astonishingly short time he was using the furniture to get about, hand over hand, like a small mountaineer. One day words were a meaningless jumble of sound; the next, his eyes told her that he knew there was more to it all. She regretted profoundly Luis's loss of this time and sometimes she whispered to her son in Spanish, telling him the names of things in his father's native tongue, comforting herself as much as him with the much-loved sounds.

October had passed in a blur of sadness and soon she must leave the apartment. Ronald's expedition had been extended but now he was coming home. It was already Hallowe'en and the advance of winter brought the Canaries more vividly to mind. In her imagination they remained elusive, bathed in endless sunshine like some mythical archipelago. Hera's Orchard, she thought, where the dragon guarded the golden apples. She thought often of La Gomera, remembering that this time last year she had been enfolded in the loving cocoon of her husband's family, wishing herself back in time, wishing that she had done things differently.

I should never have come home to have the baby, she thought. But what was the use of trying to turn back time? What was done was done. She thought about Luis almost all the time, wondering where he was and what he was doing. She wondered how he was managing in the restaurant. Very well indeed, she suspected, knowing in her heart that when it came to running a business he would be astute and imaginative. Perhaps he wouldn't miss her at all. She tormented herself with the thought that perhaps he had found somebody else by now, somebody who spoke his own language.

In the evenings, when Eduardo was asleep, she would sit watching the television and waiting for his call. At first she was sure that tonight he really would phone or text or email her, but as the evening wore on she would grow more and more despondent, sad when she went to sleep and waking to the instant perception of misery. She was relieved when Ronald contacted her about the flat. She smiled at the diffidence of his email. 'Would it be alright?' he asked, carefully. She packed up all her belongings, including some of Luis's winter clothes that he had left behind, gave the flat a last clean, and moved in with her mother again. It was when she was packing that she remembered the little blue elephant for the first time. She wondered if it had been dropped out of the pram. Certainly Edward had not noticed its absence, but later she began to wonder if Luis had taken it with him as a memento of his son, and she didn't know whether to be happy or sad at the realisation: was it a gesture of hope for the future, or a souvenir of a lost child?

Annie was loving and protective, hurt by the inexplicable break-up of her daughter's marriage, partisan in her loyalty to her daughter but at the same time unable to believe ill of Luis. So she struggled with her own emotions and took refuge in caring for her daughter and grandson, cooking meals, making countless cups of tea. Winter was fast gaining ground. One week it had been warm, a dazzling golden autumn. Then came a couple of frosty nights followed by a week of winds and all of a sudden the trees were bare and the year seemed half dead, creeping towards its bitter end. Of all months, she had always hated November most.

Once she was installed in Annie's house, Margaret had to face the ordeal of meeting Fiona again. She had avoided her sister-in-law ever since Luis's departure, but it seemed that Fiona had at last discovered her conscience. She came round to the house and was so obviously upset that Margaret, always generous, felt forced to speak to her.

'I'm sorry, Maggie,' Fiona said. 'I never meant for all this to happen. I never realised what a Pandora's box I'd be opening.'

'Why did you do it?' asked Margaret despairingly, unable to maintain the righteous indignation she had intended. 'Oh, don't cry for goodness sake. You'll start me off and I've done enough crying, believe me. Don't upset yourself so much. What's done is done.'

'I'd give anything to have it undone. I never thought he'd react like that. I never thought he'd blame you. I wanted to hurt him a bit. He hurt me. He led me on, Margaret and then told me what a fool I was being. He wasn't nice to me.'

'But then you're not always nice to other people, are you? He didn't really lead you on. He was making fun of you, I know. And that wasn't very nice of him, I admit. But you shouldn't have been so daft about him. He was my husband.' She realised with a shock that she was speaking in the past tense. 'What am I saying? He *is* my husband, still. Oh, God help me! I love him so much!' She sat down suddenly. 'Oh, Fiona, it was unforgivable.'

'I know.' Fiona threatened to burst into tears again, but Margaret forestalled her. She found it impossible to fully forgive her sister-in-law but equally impossible to maintain the cold indifference she had intended. It had been at least partly her husband's fault as well, damn him.

'Ian was very cross with me.'

'I'm not at all surprised.'

'He thought it was a terrible thing to do. I've never seen him so angry. And embarrassed. But I honestly didn't know it would cause such chaos! And I did feel quite hurt.'

'I wondered why we hadn't seen much of Ian. Tell him to come. There's no point in us all falling out about it.'

'He thought you wouldn't want to see him. He said unless I came first and apologised he'd never be able to look you in the face again.'

'Well you have. And your apology is accepted. So tell him he can come.'

Soon after this, Cristina flew to Scotland from Barcelona for an un-expected visit. She was planning to go back to La Gomera in December, to pack up some more of her belongings. The job in Sitges was going very well, but this visit couldn't wait. Her boss, Isabella, had agreed and sent her off with her blessing. She was staying with Suzie and Laura for a couple of days and she arrived at Annie's house brandishing a letter, clearly a woman on a mission. Margaret found the girl's physical resemblance to her brother disquieting, but comforting. Cristina plainly had news, and when Annie left them alone together she pulled a hand-written sheet out of the envelope. Margaret recognized Luis's jagged black handwriting.

'What does he say?' she asked. She felt as though her heart was beating so hard that it threatened to choke her.

'He says that he is very sorry. Sorry for behaving like a fool. He was jealous and stupid and he regrets it very much. It must have cost him blood, sweat and tears to write this.'

'Did it?' Margaret had gone very pale. 'And does he mention me?'

Cristina looked at Margaret, puzzled.

'Yes of course. It's *all* about you. He sends all his fond wishes to you, and his love and kisses to Eduardo. He says ...' she looked down at the letter ... 'he says I must be sure and see Margarita and tell her how very very sorry I am. Be sure and tell her that. He underlines it three times.'

'And is that all?'

'Isn't that enough?'

'I don't know.'

Cristina looked at her in exasperation. 'Margarita! It is a gesture. A loving gesture. Don't you understand?'

'Not really. He sends love to Eduardo, but not to me. What do I get? Best wishes?' She laughed bitterly and turned away.

Cristina put a hand on her shoulder and shook the letter at her. 'You don't understand him. You love him, I know, but you don't understand him at all. He can't bring himself to contact you only because he's afraid of rejection, so he contacts me instead. He's very nice to me. Be sure and tell Margarita, he says. This is an apology.'

'It doesn't sound very like one to me.'

'I think it is the nearest thing to one you will get. For now, anyway.

He's too afraid of being rejected at this moment. He can't bring himself to speak to you directly.'

'And how am I supposed to feel?'

'See sense, Margarita.'

'Why should I? It's his damned macho pride. You of all people should know that, Cristina.'

'I do. But then he isn't my husband. I love him as my brother, but I don't love him and need him the way you do.'

'Why can't he set it aside for once? Why can't he ask me himself? Why can't he phone or write to me and tell me that he loves me? Tell me he wants me back again. Why can't he do that? Why does it have to be me who gives in all the time?'

She wouldn't speak about it any more that night and a little while later Cristina left, disappointed and frustrated. At the door she took Margaret's hands in her own and looked long and hard at her. At last she shook her head.

'I think he has hurt you too much,' she said. 'Over nothing. Nothing at all. Unless you can find it in your heart to forgive him there is no hope for you. For either of you. And don't forget, Margarita, there's a child involved in all this as well.'

That night Margaret dreamed about Luis. She dreamed vividly that he came to her bed and made love to her. She could smell him and feel him all around her. Her body tingled with desire for him and she moved to accommodate him, accepting him thankfully. She felt his lips on her face and on her breast and then he was deep inside her moving with a perfect, satisfying rhythm, like the rhythm of his own perfect music, and as he came he called her name, three times, like the words of a song. But she herself was left unsatisfied, and when she woke, she felt the narrowness of the bed she had slept in as a teenager.

Eduardo was crying. He had not seemed genuinely at ease ever since Luis had left and she believed that, young as he was, he was missing the father who had been a part of his life since the moment of his birth. The following day she was scrolling through photographs on her phone and uploaded a whole file of baby pictures to her mother's laptop. She steeled herself to look at them. Frozen in time, she saw Luis's brown arms stretched above his head, holding Eduardo high into the summer air of the Botanical Gardens, Luis fast asleep with the tiny Eduardo spread-eagled frog-like on his chest, Luis proudly pushing the pram or gently towelling his son dry after a bath. How could she deprive her son and herself of such love for the sake of a silly misunderstanding? Not even that, really. The quarrel had been the least of it. It had been the culmination of something, the fear of the unknown perhaps, the challenges involved in a cross cultural marriage threatening to overwhelm her. Both of them perhaps. The very speed with which they had met, married and had the baby. There had been so little time to adjust. She had spoken to Suzie about feeling for footholds in the dark, about being an explorer in an alien land. It had all seemed so positive and exciting then. Could it not be so once more?

'How can I let this go on?' she said aloud to Eduardo. He was sitting in his buggy, waving a piece of crusty bread in the air. He was teething and liked to gnaw on it. 'I can't, can I? I can't let this go on. I have to try again, no matter what the cost.'

That same evening, as though sensing the change, Maria telephoned from La Gomera. It had taken a great deal of courage on her part. She spoke in a mixture of Spanish and English.

She said, very simply, 'Margarita, when are you coming home?'

Margaret didn't know how to reply. Instead of answering directly, she said, 'How is Luis?'

'Terrible. Not well.'

'Why? Isn't the restaurant going well?'

'It is going very well, but everything he has done, he has done for you. Now, he just seems beaten. You must come. He's my son and I can't stand to see him so hurt, even though I think he has brought this on himself. I think you must be the grown-up in this situation even if he's behaving like a child. You must do it for all of you. If you love him at all, please come.'

Margaret looked down at her own son. She knew that feeling too. She could not bear for Eduardo to be hurt, would withstand any pain herself rather than have him suffer.

'I'll come,' she said at last. 'Oh, but Maria, will he want me?'

'He wants you. Desperately. Come as soon as you can. Send me word of your flight and he will be there. He will be there to meet you. In the name of the Blessed Virgin herself, I promise.'

When she hung up, Annie put her head round the door.

'You're going back then?' she said. 'Back to La Gomera?'

'I have to.'

'I think so too.'

'Do you?' Margaret was surprised. She had always imagined her mother to be half afraid of her possible departure.

'Oh, I'll be sorry to lose you, but I'll be sorrier still to see you and that little one stuck in limbo over here. I'm only surprised you didn't go weeks ago.'

'I think I've been a wee bit mad. I think I caught a dose of my husband's temperament. It hasn't done me much good, has it?'

'You go back to him, there's a good girl. I would.' Annie went through to the kitchen and put on the kettle. It was her immediate response to any crisis, any resolution of that crisis.

'He's a lovely man. A good man,' she said simply. 'I'd have gone weeks ago.'

'Would you?'

'Oh yes.'

'I wish you'd said.'

'He just wears his heart on his sleeve, that's the problem. He can't pretend anything he doesn't feel. We bottle it all up inside. He can't do that. The way he feels is the way he acts. Probably over-acts! And often thoughtlessly. There's nothing to it. It's all show. I would have thought you'd have realised that a long time ago. Before you married him.'

'I did realise it.'

'Then why won't you make allowances for it? I'm sure he makes allowances for you in all kinds of ways. I'm sure he did when you were expecting. At least you know nothing will ever go on behind your back. He couldn't manage it.'

'I don't suppose he could.'

'I would have thought after Alastair that would be just what you needed. After all, if your Luis wins, does that mean that you lose? If you give in and go back, nobody loses this particular battle, I'd say.'

'Why haven't you said any of this to me before?'

'I thought you'd come round to it yourself. I didn't want to start interfering, Margaret. There's been enough interference between members of this family without me putting my two penn'orth in.'

'Oh mum, I wish you had.'

'You'd better see how soon you can get a flight, hadn't you?'

CHAPTER TWENTY ONE

If the sea were a road
and I were a walker
I would pass it on my knees
just to see my lover.

Margaret managed to arrange a flight from Glasgow for the following week, booking from a local agency that Laura sometimes used for business travel.

'If there's a flight to be had, they'll find it for you,' said Laura.

'About time too,' added Suzie.

'It's as well you came now,' the helpful assistant told her. 'Once we get into December it's very busy with all the Christmas visitors. You might not have managed to get a flight at all until January.'

'I think I'd have swum,' she said ruefully.

'It's that important, is it?'

'You don't know the half of it. I have to get there.'

Now that the decision was made, she was almost light-hearted. She wrote a long letter to Maria, explaining a great many things, and giving her the time of her flight. She wrote several messages to Luis and then deleted them all. She would speak to him face to face, risking no further misunderstandings. She had already got a passport for the baby when they were planning to go back to the island together, so that was no problem.

Suzie came to say goodbye.

'I only hope he wants me. What if he doesn't want me now?' Margaret had confessed this doubt to no one else, not even her mother.

'Of course he wants you. He's desperate to see you. Sad and sorry. It serves him bloody right but no one should have to go on suffering for their mistakes for ever. We'll come and visit, once you're all sorted. I really want to see your Golden Apple. I was beginning to believe it didn't exist at all. The Garden of the Hesperides. Hera's Orchard. Immortality and all that.'

Annie and Ian took them to the airport. Fiona stayed at home. The reconciliation was a precarious thing. It was very cold now and as they walked from the car to the terminal, Margaret pulled her jacket closer around her. Eduardo was muffled up in woollen trousers, sweater and a blanket. She could take off the layers, change him into lighter clothes on the flight.

Ian kissed her and Annie held her close.

'You will come back soon, won't you? At least for a holiday?'

'For lots of them. And you'll have to come to see us, mum. You promised, you know.'

'That's what Luis said. But what about the budgies?'

'We'll look after the budgies, mum,' said Ian. 'The kids would like it. They've never had pets.'

'Would Fiona allow it?'

'She'd have to allow it.'

Margaret was surprised by the firmness with which her brother spoke. Perhaps the worm had turned. Not before time, she thought.

'On my own?' said Annie.

'Why not?'

'Well maybe I will then.' Annie felt quite cheerful all of a sudden. The prospect was very exciting. She had signed up to Duolingo Spanish. Perhaps she would find some language classes. 'Maybe after Christmas. Just for a week.'

'That would be good. Two weeks would be better. It's much nicer in January on La Gomera than it is here.'

'And I could help out perhaps. In the kitchen. Or I could look after Eduardo for you.'

'I don't see why not.'

Ian too was feeling unexpectedly elated and excited by his sister's departure. Much to his own surprise, he had missed Luis. Margaret went through the gate, looked back and waved. Annie was holding onto Ian's arm and dabbing at her eyes with a tissue.

When the plane rose above Glasgow, Margaret thought how beautiful it looked in the darkness with the lights so geometrically precise below her. She was glad that she had come back because she knew now that, shabby as it seemed, she loved this place, even if she didn't want to live here. At least her appreciation of La Gomera would be rooted in reality and not a dream, a romance. She had made a deliberate choice and she thought that although she would come for holidays, she would probably never live here again. It was as though the plane were a spaceship, and she had risen high above her own safe, familiar world, casting herself off into a dark but exciting future.

She was glad to be leaving home. She was glad to be going home, but the closer she drew to the islands, the more uneasy she became. She had heard nothing from Luis and only had Maria's word for it that he would be waiting for her. She clutched Eduardo's hand as an insurance against possible disappointment. She had been lucky, she thought, to book an evening flight, because he slept almost all the way to Tenerife. It would have been different in the daytime. He was already talking, after a fashion, burbling away. Soon he would be walking. He was an active little boy.

In Reina Sofia airport, the luggage seemed to be an age in coming. She held Eduardo firmly in her arms, though he protested, but she daren't put him down lest he should crawl away from her. He could move quickly these days. It was getting very late. She was so tired now that her eyes were dry, her skin tingling.

From time to time, various cryptic announcements burst from the loudspeakers, causing the passengers to rush from one luggage carousel to another. Desperately she heaved her beloved burden after the crowd.

'Mam! Mam!' he said, grasping fistfuls of her hair in his starfish fingers.

She managed to smile at him as she stood with her travelling companions and watched a crowd of soldiers taking their luggage off a nearby carousel. There were about thirty of them, very young and fresh-faced, and their task was not made any easier by the fact that all their kitbags were identical. They fussed about like ants with a surfeit of crumbs. She suppressed a giggle that turned into a sob.

It was ten o'clock, a warm night in Tenerife. What on earth would they do, she wondered, she and the little boy, if Luis were not there to meet them? Would they be able to find a hotel so that they could take the ferry over to La Gomera the following day? Then, she could at least make her way to Maria's house. Maria would be waiting to welcome her, she knew. But what would she do tonight? By the time the suitcases and the folded buggy came round, she had convinced herself that Luis definitely would not be there. All her high hopes at the start of the journey had sunk to nothing.

A fellow Scot, an elderly holidaymaker, helped her to load her cases on to his own trolley.

'You can't manage a trolley and a buggy,' he said.

Margaret put Eduardo, protesting, in his buggy and pushed him along beside her saviour and his wife. When she had stepped off the plane, and before getting onto the bus to the terminal building, she had inhaled deeply, smelling Tenerife, the warm night air, the scent of flowers. She had been able to recognize it even above the overpowering aroma of aviation fuel. Now she scented it again and was smitten with a physical longing for Luis so powerful, so sensual that it almost knocked her off her feet. He was in her blood. She could feel him coursing through her. She stopped the buggy and leaned on it for a moment to catch her breath and steady herself. Wherever he was she must go and look for him. Whatever happened she mustn't give up. Not now she had come so far. And surely he wouldn't be able to resist his son?

Another fear, long buried, atavistic, maternal, suddenly gripped her. What about the baby? Would Luis, seeing the little boy he undoubtedly loved, want to take him and keep him, discarding her. Ian, in spite of his approval of her journey, had felt it his duty to caution her about taking Eduardo back to Spain.

'He could keep him there and send you packing. You wouldn't really have much of a leg to stand on. Legally speaking, anyway. Well, I suppose you would. But it might be difficult. And expensive.'

She had scoffed at the idea then, but it had stayed with her, to emerge now when she was at her most vulnerable. Maybe she should have left her son in Scotland and come alone. Just to make sure. But wouldn't that have been one more nail in the coffin of their relationship, their marriage? He had always been telling her to trust him.

'*Soy un buen hombre,*' she thought. Was he?

'Are you alright, hen?' Her Samaritan of the carousel was behind her, accompanied by his wife, a kindly woman, tut tutting at her plight.

'Yes. Thank-you. I'm fine. Just a bit tired.'

How could she tell them, I have to stop and think about my husband for a minute? The word itself brought her up short. Her husband. For so many years that word had brought Alastair to mind. At first, even though she was married to Luis, it had still brought Alastair to mind. That had been a part of the problem. Now all she could think about was Luis, his sensual mouth, his dark eyes, his long, capable fingers. His laughter. They had laughed so much. His capacity for clowning around. Above all his energy and the warmth of his body that seemed to radiate through his clothes, a glow that warmed her like sunshine whenever she was close to him, a warmth that melted something in her. She remembered that first day on Teide, remembered him gently patting her back as she wept, soothing her, a complete stranger, with kind words and gestures. Oh yes. He was a very good man. A generous man, generous with his love, his friendship, his simple kindness. She wanted him so much. She felt desire ignite again in the pit of her stomach and spread through her whole body but then came the awful fear that he was lost to her for ever, that his love for her had withered away, had shrunk and died in the cold winds of Scotland, much as the vivid blossoms of this place might, if transported to that chilly shore.

He must have been unhappy as only a Spaniard knew how to be, courting misery almost as assiduously as he had courted her. Would he have retreated into himself? Gone from her for good? It was unthinkable. In spite of all their years together she had never felt like this at the idea of losing Alastair. She had regretted the wasted time, not the man. Now at the idea of losing Luis for good, she felt sick and faint, and realised that she had never really accepted the finality of their separation. If only they could have another chance, she could love him, like the island, like this country itself, for a whole lifetime and in a hundred different ways, and never grow stale, never have enough.

Suzie had been only half right. If she was charmed, she had accepted it willingly, gone into it with her eyes wide open. The differences between them existed, but then one might have thought that she and Alastair would have been close enough, with so many interests in common. Yet there had been a yawning space between them, perhaps between all men and women. On La Gomera, people had evolved a way of communicating with each other that was both practical and beautiful. She and Luis had begun to do the same. Could they not continue? Could they not construct a whole new language of affection and compromise? What was it her mother had said, with surprising perception? 'If he wins, nobody loses this battle.'

All this came to her, washing over her in a great wave of realisation as she walked into the open concourse of the airport. She looked into the crowd. There were taxi drivers, tourists waiting for friends, the odd Canarian meeting a returned traveller. She scanned the crowd hopefully but saw no familiar face, only the vague mass of anonymous countenances returning her stare without recognition or affection. She gazed until her vision became blurred by the tears that threatened again. Eduardo stirred and sighed, as though sensing her sadness. He rubbed at his eyes with a fist and then thrust his fingers into his mouth.

'Is there no-one to meet you?' asked her fellow Scot, anxiously.

'There will be,' she said. 'Look ...' She saw a plastic chair standing against a pillar, one of the few seats in the place. 'Leave my luggage over there. I'll sit down and wait. I thought my husband was meeting me. He'll just be late.'

Somewhat reluctantly they agreed, settled her and the child with her bags around her and left her, but not before giving her the address of their apartment in Las Americas.

'If he doesn't arrive, you get a cab and come to us for the night. We have a spare room. We can't have you and the wee lad spending the night in this place.'

She was moved by their kindness. Always now the thought of her son and her responsibility for that small life intruded on her other emotions, steadying her, giving her purpose. Gratefully she accepted their offer, glad of their generosity.

'But I'm sure he'll come,' she said with more certainty than she felt.

They left her to find their own taxi and she watched their retreating backs with misgivings. What must she do? How long must she wait? Could he possibly be coming now? Might she have somehow missed him in the crowd? She blew her nose and then lifted Eduardo out of his buggy and onto her knee. He leaned his head against her breast and stared out at his unfamiliar surroundings with round blue eyes. She rested her chin on the top of his head, smelling his sweet hair, closing her eyes for a moment, blocking out the busy concourse, blocking out the misery.

When she raised her head again, she saw that Luis was coming towards her, threading his way through the crowds. She sat for a moment, unable to move. As he drew closer she could see an expression of passion fuelled by concern, of hope dulled by fatigue on his dark face which must match something very similar on her own. And she knew that, whatever he might be going to do, he was not going to reject her. He had lost weight. His cheekbones were sharply delineated giving his face an air of stern severity. But then, when he saw her, he smiled. Like sunshine, she thought. He was the sun in her sky.

She stood up and as she did so, Eduardo began to cry quite quietly but determinedly, like some small animal. The sound of his weeping tore at her as it always did, an inescapable biological imperative. He was tired and hungry and a little afraid. She held him and shushed him and patted him and then she found that she was holding him out as an offering to Luis. She saw that he too was holding something: a big tightly packed bunch of Tenerife roses. He had stopped to buy them and it had made him late. A security policeman watched them, tensing for a moment at the man's wild progress towards the woman and child, but then relaxed, his features dissolving into a smile at the obvious profusion of love there in the grubby concourse.

Luis did not speak or perhaps he could not, but held her and the child close in his arms. Eduardo turned his face, the skin so fair that it seemed translucent, like some exotic flower, turned it up to Luis and smiled in return.

Oh wise child, thought Margaret.

'My darling,' he said. 'I'm so sorry. So very, very sorry. Oh my best love. *Mi mejor amor*! My life! You came!'

There were tears in his eyes as he looked from one to the other but he was not ashamed of them.

'Eduardito,' he said. 'Margarita!'

Outside the high trilling of the cicadas hovered on the very edges of sound. Outside the sweet flower-heavy night waited to claim them. She felt the irresistible pull of it and was ready to let herself go. She thought of another child, perhaps, a child of the islands, but for now this was enough. She and Luis and Eduardo. She felt her own inevitable surrender and her liberation. His too. The prize, the golden apple, was theirs for the taking.

Poised there on the brink of a lifetime, they enfolded each other with the little boy in the middle, each indistinguishable one from the other, like the sweet flesh of some golden fruit, like the tightly furled petals of a rose.

THE END

Acknowledgements

Many thanks to Dolores Torres Medina and her family for so much invaluable information about La Gomera, for recollecting traditional poems and songs of the islands and for much appreciated assistance with translation. Many of these songs can be found in the original Spanish in *Cantares Tradicionales Canarios Uso y Significado* by Francisco J Castro Perez. Some of the later translations are my own.

Posthumous thanks to an enterprising Victorian lady traveller called Olivia M Stone, whose two volumes written about the Canaries in 1883 and 1884 and published in 1887, Tenerife and its Six Satellites, have proved to be an invaluable resource, full of precise and enchanting details, not just about the landscape, but about the people of the Canaries at that time: their way of life, food, dress, customs and music, all lovingly depicted. They contain everything a fiction writer's heart could desire in the way of information.

Chapter headings involve a mixture of traditional Canary Island songs, and quotes from the above books.

Thank-you to Edgar Salsas Boada (our dear T-shirt Boy) for some help with Spanish phrases and expressions and to Martin Hannah who knows about guitars, and gave me the information I needed at exactly the right time. Thanks too must go to the people of *Las Islas Canarias* for proving to be such an enduring inspiration, and to my husband, Alan Lees, whose sailing career took us and later our baby son to these most beautiful islands. A special mention must be made of my late, sorely missed friend Anna Goudie, who first told me how much she loved the story, and last but by no means least, Eileen McKoy, who has been waiting for this second book for far too long.

About the Author

Catherine Czerkawska is an extensively published writer of fiction (novels and short stories) non-fiction, poetry and award-winning plays for BBC radio, theatre and television. Born in Yorkshire, of Polish and Irish parentage, she has spent most of her life in Scotland, with time also spent working in Finland, Poland and the Canaries.

Her many novels include The Physic Garden, set in early nineteenth-century Glasgow, The Curiosity Cabinet, The Posy Ring, Ice Dancing and The Jewel, a meticulously researched novel about the life and times of Robert Burns's wife, Jean Armour. Bird of Passage and The Amber Heart are family sagas of cruelty, loss and enduring love. A Proper Person to be Detained and The Last Lancer are poignant true histories that take us from 19th century Ireland and WW2 Poland to the industrial heartlands of England and Scotland.

Her stage plays include two full length plays commissioned by Edinburgh's Traverse Theatre: Wormwood, a play about the Chernobyl disaster, staged in 1997, and Quartz. She has written plays for Glasgow's Oran Mor, as well as various community theatre projects, television drama and more than 100 hours of drama for BBC R4.

Her other interests include antique textiles, collecting vintage perfumes, local and social history. She has served on the committee of the Society of Authors in Scotland and spent four years as Royal Literary Fund Writing Fellow at the University of the West of Scotland.

https://www.catherineczerkawska.co.uk/

Look out for the next Canary Island novel:
The Golden Apple, in early 2026.